PRAISE FOR ELIZABETH THE FIRST WIFE

"Lian Dolan has created the perfect blend of vulnerability, complication, and wit in this outstanding second novel. Our main character Elizabeth is definitely the kind of friend you'd be lucky to have! With timeless storylines that play out on the stage and in the real world, this is a purely enchanting read."

— ROBIN KALL, HOST, READING WITH ROBIN

"I loved *Elizabeth the First Wife*. Lian Dolan's Elizabeth is smart, sassy and just As You Like It. This is a love story about moving on from young love and finding the right spot for yourself, in work and in relationships, interspersed with fun insights about the Bard. You'll laugh out loud at the pop culture comparisons between Shakespearean couples and today's notorious duos. Romance, celebrity, and Shakespeare—there's nothing better than that."

— KAIRA ROUDA, BESTSELLING AUTHOR OF HERE, HOME, HOPE AND ALL THE DIFFERENCE

"Elizabeth is a smart and lighthearted yet complicated woman whose journey will enthrall you. And with the references to Shakespeare, it will have book clubs talking for hours."

— MARI PARTYKA, MANIC MOMMIES BOOK CLUB

PRAISE FOR HELEN OF PASADENA

* A full year on the *Los Angeles Times* Bestseller List

* #1 Mover & Shaker on Amazon.com

* Finalist for Best Fiction, Southern California
Independent Bookseller Awards

"A compelling narrative and a memorable cast."
— PUBLISHERS WEEKLY

"A send-up of a 40something mom who finds herself suddenly
widowed, broke, and forced to reinvent herself...opinionated,
energetic, and sassy."
— MANDALIT DEL BARCO, NPR

"A knockout debut...it mixes up the classics and class structure
in a deliciously witty romp."
— CAROLINE LEAVITT, NEW YORK TIMES BESTSELLING AUTHOR OF
PICTURES OF YOU

"Every reader will see something of herself in Dolan's likable
heroine, Helen of Pasadena. Offering up every woman's worst fear,
Dolan pulls the rug out from under Helen, and we get to watch as
she recovers and reinvents herself with wit, charm, and smarts."
— SALLY BJORNSEN, AUTHOR OF A SINGLE GIRL'S GUIDE TO
MARRYING A MAN, HIS KIDS AND HIS EX-WIFE

LEARN MORE ABOUT LIAN DOLAN AT WWW.LIANDOLAN.COM

ELIZABETH
the FIRST WIFE

LIAN DOLAN

PROSPECT PARK BOOKS

Published by Prospect Park Books
969 S. Raymond Avenue
Pasadena, California 91105
www.prospectparkbooks.com

Distributed by Consortium Book Sales & Distribution
www.cbsd.com

Library of Congress Cataloging-in-Publication Data

Dolan, Lian.
Elizabeth the first wife / By Lian Dolan.
p. cm.
ISBN 978-1-938849-05-3 (pbk.) -- ISBN 978-1-938849-06-0 (e-book)
1. Women college teachers--Fiction. 2. Divorced men--Fiction. 3. Man-woman relationships--Fiction. I. Title.
PS3604.O427E45 2013
813'.6--dc23
                                    2013003791
10 9 8 7 6 5 4 3 2

DESIGNED BY KATHY KIKKERT

Printed in the United States of America on FSC-certified, sustainably produced paper

IN MEMORY OF MY PARENTS

EDNA KLARMAN DOLAN
JAMES JOSEPH DOLAN

Boy Meets Girl, Shakespeare-style

MIX & MATCH YOUR ROMANTIC PLOTLINE

BOY	GIRL
Troubled Prince	Young Maiden
Exiled Duke	Fairy Queen
Banished Black Sheep	Frosty Countess
Handsome Rogue	Shipwrecked Cross-dresser
Alleged Pirate	Sharp-tongued Shrew

FALL IN LOVE
At a Ball
On an Island
Against All Odds
With an Ass

COMPLICATIONS ENSUE

Mistaken Identity	Prolonged War
Murdered Relative	Fatal Miscommunication
Vengeful Mother	Filial Ingratitude
Bad Fairy Dust	Jealous Rage
Unfortunate Duel	Political Ambition
Forged Letter	Crazy Sister

AND IN THE END...
They marry
They die
They rule

CHAPTER 1

"So, is this a relationship built on manipulation or intellectual attraction?"

Please God, someone have an answer. *Anybody.* Nobody. I looked out at my class of twenty-four students, only about sixteen of whom were feigning interest in the material. Not a single hand was raised, not even Lydia's, which was a bad sign. Lydia was my prize student in Shakespeare 401, my upper-level English class at Pasadena City College. A bright young Korean second-gen with UC Berkeley dreams, she was my go-to responder on days when even I didn't feel like discussing the Bard. Lydia would pull some question out of thin air and keep the discussion going until the bell rang or Antonio's cell phone went off *(Party Rockers in the House Tonight!),* whichever came first.

But on an unusually hot and smoggy Tuesday in April, even Lydia couldn't have cared less about *The Taming of the Shrew.*

God, I hate this play.

Which is why I taught it, to make my point that even a writer as brilliant and timeless as Shakespeare can miss the mark. But apparently, not a single student in my class was interested in my reverse (perverse?) psychology. Not Morgan, the spectacularly beautiful private-school girl who spent one semester at NYU then fled back to Pasadena after discovering that college in NYC was not at all like shopping in NYC. Not George the Ukrainian (his moniker, not mine), who wanted to become a teacher after driving a truck for ten years. Not Emilia, the young single mom who was somehow putting herself through school and working at Bed Bath & Beyond. My usually lively class was otherwise occupied. It was the last week before spring break and, clearly, they were all mapping out the quickest route to the frozen yogurt emporium post-lecture.

"So no one has an opinion on one of the most famous relationships in all of Shakespeare? Kate and Petruchio. Fire and Ice. Sexist Pig and Cold-hearted Be-yotch. You read this scene and you thought, what? Fine, great. I gotta get me a guy like that."

Laughter rippled throughout the classroom, reminding me why I get up in the morning. "Professor Lancaster, I have no idea what's happening in this play," Nico Andregosian piped up. Nico faithfully wore his high school letterman's jacket every day to class, despite the heat and without irony. Nico wasn't headed to Berkeley anytime soon, but he did help me change a tire last week. Another reminder of why I got up in the morning. "I don't get this at all."

"Did you actually read it, Nico?"

"Yeah, kinda. But it's crazy, about the sun and the moon."

This is where the class gets good, I thought. Where I, Elizabeth Lancaster, community college English teacher and theater enthusiast, feel most in my element. "Okay, let's do this. Let's read it together, Nico. You and me. Like I always say, Shakespeare's words are meant to be spoken, not studied at arm's length. It's living, breathing dialogue. And in this scene, the sexist pig is trying to convince the cold-hearted be-yotch that the sun is actually the moon. It's his way of exerting power, and she is employing her own manipulative techniques to shut him down. Raise your hand if you've done this in your own relationships. Who's played mind games in a romantic relationship?"

All the hands went up except Sahil's, whose closest personal relationship has probably been with his PlayStation controller. "That's what I thought. Get up, Nico. You're Petruchio and I'm Kate. Let's go."

He heaved his squat body out of the chair, as his classmates hooted. His buddy from high school, Aron, hissed, "Duuude." Nico's reluctance was skin deep. He was a ham at heart. "Please, don't make me do this."

I took a swig of Diet Coke and did my best faux-ghetto "Oh, it's on." The students whooped, like I knew they would.

Nico began haltingly, adding several more syllables than in the original. *"Come on, a' God's name. Once more, um, um, toward our father's. Good Lord, how bright and goodly shines the moon!"* He inserted a dramatic hand gesture for emphasis, then gave me a triumphant look.

Oh, it was on. I tapped into my Inner Shrew, which wasn't hard. I was a single, mid-30s woman with emerging bunions, a leaking roof, and a love life that had been in decline since the early aughts. Not to mention that I had a mother who kept setting me up with every divorced dad in Pasadena and a sister who insisted I needed to keep "putting myself out there" even though she has no idea how rough it is "out there." Why couldn't they just leave me alone with my books, my vegetable garden, and my growing collection of European comfort shoes? I happened to like my life. Why didn't my family? Oh, yes, at that particular moment in time, I was feeling extremely shrewish. Watch out, Nico. *"The moon! The sun—it is not light now."*

Nico rose to the challenge, playing his Petruchio with a touch of *Jersey Shore. "I say it is the moon that shines so bright."*

The classroom door creaked as it opened. I didn't bother to turn to see who'd arrived thirty minutes late to class. Besides, the audible gasp from a dozen young women told me it was Jordan. He was easily the best-looking boy in the room and a star baseball player who was hoping for a decent transfer offer. Jordan slid in late most days, hoping for attendance credit and a chance to flirt with Shiree. But I paid no attention to the rumble from the other students, because I was in the zone. *"I know it is the sun that shines so bright."*

Nico's jaw dropped open, apparently stunned silent by my confidence. But the scene wasn't nearly over, so I gave him the universal "it's your turn" sign with my hands. He stammered, unable to get out the next line. And then I heard the next lines come from behind me. *"Now by my mother's son, and that's myself, It shall be the moon, or star, or what I list...."*

I turned to face the owner of the familiar voice. Good God, just what I needed.

No wonder the girls gasped. There, resplendent in jeans and a black T-shirt that probably cost more than my car, was Francis Fahey. Or as the world knew him, FX Fahey, the third-highest-grossing action star behind Harrison Ford and Tom Cruise. His *Icarus* franchise had spawned video games, fast food tie-ins, and a legion of fans that believed the laid-back actor to actually be the futuristic-cop hero. Clearly, FX was used to being the center of attention, and he owned the classroom the minute he entered. He strode up the center aisle, grinning effortlessly, like he was just returning from the grocery store with a six-pack of beer instead of invading my workplace after a decade with no face-to-face contact. Oh, he was enjoying the moment. *"Or ere I journey to your father's house. Go on and fetch our horses back again. Evermore cross'd and cross'd, nothing but cross'd."*

I wanted to kill him. *"Forward, I pray, since we have come so far, and be it the moon or sun, or whatever you please."* Now he was close enough to touch, and I was tempted, because his T-shirt, stretched poetically across his chest, appeared to be made of the softest cotton ever spun. I needed to physically stop myself from petting him. Be the shrew. Be the shrew. *"And if you please to call it a rush-candle, henceforth I vow it shall be so for me."*

FX leaned in, his chin barely grazing the top of my head. He smelled like lime. *"I say it is the moon,"* he whispered for all to hear. The students responded with catcalls and an "Oh no, you didn't."

I stepped back, a gesture of stagecraft and self-preservation. *"I know it is the moon."*

FX closed the gap. *"Nay, then you lie; it is the blessed sun."*

"Oh, snap, Professor," Nico interrupted from his seat, where he had returned to watch.

"Then God be blest, it is the blessed sun. But sun it is not, when you say it is not; and the moon changes even as your mind." I brushed away a lock of brown hair from his forehead, in what I believed to be a saucy fashion. That was a mistake. *"What you will have it nam'd, even that it is, And so it shall be for Elizabeth."*

FX broke character, beaming, "Don't you mean, '*So it shall be for Katherine*'?"

Busted. "What did I say?"

"You said Elizabeth. That's you. I think you meant to say Katherine, because while Kate might agree with Petruchio to shut him up, Elizabeth Lancaster would never agree with me for expediency's sake."

Oh, snap.

"You haven't changed a bit, Lizzie," FX said, looking around my tiny office, taking in my decorating style, which I referred to as Oxford in Southern California. Basically, my look included a couple of walls of leather-bound books, some gold-framed flea-market oil paintings, and one of those good-luck Chinese bamboo plants that a student had given me years ago and I didn't want to tempt fate by tossing out. He wandered around, touching everything like a five-year-old at Target. "You look good."

Compared to whom? The Brazilian supermodel he'd been living with, or the supermodel's nanny he was sleeping with, according to *Stun* magazine?

"Thanks. So do you, Francis." His amused look told me that only his mother still called him Francis. "Sorry, FX. Or is it really just X now? That's how Matt Damon referred to you on *The Daily Show*."

"On set, it's X. Short, simple. Kinda boss. Remember when you helped pick my stage name? The X was your idea." Of course I remembered. We were lying on a futon, the only piece of usable furniture in our tiny, oven-like apartment on the Lower East Side, just before the gourmet cheese shops and a John Varvatos boutique invaded the dodgy neighborhood. It was the summer FX landed his first professional acting gig with the Public Theater, and I followed along, as an intern to the artistic director. There was already a Francis Fahey and a Frank Fahey registered in the union, so I suggested replacing his actual middle name, Christopher, with the more traditional match to Francis: Xavier. FX Fahey was born. That was a name, I declared, that made him sound like a member of the IRA. Back in those days, terrorists were cool.

"I remember," I answered, but I didn't want to remember all of it, so I moved on. "What are you doing here? How did you find me at work?"

"I have people, Liz. That's their job."

"You couldn't have just Facebooked me, like everybody else I haven't seen in a decade?"

"I'm an actor. I like to make an entrance." He smirked. "Plus, I was in Pasadena for a photo shoot, so I thought what the hell? I'll swing by."

Ah, I was convenient. Got it.

FX was studying my framed diploma collection: BA from

Wesleyan; MA and PhD from UCLA; First Aid/CPR certification from the Rose Bowl Aquatic Center. He turned, "You have to admit, we were good in there. I think your students were impressed."

"They've seen me do Shakespeare. Pretty much every class."

"I meant with me. I think I impressed them." Was FX Fahey seriously looking for props from a classroom of nineteen-year-olds and George the Ukrainian? Still insecure about his talent, I noted. He carried on, "Remember the last time we did that scene together? I think we were better today."

I did remember, and it filled me with embarrassment and a touch of nausea.

FX picked up a silver-framed photo of my family taken several years earlier. There was my father, the man of the hour that night, Dr. Richard Lancaster, in white tie with decorations, standing stiffly next to my mother, Anne, who was flashing a triumphant grin. My mother was clearly at her spousal zenith that night, taking her victory lap wrapped in peach silk taffeta and her grandmother's diamonds. Next to my parents stood my two sisters, Sarah and Bumble, as different as night and day, but both in black sequins, flanked by their husbands, solid citizens each. And then there was me, on the end, in a vintage Lanvin gown and excruciatingly painful heels, posed next to the King of Sweden. FX didn't seem to notice the royalty. "How is your dad? He gave me all that grief for years because I didn't know who that famous science guy was, what's-his-name?"

"Feynman. Richard Feynman."

"Yeah. Wasn't he the founder of *Popular Mechanics* or something?"

I thought for a second. "You must be thinking of *quantum* mechanics. And actually, Feynman worked on quantum electro-dynamics. He was a theoretical physicist and a friend of my father's."

"Quantum Mechanics! That's a good name for a movie. Does your dad still talk about me?"

"FX, my dad won the Nobel Prize in Physics a few years ago. He never talks about you." I snatched the photo out of his hands with a little too much impatience.

FX threw up his hands in admiration, "See, nobody puts me down like that anymore! I've missed you, Lizzie. Wow, a Nobel Prize. That's pretty impressive."

Yeah, kind of. I didn't have the heart to tell him that the last time my father noticed an ad for one of his movies on the side of a bus, he pointed at it and said, "Isn't that what's-his-name?" My father exists in a world without TMZ and always has. When your day job involves determining the origins of the universe, you simply can't be bothered with the mundanity of pop culture. Or a boy your daughter used to know. "Did you just stop by to run lines, or did you need something?"

In one graceful move, he grabbed my extra chair, pulled it closer to my desk, and sat down on the edge of the seat, "I have a proposal for you, Professor Lancaster."

Our knees were almost touching. *A proposal?* I was afraid to open my mouth, convinced unfortunate squeaking noises would come out. Like the Tin Man in *The Wizard of Oz*, only not so charming. So I used my timeworn technique of lifting my eyebrows and lowering my chin, as if to say, "Go on."

It worked. One of the world's biggest movie stars continued. "I want you to come to Ashland with me this summer for the Shakespeare Festival. I'm doing a production of *A Midsummer Night's Dream*. You, me, Shakespeare. How perfect is that, right? Remember sophomore year? I need you on the team. As a producer or consultant or whatever you want to call yourself. And guess who might be directing?"

I managed a shrug and a head shake.

"Taz Buchanan. Freakin' Taz Buchanan. The original director dropped out because the surrogate delivered early and he and his partner are home with twins. But then I ran into Taz in a bar in

London and the next thing you know, boom, he's interested. I go to New York next week to seal the deal, I hope. But I need your help. We have two months to pull it together. A couple weeks of rehearsal with an eight-week run. Please say you'll do it."

Of all the proposals that might have come out of FX's mouth— Let's go for a beer! Can you dig up my Counting Crows CDs? Would you be a character witness at my trial?—this is the one I least expected. I finally found my voice, "That is a proposal. But why me? Don't you have people who would be better suited?"

He shook his head. "Better suited? Just your use of the phrase 'better suited' makes me realize how perfect you are for this." He relaxed back into the chair like my acceptance was a done deal. "And Taz Buchanan? You've gotta want to work with him, right?'

Yes, FX, I often fantasize about working with brilliant but temperamental directors like Taz Buchanan in my role as faculty advisor to the campus Theater Appreciation Club. "Ah, that possibility has never really come up in my career," I responded, then shook my head a little. "FX, what's the real story? Are you down a babysitter? Is that why you want me?"

His face got serious. "I did not sleep with that babysitter. Seriously, have you seen her? She's like sixty. Or fifty anyway. Things are over with Bebe, but not because of any babysitter. Although, I could use some time out of the limelight...."

Now we were getting somewhere. Here was the thing about FX—despite the box office, despite the perfect dimple on the perfect chin, despite the ease with which he glided through the world, he was not a bad guy. And, much as I hated to admit it, he was impossible to dislike. Not liking FX was like not liking bunnies.

"What's going on?"

"I have a movie coming out in the fall. It's really good, Liz. And I'm...really good in it." I knew, of course, about his movie. Starting with last year's Super Bowl ad, *Dire Necessity* had been called everything from "a masterpiece" to a top Oscar contender months before its premiere. It starred FX Fahey as General George Washington in the days leading up to the crossing of the Delaware. Only in Hollywood could somebody with unrelenting bone structure and a personality like a yellow lab be cast as a brilliant soldier with a pockmarked face and wooden teeth. But according to the story I read in *US Weekly* (I was at the nail salon), FX Fahey quite simply embodied the leader of the Continental Army. Or so said his PR person. He was also getting credit as a producer on the film, a first for him. "This is a big deal for me, and I want to make sure everything that could happen, does happen."

FX gave me the same openly sincere look he threw my way during our first-night freshmen mixer at Wesleyan, fall of 1993. Back when he was simply Francis, a Seattle-bred, Nirvana-loving aspiring English major in a flannel shirt and Doc Martens. "I want to change my generation with my poetry," he had said that night, as if he really, really meant it. And I really, really fell for it. It didn't matter that most of the poetry he quoted to me was actually written by Kurt Cobain. I was in a heart-shape box for the next five years.

And here I was, falling for it again after more than a decade of being Francis-free. At least this time I wasn't wearing a thrift-store granny dress and cowboy boots. Small victories.

"I get that the movie's important. That's great, FX. But where does the Shakespeare fit in? Sounds like you need a marketing team, not a professor-slash-producer."

"Oh, I have a team. That's who wants me to go to Ashland. According to my agent, my manager, and my publicist, I need to raise my acting profile before the movie comes out to be taken seriously for a nomination." He was all business now. He didn't get this far in his career because he didn't understand the score. "Doing live theater is exactly what my resume needs now. It's real, it's brave, and, you know, Shakespeare is classy. Not every action hero can do that shit. Can you imagine Channing Tatum as Hamlet?"

"Well, *Midsummer* is not exactly *Hamlet*, but I guess I see the point." But I was still vague on what my role might be in the FX Fahey Road to the Oscars. "You know, FX, I haven't worked on anything but student productions in the last ten years. Sure, I've led some tours to Ashland for students and friends of my mother, but Taz Buchanan and the Oregon Shakespeare Festival are both kind of out of my league."

The Oregon Shakespeare Festival, or OSF as it was commonly referred to, was one of the top repertory theaters in the country, thanks to consistently excellent directing, acting, and production values. It produced about a dozen plays a year, everything from four or five Shakespeare titles to new plays by emerging writers. Hundreds of thousands of theater fans made their way to the tiny charming town of Ashland during the season to sit under the stars and feel the power of live theater. It wasn't a place for amateurs.

"You'd work for me. You'd be my person. I need you to keep me on track, to make sure I don't do anything too stupid. To be the voice of good judgment, like you always are." FX noticed my raised eyebrows. "Onstage. Only onstage, not offstage. I'm a big boy. I'll lay low when the curtain comes down. I'm totally focused on this. We have, like, no time to produce this thing, and Taz is Taz. I just need to know the production won't go off the rails. Creatively. And I know you won't let that happen. You care too much about this stuff. It's just, I mean, I haven't done live theater, you know, since...."

Ah, yes, since what Frank Rich, the *New York Times* theater critic at the time, called "the most self-indulgent three hours ever produced for the Broadway stage," otherwise known as FX's turn in *Coriolanus* in 2002. (And that was one of the better reviews.) He offered up his performance as a "gesture toward healing in the post–September 11th world"—a fatal miscalculation about his worth to the American psyche. He paid for his hubris for years, with mocking referrals and unrelenting ridicule. I admit, at the time, it pleased me. Since then, the green screen has been his friend, and he hasn't stepped foot on a stage other than at the Golden Globes. Now, to get his Oscar nomination, he was ready to conquer his demons, but he thought he needed me there.

I was flattered.

I shuffled papers around on my desktop, stalling for time. "What role are you playing?"

"We're doing the dual-role interpretation. I'll be Theseus and Oberon."

Perfect, the King of Athens and the king of the Fairies. One powerful in reality; the other powerful in the dream world. Now I was impressed, damn it. And interested.

"I have to think about this. I do have a life here, you know. I have a lot going on. A lot."

I had nothing on my calendar for the summer. Seriously, not even a dentist appointment. State funding for community colleges was so bad that all my usual writing classes had been canceled for the summer. I was actually considering starting a college-essay advising business to take advantage of all the wealthy Pasadena parents who didn't want their kids to do time at PCC and had the money to buy their way into a small liberal arts school in Ohio, thanks to tutors. But I hadn't even put up a flyer on the community boards at the trendy coffeehouses yet. Still, FX didn't need to know all that. "It's not so easy to pack up and relocate for the summer."

He nodded. "I'm sure you're booked, and I know it will take some rescheduling. I'll take care of everything, and I mean that. Housing, transportation, and whatever you want for a fee. Really. Whatever."

Good to see a touch of guilt surfacing. FX handed me a card with his agent's contact information. "I need you, Liz. Think about it and then call my agent. We'll set up a meeting. We'll sign a contract and iron everything out. This is a real job offer."

"Not an au pair position. I get it. I'll think about it, FX." There was a knock on the door and one of my students, Julio Jimenez, popped his head in. It was time for our weekly advisor meeting. God bless Julio. I stood up to signal the end of our conversation. "Give me a couple of days."

FX gave me a double-cheek kiss. Yup, limes with a little bit of mint. "Come to Ashland, Lizzie."

As FX shut the door, Julio stared him down. "Hey, was that…?"

"Yes, it was."

"Cool! How do you know FX Fahey, Professor?"

I spun my chair around to look out the window facing the quad. "I was married to him."

POWER COUPLE #1

Kate & Petruchio

FROM *THE TAMING OF THE SHREW*

HER: Take your pick: either Acid-tongued Shrew in need of a Good Man or Smart Ambitious Woman with limited options in sixteenth-century upper-crust society.

HIM: Swaggering, Arrogant Gold Digger with six-pack abs. Loves money more than love.

MEET CUTE: Lust at first sight. Blind date arranged by father looking to marry off old-maid daughter. Verbal sparring establishing the two are intellectual equals. Did I mention lust?

HISTORICAL NOTE: The meeting of Kate and Petruchio has inspired every rom-com since the dawn of time. And the taming of Kate by Petruchio has aroused hatred in every feminist who ever read the play.

RELATIONSHIP LOW POINTS: Forced arranged marriage; disastrous wedding (groom arrives late, wears a ridiculous outfit, and forces bride to leave without dinner); and harsh wife-taming process that includes starvation and sleep deprivation.

WHY THEY WORK: Smart is sexy. Sex is sexy. And no one else will have them.

HIS BEST LINE: "Why there's a Wench! Come on, and kiss me, Kate."

HER BEST LINE: "Asses are meant to bear and so are you."

SHAKESPEAREAN COUPLE MOST LIKELY TO: Swing.

WHO PLAYS THEM IN THE MOVIE: Emma Stone and Justin Timberlake.

CHEMISTRY FACTOR: 4.5 OUT OF 5

CHAPTER 2

"Do not get sucked in."

My big sister Bumble was nothing if not cynical and jaded. She prided herself on being the least gullible human being in Southern California. Maybe that's why she went into public relations. Or how she ended up married to a congressman. Those four years she spent at a women's college did wonders for her sense of self. She was only fifteen months older than me, but she thought of herself as light years ahead of me on her life path. Now her goal was to self-actualize me, one pep talk at a time. She'd been trying for some time, with hit-and-miss results.

"He played you once with something we in the business like to call 'wedding vows,' and now, what? You owe him nothing." She was so worked up that she almost popped a button on her plum Ryan Roberts jacket, and that would have sent her over the edge. "Mr. Movie Star wants you to make sure he doesn't do anything stupid so he can win an Oscar? Oh, so he comes running back to his ex-wife. Like you're his rehab minder."

"I think maybe he respects my professional opinion," I suggested meekly, as I watched her straighten up my living room with her prototypical efficiency and disregard for my personal wishes. "Plus, I'd have time to work on my book—you know, the one that publisher wanted me to think about."

"Oh, sure. Great idea. A summer with FX will really clear your head so you can get that book proposal together. The one you've been talking about for three years," Bumble countered, restacking my coffee-table books with expertise and speed.

"Please stop cleaning my house," I begged. That did nothing to slow her down. She moved onto rearranging the furniture.

Bumble Lancaster Seymour was a force of nature, the type of operator who could squeeze anything out of you and then make you feel like you have to write her a thank-you note for the privilege. (*Dear Bumble, I know I asked you to stop cleaning my house, but you were right and I was wrong. It does look better your way. With love, your sister Elizabeth.*) Christened Beatrice, she'd never been called by her given name. "Bumble Bea" is what the family called her from the get-go, because she never stopped buzzing about. Eventually, the Bea fell by the wayside, and she's been Bumble since toddlerhood. Though why, at the moment, she was so intent on repositioning the objets d'art on my bookshelves, I wasn't sure.

"Listen, Francis-slash-FX-slash-Icarus broke your heart. He married you and then screwed around with the first co-star he could find."

"Thanks for not mincing words."

Bumble carried on, taking out her long-held anger on my pillows, which, frankly, didn't deserve it. "And then he walked away without paying you a dime. Not a dime. Do you think that timing was a coincidence? Don't you think he knew he was about to sign a three-picture deal? The ink was barely dry on your one-page divorce agreement that was, air quotes, mediated by whom? Some barista in the Village? And the next thing we know, there's FX Fahey walking down the red carpet to a giant payday. He did you wrong, really, really wrong, Elizabeth. I don't know why you care if he has professional success." During this rant she was refolding our grandmother's antique Hawaiian quilt.

"That was a long time ago, okay? The divorce or how it went down is water under the bridge. Yes, I'm sorry I married him at twenty-two. We never should have gotten married. Then when it ended, it would have just been twentysomethings going through the inevitable post-college breakup. But what happened happened." That was my story and I was sticking with it.

Bumble artfully placed the quilt over the arm of a mushroom-colored Pottery Barn couch she had helped me select. "How come Gigi left you her house and this great quilt? I think I deserved the quilt."

"Because I gave Gigi that quilt. I found it at the Rose Bowl flea market. And you got all the artwork." Dang, the place did look better after Bumble's whirlwind restaging.

"Good point. And now that Helen Frankenthaler is dead, those things are worth a fortune," she crowed, pausing for dramatic effect. "All I'm saying is don't get sucked in." The doorbell rang and Bumble squealed a tiny bit. "He's here. Try to impress him."

Pierce DeVine, nee Paulie DeVito, decorator to the stars, or at least the Pasadena elite and their adult children, could only be described as "gleaming." Literally, he was the shiniest man I'd ever laid eyes on. His dress shirt was blindingly white, his blue blazer looked like it was sewn on him moments before walking in the door, and his pressed gray flannels must have once belonged to Cary Grant. His tanned complexion said Weekend Home in Montecito, but his blue eyes showed no signs of the fine lines that normally appear when that is the case. Were his teeth actually sparkling? No wonder Bumble felt the need to redecorate my home before his arrival.

I was not worthy.

Or was I? I could swear the gleaming Pierce DeVine was intrigued, despite the fact that my hideaway lacked the grandeur, formality, and property-tax bill of his usual transformations. He was taking in La Casita de Girasoles, or the Little House of Sunflowers, the moniker my great-grandparents had bestowed upon the home, with some admiration. La Casita was a classic California hacienda-style house, with wood-beamed vaulted ceilings, Saltillo floor tiles, and thick adobe walls that danced with light and shadows. A massive stone fireplace dominated the living room. Handmade square-frame windows and oversize doors drew the eye out to the courtyard, which was anchored by a mature olive tree and my humble breakfast table, where my coffee cup still sat from the morning. I hoped he wouldn't mark me down for my sloppy housekeeping.

"Tell me the story of this home," Pierce demanded, his manicured hands performing some sort of interior designer sun salutation. He nodded in my direction, summoning speech.

It was a lecture I'd given many times since moving in three years ago, the house inspiring that question from most guests. But I gave him the short version, because doubtless he'd walked into countless other gems in the area. My house had the same back story as scores of homes in the area: Easterners moved to sunny Pasadena in the 1920s; they started a business and it flourished; the money flowed; lovely house was built; life was good until the about late '70s, when smog and crowds took over; original homeowners died and history was up for grabs; some homes survived yuppie remodels with character intact, and others got the popcorn-ceiling treatment.

Luckily, my casita hadn't really changed hands. "The house was built in 1926 by my great-grandparents on my mother's side. According to my grandmother, her parents wanted to build the most

California house they could, to let in sun and clean air. That's why they used a hacienda layout. Very little has been done to this house since 1926."

"Very little," Bumble concurred, clearly working up to her rant on my inferior counter space.

I shut her down, "My grandmother Gigi lived in it her whole life. She was the only Bosworth child, married young, had my mother, but then was widowed in World War II and moved back in with her parents. She never remarried and stayed here until her death a few years ago."

"Some days, that sounds like a good life to me," Bumble interjected. "Alone but in charge."

I carried on, "Our grandmother was a great entertainer and patron of the arts. The house was always in use for fundraisers or musicales. People loved coming here. Gigi was legally blind in the last decade of her life, so we literally couldn't change anything about the house for her sake. When she died, she left the house to me."

"Not that the rest of us minded," Bumble added, repeating her standard beef about the will's inequity. The truth is, Bumble really didn't mind. She and the Congressman lived in a massive center-hall Colonial in the upstanding Madison Heights neighborhood. But Bumble liked to give the impression that we were the Most Interesting Family in Town, so she carried on for the sake of a controversy. "Elizabeth here was our grandmother's favorite. She lived in the guesthouse for years during grad school. The two of them loved books and plays. She even suffered through the musicales, because who doesn't love the lute? And God knows, when my grandmother lost her sight and her friends started to die off, Elizabeth would sit with her for hours and describe what all the actresses were wearing on *All My Children*. She earned this house in the end."

"I feel the spirit of your grandmother in this home. And your light shines through as well, Elizabeth. You are a nurturer and an emotional sponge. You soak up the needs of others. So let's take care of your needs now." Pierce ran his hands over the adobe walls, caressing each dip. "I hope you know how special this house is. It's like a virgin, touched for the very first time."

Bumble muffled a laugh and shot a look in my direction. Yes, Bumble, I get the virgin analogy. I'm like the house.

I turned to face Pierce again, his personal luster diminished slightly with the Madonna quote. But I had to admit that he seemed to really care about my hacienda, so much humbler than the cavernous old Pasadena houses he usually gutted and retiled in white. I started with my modest list. "I don't want to change too much. But the kitchen needs a little work."

"A little work?" Bumble snorted. "I'd tear the whole thing out, blow out a wall and make this one gigantic entertaining space. Wouldn't you, Pierce?"

Pierce's glass-blue eyes turned cold for an instant. If Bumble hadn't been the wife of a member of the House Ways & Means Committee, she would have been toast. But then his face softened. "You, my dear Bumble, need your home to be a showpiece, because you and your handsome husband thrive at the highest level. You create the noise of life. You're noise creators. But this home is quieter and needs a careful touch. Listen to the silence." He gestured again, signifying the end of his pontification, and then closed his eyes, presumably to commune with the silence.

As commanded, we listened to the silence, but really, all I could hear was the freeway in the distance, a fact of life in Southern California. I kept my mouth shut for a moment to honor his meditation, then carried on. "Yes, I want to preserve the peacefulness, but I'd really like a dishwasher. And maybe a stove that doesn't have to be lit by hand. And I'd love a prep sink. And if I could get a window over the sink to look out at my garden, that would be enough for me."

Pierce remained still with his eyes shut, and then they flew open, scaring me a tiny bit. Was he possessed?

"I'll do it."

Bumble squealed again and gave the Shiny One a hug. "Oh, Pierce, thank you. I know this isn't your usual high-profile project, but I know you're ab-so-lute-ly the only one who can do justice to this house."

Wait, what had just happened? I thought I got to choose the designer, not vice versa. Once again, I was reminded that my world and Bumble's rarely coincided, even though we lived only one zip code apart. "Um, thank you?"

Pierce DeVine reached for both my hands, "No, thank you. This is a journey we take together."

I never should have opened the box. Honestly, I should have thrown that box out a long time ago, finally admitting defeat, like I did with my extensive wardrobe of DKNY blazers with shoulder pads. They were never coming back in style and I had to face facts. But I'd gone ahead and opened my Big Box of FX Memories, and now no amount of Meritage was going to wash away the pain.

Inside were flyers from dorm parties, two Eurail passes from our junior year in London, Playbills from productions we had seen together, Soundgarden ticket stubs, coasters from our favorite bars, a mixed CD of quirky love songs by quirky singer-songwriters, actual letters and love poems written by FX, a dried rose from my twenty-first birthday, and Mardi Gras beads. Nothing out of the ordinary, but everything brought back vivid images and intense feelings.

There, too, was the hand-lettered flyer from the production of *The Taming of the Shrew* we performed in the Shakespeare class we took together second semester sophomore year. Elizabeth Lancaster as Kate. Francis Fahey as Petruchio. After so many months of staying up all night writing his history papers while he played Nerf basketball in the hall. After so many months of searching for him every time I walked into the library or a party. After so many months of watching him be the center of attention and go home with other women. All it took was one scene *(I say it is the moon…)* and Francis Fahey finally fell for me. The night after we performed in front of the class, he pulled a *Say Anything* outside my room, complete with raincoat and Peter Gabriel. (He was from Seattle, after all.) It wasn't original, but I didn't care. I was already in love with him.

If I was the scrapbooking type, I might have stuck all the items in an album entitled: College Kids Fall in Love. But I'm more of the unmarked-box-in-the-closet type, and maybe that's why the FX sighting today had me so unnerved.

I studied the photo of us leaving the courthouse in Lower Manhattan the day we got married. Our friend Margot had captured the event in a series of Polaroids, but the other photos had long since disappeared. (Or maybe I cut them up violently the night FX told me he needed to "experience more to really be an actor." And by "more" he meant more sex with more women who weren't me.) But on that spectacular New York City October day in 1998, I was deliriously happy. The joy showed on my face in the fading image. I was wearing a long white crocheted dress and pink silk scarf, holding a bouquet of daisies. FX was in a tweed jacket and a purple striped shirt. The skyline in the background, the future in front of us. God, we looked so young.

Why wait, we'd thought. We're in love, and this is forever.

Seventeen months and twenty-six days later, we were divorced. My heart was cleaved in two.

Then the Lancaster clan stepped up. Bumble came to collect my remains from New York and move me home. Sarah practically wrote my grad school applications during all her spare time in med school. My grandmother cleaned out her guesthouse, gave me her old BMW, and signed me up for water aerobics. My father showed up every Friday afternoon, racket in hand, to smack around the tennis ball. Even my mother recognized the fragility of my state; she never once said, "I told you so."

I wish I could say the first year or two post-FX was a blur, but it wasn't. It was excruciating. Every day took me back to him, to his laugh, to the feel of his skin. It was like full-body plantar fasciitis: Every step felt like I was walking on a million knives. I didn't know heartbreak could hurt everywhere. I had multiple copies of Liz Phair's *Exile in Guyville* and Alanis Morissette's *Jagged Little Pill* for car, home, and office use. But even a daily dozen playings of "You Oughta Know" couldn't quicken the healing.

Then one Friday morning I opened the *L.A. Times* and there it was: the first big article about FX, splashed across the front of the Calendar section on the day of the release of *Icarus: The Beginning*. The writer described FX as "single." Not "divorced" or even "on the rebound," just "single." I didn't even get the ultimate *Hollywood Reporter*–style insult: "Ex-wife is non-pro." There was no mention of me at all, no mention of us. Like we never happened. I stayed in bed for the weekend, with my grandmother's blessing. On Monday morning, I packed up the stuff and shoved it in a closet and went to work on finishing my PhD in record time.

Eventually, the pain dulled and the embarrassment faded. At some point, I realized I could look at the giant billboards on Sunset with FX's image without retching. I could flip through *US Weekly* at the nail salon and breeze right past the shot of FX and his latest model. Finally, I watched the entire *Icarus* trilogy in a single day, like ripping off a Band-Aid, fast-forwarding through the inevitable scenes where he got the girl.

The first and only time I ran into him after the split was in a completely generic chain restaurant near UCLA, after the third *Icarus* film had made $100 million on its opening weekend. He was getting four carne asada tacos, and I happened to walk in for a chicken bowl. We talked for two hours, until the manager asked us to buy another meal or leave. As we said goodbye, he gave me the patented FX Fahey eyes and said, "I'm sorry, Elizabeth."

I said, "I forgive you." And by then, I had.

He called five years ago when his father died of a sudden heart attack. Jack Fahey spent forty-five years at Boeing, working his way up from janitor to supply chain executive. He dropped dead two weeks after his retirement party. FX called and asked if I would go to the funeral with him. He was a wreck. "You knew him, Liz. People in Hollywood, the people I work with, they don't really get normal families. If you're not in the business, you don't really exist. My dad was just my dad. I'm not sure I can handle normal anymore. If you're there, I can do it."

I almost said yes, but then I came to my senses. I could imagine the look on his mother's face if I returned home with the prodigal son at her darkest hour. It would have been the same look she gave me the one Christmas I spent with the Fahey family in Seattle during that tiny window between our wedding and our divorce. May Fahey loathed me. She cornered me in the pantry of their warm and lovely home after dinner on Christmas Eve and hissed, "How could you? How could you marry my only son and not invite me, his mother, to the wedding?"

I've never felt worse in my entire life. Never. It was as if the folly of the entire marriage was summed up in that one thought. Of course it wouldn't last; his mother wasn't at the wedding.

So I told FX that he had to do the funeral alone. "You know I can't go with you, but you'll be fine, FX. You'll see. You'll get home and you'll be you again." I meant it. His vulnerability had touched me deeply.

He sent me an e-mail a week later. All it said was: You were right. I could do it. Thanks. Love, Francis.

I still had the e-mail in my inbox.

I pushed the walk down FX Memory Lane aside and worked on dinner. *Focus on the present, Elizabeth.* I chopped my kale with determination, shredding it for a marinated salad. I tossed the greens into a bowl with avocados, mushrooms, sesame oil, and lemon juice, left it to sit for a half hour, and poured myself another half a glass of wine.

FX was back with another request. Maybe Bumble was right. Why should his lack of confidence be my problem?

As much as I wanted to go for the work, the experience, and the clean Oregon air, letting FX back into my life was not productive. One trip into the past confirmed what I already knew: FX knew how to push all the buttons, good and bad. Especially the good.

I didn't want to risk…well, anything. I had a life, a small and well-ordered life. It suited me. That was enough. I couldn't go to Ashland. No way.

My phone beeped and a text came in from my father: See you for lunch? For a guy who could barely change a lightbulb, his delight in texting amused me. Maybe he loved the efficiency and immediacy, because he was never a big fan of small talk.

I responded: Usual spot. Usual time.

I would let FX twist for a couple of days, then call his agent and decline. There, decision made.

RIGHTEOUS ROLE MODEL

Portia

FROM *THE MERCHANT OF VENICE*

WHO SHE IS: A rich, intelligent heiress who is forced to auction off her hand in marriage in a bizarre lottery as stipulated by her father's will. She's also a total babe. Lauded as a free spirit who must abide by rigid rules when it comes to finding a husband, and one of the Bard's most complex female characters. In the end, she gets her man, has her day in court, and enjoys the respect of society.

WHAT TO STEAL FROM PORTIA:

❧ Gracious, quick-witted, and sets high standards for her romantic partners.

❧ Epitomizes independence in her life choices, as much as a girl could in Elizabethan England.

❧ Cross-dresses for good! She impersonates a lawyer's apprentice and saves the life of her beloved's BFF. Both guys owe her big time.

❧ Awesome name.

WHAT TO SKIP: Scholars think she represents the blunt, barbaric Christian Primitivism of the play.

HISTORICAL NOTE: Shakespeare created Portia in homage to Queen Elizabeth herself. Also, in letters to his beloved wife, John Adams calls Abigail "Portia." (In turn, she calls him "Lysander" after the young swain in *Midsummer*, which is kinda creepy.)

BEST QUOTE ON RELATION-SHIPS: "I am glad this parcel of wooers are so reasonable; for there is not one among them but I dote on his very absence, and I pray God grant them a fair departure."

WHAT SHE MEANS: There are tons of fish in the sea. Unfortunately, I don't really care for any of them. I'll wait until the right guy comes along.

PORTIAS OF TODAY: Arianna Huffington, Ivanka Trump, Martha Stewart, Alicia in *The Good Wife*.

CHAPTER 3

The campus of the California Institute of Technology, known as Caltech to the world, wasn't beautiful, but it had its highlights. It was a hodgepodge of history, gravitas, and some unfortunate expansion during the '70s. A recent building-and-renovation spate had improved the balance of the campus somewhat, but very few of the three thousand–plus students, grad students, and professors really cared about the aesthetic of the institution. For them it was about the work, plain and simple. The quirky design, the jumbled labs that remained unchanged for decades, and the lecture rooms that still reverberated with the teachings of more than thirty Nobel Prize recipients, dozens of National Medal of Science honorees, and the occasional MacArthur Fellow better served the work than some picture-perfect campus.

As my mother always said, "All these Techies need is a slide rule and three meals a day, and they're happy. The rest is meaningless to them." I laughed thinking about my mother's assessment as I watched my father approach our table for our weekly lunch at the Athenaeum. The "Ath" was the private dining club on the Caltech campus that catered to the faculty and administration of the school, as well as a select list of community leaders from Pasadena at large. As opposed to my little office at Pasadena City College, the Athenaeum actually was Southern California meets Oxford, the building being a fine example of grand Mediterranean architecture filled with the handsomely worn appointments of a well-endowed club. It was built in 1930, with money cashed out of the stock market just before the crash, to serve as a social, ethical, and intellectual center for the city. The first event held in the club was a dinner in honor of Albert Einstein, newly arrived for a stint at Caltech. Many more illustrious dinners had been held over the decades, including, but not limited to, my sister Bumble's wedding.

My father, Dr. Richard Lancaster, fit in perfectly, thanks to my mother's refusal to allow him to descend into that scruffy academic look of short-sleeved, buttoned-down shirts and Birkenstocks favored by too many on campus. Instead, my father wore a daily uniform of a tweed jacket, white polo shirt, pressed khakis, and clean pair of Jack Purcell sneakers. He nodded in greeting to his fellow faculty members at their coveted "round tables" in the center of the large room—the engineers, the biologists, the applied mathematicians. The seating in the dining room was a neatly organized universe of hierarchical lunch buddies with some of the world's highest IQs.

Normally, my father sat with his fellow physicists to talk shop about string theory or nucleosynthesis or gravitational wave detection. But every Wednesday for the last five years, we shared a table for two and talked about movies, the news, academic politics, and tennis. Tennis was the only sport he played and the one sport he followed religiously. Now, we played and talked tennis together. I wish I could say it was something we'd done since my childhood, but honestly, it wasn't.

I had no interest in my father's life when I was growing up, except that it would occasionally take us to fantastic European destinations during summers, thanks to conferences and guest lectures. I would answer questions about him with vague statements like, "He's a science teacher" and "He works in a lab." Unlike my older sister Sarah, herself a scientist, researcher, and doctor, I couldn't understand my father's work, and unlike Bumble, a spinner of reality, I didn't appreciate its magnitude until I was in college. When I was in real grade trouble in Physics for Non-Science Majors, I managed to pass simply by dropping my father's name.

I think I can say with complete confidence that my father had very little interest in my childhood life, which was filled with school theater productions, books about history, and long sessions in front of the mirror, wondering why Bumble got the bouncy blond hair and I got the straight brunette stuff. We never really clashed, he and I, because we had so little in common.

But over the last decade, we'd found a connection, mainly because of our shared admiration for Roger Federer and my improved backhand. Best of all, even though I was at a community college and he taught at one of the most elite schools in the world, we had become colleagues of sorts.

"Hello, Elizabeth. Am I late?" Never, but he asked every week anyway.

"No, I was early. I'm ahead of you on iced teas, so order up."

He laughed and gestured over his shoulder. "Your mother's right behind me. She stopped at the desk to take care of reservations for some dinner months from now, that sort of thing. Probably telling the dining room what to serve that night. She'll be joining us today apparently. I'll flag down Ursula and have her move us to a bigger table."

Perfect. My mother. Or, as I thought of her, the Community Volunteer/Dynamic Faculty Wife/Self-appointed Arbiter of All that Is Right and Good. I wasn't in the mood. An encounter with Anne

Lancaster required me to be on my A game emotionally and sartorially. I was only at about a B-minus on this particular Wednesday. The FX situation had disturbed my sleep, and I wasn't ready to go public with his offer or my decision.

Add to that my newfound Pierce DeVine relationship, which would annoy my mother to no end, because she'd been trying for a year to get me to meet with her "lovely and tasteful" decorator Chantal, a woman in her mid-sixties whose devotion to chinoiserie far outweighed any consideration of comfort, practicality, or her clients' actual design preferences. My personal style didn't exactly scream, "Yes, I need more cane and bamboo chairs and a tufted ottoman!" I thought that was obvious to even the casual observer, but not to Anne Lancaster. I'd been dodging her offers to have Chantal swing by for a consultation, but now I'd have to come clean.

Plus, I was wearing Frye boots, and I knew my mother would surely comment on them.

Ursula, a server with decades of experience, moved us quickly, resetting my iced tea. "There you are, Doctors Lancaster. I assume you'd like the lunch buffet, but if you need anything off the menu, just let me know. I'll direct Mrs. Lancaster to your table."

"Let's go get our lunch," my father said gruffly. "It could take your mother an hour to make her way across the dining room. She'll stop at every table."

I knew he was right, especially when I spied the Caltech president, his impressive wife, and the mayor of Pasadena lunching together in the path of Hurricane Anne. That was twenty minutes right there, while she roped them all into one of her causes. She was chairing the Showcase House for the Arts this year, the mother of all local charities. My guess was that she'd sign up the trio to attend the opening reception, as all the proceeds went to music education—and really, who could object to music education? Well, Bumble's husband wasn't a fan of the arts, and he voted that way whenever he had the chance, but other than Congressman Ted, most citizens could agree that music education was a worthwhile cause.

By the time my father and I returned, my mother was seated and waiting, a trio of buffet salads in front of her. Ever since my father won the Nobel, she'd used her celebrity status to entice the servers to go through the lunch buffet for her and compile *"a mélange de trois salades"* rather than wait in the five-minute line herself. It drove me crazy, as the Ath was noted for its egalitarianism, but my father pretended not to notice.

"Hello, Elizabeth dear. I thought I threw those boots out when you went to grad school," she said, because she just couldn't help herself, and then she added with glowing eyes, "At least you're wearing shoes. Which is more than I can say for Sarah's twins."

Here we go again. My big sister Sarah is literally one of the finest people on the planet. She's a pediatric oncologist and researcher who works tirelessly to cure freaking cancer. She married the cute boy who sat next to her in calculus class in high school, Steven Chen, who is also a doctor. Sarah then gave birth to two wonderful daughters, Hope and Honor, names that would under most circumstances be considered highly pretentious. Except that Sarah is one of the finest people on the planet.

But in my mother's eyes, Sarah was committing an inexcusable offense by sending her kids to Redwood, the private school favored by Pasadena's moneyed artsy crowd who shunned test scores, dress codes, and mandatory footwear. The school and their child-rearing philosophy was a complete affront to All That Was Right and Good according to Anne Lancaster.

"I was at one of their pagan celebrations today...."

"I think it's called Earth Day, Mom."

"That's it. And none of the children were required to wear shoes. Never mind the uncombed hair and the pajamas that most of them seemed to be wearing. I just don't understand. Is proper footwear so awful? Did I ruin you girls with Stride-Rites? Richard?"

My father had stopped paying attention about the time he heard "pagan celebrations," so he resorted to his fallback conversational gambit. "Hmmph."

"I would just think that as a medical doctor, Sarah would be more concerned with her children's arch support and less concerned with free-form and, frankly, awful poems about trees," she summed up before moving on. "So, did your father tell you?"

My mother specialized in a verbal gambit I'd come to describe as the Hanging Tease. In short, it was as if every fact my mother had at her disposal was part of some gigantic galactic secret that she was the first to know. *Did you hear about the dean of admissions? Can you believe what happened at the committee meeting? I suppose you know about the new girl at my salon?* My answer to every Hanging Tease was always, "No, why would I know about that?" But what I really meant was, "No, why would I care about that?" My clear disdain never stopped her from teasing me anyway.

"No, Dad didn't have a chance to tell me much of anything yet."

"Richard?" She looked at him with mounting excitement. Richard did not respond in kind.

"My old college roommate is now the president of Redfield College," he admitted with some trepidation. "If you wanted to send him your resume...."

Aha. That's why she'd shown up uninvited. To remind me once again that teaching at a community college was somehow beneath the Lancaster family. Oh, my mother believed in equal education for all, but some education is more equal than others. And clearly Lancasters should be teaching/attending/being honored by the *more* equal schools.

My mother had been the smartest girl in her class at the Eastmont School for Girls in Pasadena. She went on to graduate summa cum laude from Scripps with a degree in biology. Having never been in a classroom with boys until grad school, she was shocked to discover that women were not held in universally high regard. She met my father, then a doctoral candidate at Berkeley, when she was completing her masters as the token female in her department. In another time and place, like if she'd been born twenty years later, she herself might have been the Nobel laureate. But the women's lib movement didn't make it into the sciences early enough to get her off the faculty-wife track and onto the faculty. She taught middle school science for several years before "succumbing to motherhood" (as she liked to say when we were in earshot) when my father's postdoc took him to Oxford. Now, she spent an inordinate amount of time on worthy community projects in the sphere of education, science, and children. But it wasn't quite the same as actually being a professor.

Hence her focus on my career.

"Thanks. I'll think about it, Dad," I responded, turning to face him directly. There, addressed and tabled. Moving on?

No such luck. "Why would you not at least explore the possibility? Redfield is a very fine school where they appreciate Shakespeare." Anne Lancaster would not be silenced with a "thanks, but no thanks" response.

Of course, she was right about Redfield, a small liberal arts college outside of Portland, Oregon, that had seen its ranking rocket up the charts in recent years, thanks to hefty donations from moneyed alumni in the Pacific Northwest, which allowed the school to attract high-profile professors in the math and writing departments, not to mention a very good lacrosse coach. It was now on the radar of prep-school guidance counselors and savvy East Coast parents looking for a West Coast alternative to Middlebury and Colby. A decade ago, Redfield might have been a dream school for me, but now I was too entrenched in my job and my life in Pasadena to seriously consider a move.

"My students appreciate Shakespeare, and so does the administration. I like what I do and where I do it. I have a chance to teach kids who will go onto some very fine schools themselves. They're smart kids, too." This was my broken-record answer to her frequent queries about my "stalled academic trajectory." "Plus, do you know how many women with doctorates in English are wandering around looking for work? I'm lucky to have this job."

"I know. It's just that you're always fighting to keep your classes on the schedule. You have to teach those remedial writing classes just to earn a living. The whole community college system is a mess because of all the budgets cuts. Maybe a private college would be a more stable environment. Not so much scrapping for respect."

"I like scrapping," I said, taking a swig of iced tea for emphasis.

"Atta girl," my father said, clearly eager to change the subject himself. "See, Anne, I told you she wouldn't go for it."

"You act like I'm suggesting she fly off to Timbuktu. It's just that you could be so much more…never mind. I'm sorry I mentioned it."

"As a matter of fact, I got a fantastic job offer this week to work in Ashland all summer with a top-notch director and cast on a very exciting new production of *Midsummer*. And I'm in discussions to write a book. I have an agent who's very interested." I regretted my words a nanosecond after they were out. Why did I weaken?

My father perked up and my mother looked about ready to burst. "How wonderful!" Anne Lancaster was on the offensive already.

I could see the wheels spinning inside her head. This was a month's worth of Hanging Teases to use while gossiping with friends at her salon. *I suppose you heard with whom Elizabeth is working this summer? I assume you're familiar with the Taz Buchanan production of* Midsummer *in Ashland? You know my daughter Elizabeth has the book coming out?*

"Let's get Ursula to bring us some champagne!" she announced, waving over the server with the grandest of gestures.

Yes. Let's.

"What you need is a husband or a dog," my sister Sarah offered the next day while tossing her yoga mat into the back of her Volvo.

Our weekly Saturday-afternoon class at Yoga Haus had managed to fully relax her and fully rile me up. I'd filled her in on the FX situation and the aftermath. "You need a distraction so Mom doesn't focus on your work. Bumble and I have other people in our lives that she can criticize, so it's like a career-discussion buffer. She never comments on my work choices because...."

"Because she's so busy commenting on the twins' footwear choices," I finished. "Or the fact that your children attend an inferior version of Hogwarts."

Sarah laughed. "Exactly. Sometimes I do that stuff on purpose to throw her off. Like the paper napkins at family dinners. I know that makes her nuts, but I do it anyway so she doesn't talk about my mediocre cooking." Sarah had the right amount of perspective. I felt I was losing mine on almost all fronts. "You know, you don't have to go to Ashland just because you panicked and told Mom and Dad that you were. You are a grownup, Elizabeth."

That was the problem. Ever since FX had shown up uninvited and put the Ashland offer on the table, I felt my emotional age regress to about twenty-two. An age, I might add, at which I made some spectacularly bad decisions, like getting married. The outburst at lunch with my parents was just another example of my maturity regression. I hadn't felt the need to prove myself to my mother in years, and then all of a sudden, boom! Look at me! I'm going to Ashland. I'm writing a book! What was next? A repeat of the Rachel haircut?

"What do you think I should do?" I asked with all sincerity. Sarah always had good solid advice. She was a good-solid-advice machine. Sign the divorce papers and come home, she'd told me. And that's exactly what I did. Teach what you love wherever you can get work, she'd said. The next month, I landed a gig at PCC teaching Shakespeare. Stop drinking all that diet soda or you'll pay for it in twenty years. I switched to green tea and have never felt better. Sarah would know what I should do.

"About Mom? Or FX?"

"FX."

"You said you'd already decided not to do it, then you had lunch with Mom. So you've made your decision, right?"

Had I? I had, but it didn't feel quite certain anymore. When I told my parents about my mostly fictional groundbreaking *Midsummer*/book deal, I'd failed to mention FX. As a result, I'd started to get excited about the prospect of actually working on a groundbreaking Shakespeare production and possibly getting a book deal. It all sounded so good in the FX-free version that I felt my resolve wavering.

"Well...."

"Elizabeth, if you want to go to Ashland, go to Ashland. You're a totally different person now than you were when you lost your mind and married your college boyfriend. You're a professor, your students love you, you have tons of friends and family who care about you. You can handle FX." Sarah rattled her keys in her signature I've-got-to-go-and-cure-cancer move, signaling the end of the conversation.

"So you think I should do it? Take the job and go to Ashland?"

"I don't think you're as vulnerable as you think you are." See, there was that super-solid Sarah advice. So I felt compelled to confess, "I had a dream last night and FX was in it. And he was naked."

"Oh, that's not good. Maybe you should just stay home and get a dog."

There were two packages at my front door when I got home, which wasn't unusual due to my Etsy addiction. But both of the boxes appeared to be hand delivered, which made me suspicious. Ever since my short fascination with all things Unabomber in college, my delight over unexpected mail was forever changed. I approached with caution.

Nothing was ticking or emitting a pungent odor, so I decided to bring them inside to extend the opening process. I enjoy practicing delayed gratification whenever I have the chance, and this seemed like the perfect occasion. The sun was setting, signaling another Saturday night alone. If I milked the gift-opening process, it could practically be considered a date. I made the most of my post-yoga glow, brewed a cup of tea, and poured a glass of wine as backup. I turned on some music and found my kitchen shears, though the ribbons looked too pretty to cut.

The first box was metallic silver with a pure white bow and a small card tucked under the ribbon. I opened it slowly. Let's light up the stage. Come to Ashland. – – FX. Also in the envelope was his agent's card again, as if I'd lost the number.

Inside the box was a beautiful hand-blown votive in a deep rose color with accent stripes of orange. Clearly, the votive was one of a kind, as evidenced by the signature on the bottom. The artist had even included a tea light. I dug some matches out of my junk drawer and lit it immediately. The votive glowed, throwing long pink shadows on my walls.

FX was wooing me. I liked it. In a professional sense, of course. But dash-dash FX? What did that mean? In a professional sense, of course.

I turned my attention to the larger, rectangular package and got excited when I saw the small logo in the corner: PDV in embossed gold. What could Pierce DeVine be sending me? My mind raced as I carefully untied the miles of gold ribbon. Antique tea towels? Heirloom tomato seeds? A photo album of himself? Unfortunately, none of the above. It was his estimate for the work.

And it was astounding.

Like fancy-sports-car astounding.

But underneath the estimate were his drawings of what my little casa would look like after it received the Pierce DeVine treatment. And those, too, were astounding. Just what I'd asked for, only better, because it was impeccable and rendered in three dimensions. A tasteful addition, a few opened walls, and a new window to look out over my garden. Plus, the almighty dishwasher I longed for. He'd sketched in my furniture, artwork, even the antique quilt. In a short note, he wrote: We will make La Casita de Girasole bloom. You'll never want to leave home. As it should be. XOXO PDV

Ah, as it should be, PDV. Pierce had managed to capture my vision completely.

All for the price of a luxury automobile.

I went through the drawings again and again by the light of the rose-colored candle. By now, I'd settled onto the couch and moved onto the wine. I wanted to live in those drawings, to grow old in those drawings. My life would be a Nancy Meyers movie, and I'd age as gracefully as Meryl Streep. I'd spend convivial evenings in my kitchen with my attractive family and friends, who were also aging well. We'd cook elaborate meals and drink wine out of oversized goblets. We'd have erudite conversations and listen to Mozart, even though I really preferred music with words. Maybe FX would co-star in my Nancy Meyers movie, as the charming ex-husband who forever carries a torch for me. And because I was so grounded, like Meryl, I could handle his attention and still attract a swarm of charming gentlemen callers. Life was good in those drawings.

I deserved to live in those drawings. I deserved that dishwasher, that life.

So I picked up the phone and did what I had to do to make that happen: compromise my integrity and ignore the gnawing feeling in my gut.

I called FX's agent and left a message. I wanted to set a meeting for Monday.

FAKE THE SHAKE

6 Great Lines Guys Should Steal

LINE: "It gives me great content to see you here before me. My soul's joy!"
FROM: *Othello*
WHAT HE MEANS: Seeing you, babe, is the best part of my day.

LINE: "Hear my soul speak. The very instant that I saw you, did my heart fly to your service; there resides to make me slave to it."
FROM: *The Tempest*
WHAT HE MEANS: Love at first sight and he is doomed. And so are you. Watch out. Could be a stalker.

LINE: "Sin from thy lips? Oh trespass sweetly urged. Give me my sin again."
FROM: *Romeo & Juliet*
WHAT HE MEANS: Seriously? You need to ask? He wants it again.

LINE: "Come woo me, woo me, for I am in holiday humor and like enough to consent."
FROM: *As You Like It*
WHAT HE MEANS: Hey, we're both here on vacation and we've both drunk too much Jagermeister. Wanna hook up?

LINE: "Whoever loved that loved not at first sight?"
FROM: *As You Like It*
WHAT HE MEANS: Pretty self-explanatory, unless it comes from your oral surgeon during a root canal. If a guy tries this one on you, definitely give him a chance.

LINE: "When you do dance, I wish you a wave o' the sea, that you might ever do nothing but that."
FROM: *The Winter's Tale*
WHAT HE MEANS: Girl, you look gooooood on that dance floor.

CHAPTER 4

I took the coward's way out.

I could have made explanatory phone calls to family and friends about why I had decided to spend the summer working closely with my ex-husband under intense circumstances in a small, remote town in Oregon. Or I could just show up at the biggest social schmooze of the year, ex-husband in tow, and let them figure it out for themselves. I chose the latter.

Really, who was going to question my sanity in front of *le tout* Pasadena? Not even my mother, the benefit co-chair, would let a scowl cross her face, so terrified was she of an unflattering photo on her night of nights.

Thanks to my cowardice, FX and I were in a Prius limo headed to the event, like we were just another couple and this was an everyday occurrence. FX, wearing his producer hat, was on the phone to Somebody at the Studio discussing the poster for the Washington movie. I listened to the conversation with one ear, amazed at how long people could discuss fonts.

Over the course of the week, I'd been sucked into the vortex that is FX Fahey. The meeting with his agent was exhausting in its Hollywoodness. There were seven people in the sleek, high-rent conference room: five men in suits, FX, and me. The Suits introduced themselves but handed out no cards, assuring that I would never remember any of their names, except Hank, who appeared to be the Number One Suit in FX's world. A credenza on the far side of the room held an array of fresh muffins, juice, and fruit salad, despite the fact that snacking of this sort had gone out of fashion in 1997. I was dying for one of those muffins, exactly the kind of oversize baked good that those of us in the public sector never had access to in our work environment. But I couldn't have six men watch me eat a muffin.

Having proven myself to be a terrible negotiator in the past with FX, I'd Googled "How to write a Hollywood deal memo" before the meeting. After eleven rewrites, I possessed a sheet of paper outlining everything I wanted, including a fee that I assumed was at least three times what FX expected to pay. After opening chitchat and some vague creative discussions, I preempted any offer that FX might have put together by sliding my deal memo across the extremely large conference table toward the Suited Ones.

"Look at you. All ready to go," FX said, picking up my memo with a smile on his face. A face sporting the perfect three-day growth.

"I have people, too," I responded. "Esquires Google and eHow."

The Suits laughed. FX nodded. "So this is it? Accommodations, per diem, and the fee. This looks doable. Hank?"

Hank, in a blue shirt–and–blue tie combo, gave it a quick once-over. "Looks good. We'll get this going. My assistant Yvonne will send the paperwork. Let me know if there's anything else that comes up. It's great to have a scholar like yourself onboard."

A scholar like myself? Yes, exactly, that's what I was: a Shakespearean scholar. I had done it! Gotten my kitchen and then some. I was satisfied but nonetheless made a mental note not to mention the ease of the agreement to Bumble. Clearly I could have gotten more, maybe much more. I didn't want her to yell at me for, once again, being taken in by FX.

As the Suits turned their backs and headed out the door, I shoved that orange cranberry muffin in my messenger bag.

My confidence was surging, so I contacted the agent's assistant who once thought my take on Shakespearean romances could be turned into a self-help book for literate women. A few years ago at a conference she'd heard me give a paper entitled *Will Shakespeare Meets Bridget Jones: Romantic Comedy Then & Now*. It was a big hit with the women in the crowd and a fun bit of scholarship for me. Over drinks in the hotel lobby, the young go-getter had said, "This is a book! It's a book! You know, like *Shakespeare in Love*. But literally." I promised to be in touch and then proceeded to do nothing for years.

But buoyed by my *Midsummer* deal, I found her e-mail address and whipped the unfocused ideas that had been bouncing around in my head for years into a laser-sharp one-page pitch for a book called *All's Fair: A Shakespearean Guide to Contemporary Life and Modern Relationship*s. I hinted at chapter ideas based on archetypal couples like Rosalind and Orlando ("Blinded by Love"); the Macbeths ("the Power Couple Corrupted"); and Silvius and Phoebe ("Straight Women Who Fall for Gay Men"). There would be lighthearted how-tos on flirting with double entendres, swordplay as foreplay, and cross-dressing to get your man. I outlined a section on Faking the Shake, or how to impress your friends with references to the Bard while knowing next to nothing about the Bard. To gild the lily, I tossed in shameless references to FX Fahey and Taz Buchanan. Without overthinking, a first for me, I hit "send" and off my pitch went to NYC.

Melissa Bergstrom-Bennett, the once assistant to an agent and now a junior agent herself, replied immediately. Her e-mail started with the headline: FX FAHEY IS YOUR EX-HUSBAND!!! WILL HE BLURB IT?

Ms. Bergstrom-Bennett said she'd love to take a look at a full book proposal. She managed to mention things like zeitgeist, Pippa Middleton, and *Downton Abbey* in her reply, which, frankly, didn't make sense in the context of my pitch, but I tried to make a connection. Make it highbrow and British, but not too highbrow, because it needed to appeal to American women. Oh, and she added, "Sex up the title, because *All's Fair* sounds like a book about divorce settlements." Got it, MB-B.

On the surface, I was making the kind of bold, brave career choices I'd never made before. But there in the Prius limo, I was starting to feel a little sick to my stomach. It was a lot to pull off, starting with this evening. Maybe my strategy for informing the world of this arrangement was a mistake. But, as my depressive colleague in the English Department always said whenever a faculty member expressed concern about something, "Will anyone die? No? So, really, how big a deal could it be?"

Right. All that was happening was a play and a book. Nobody would die during the production of either.

I hoped.

"So what is this thing we're going to?" FX suddenly piped up, tucking his phone into his pocket, typeface conversation complete. He was used to being led around on press junkets by PR girls in short skirts and headsets, so he hadn't asked any questions when I suggested that we make this appearance.

We'd spent the afternoon in his hotel suite at the W, breaking down *Midsummer* act by act. I took him through my interpretation of certain scenes and passages that underscored the notion that although the play is a comedy, it says some pretty deep things about love. I explained that Shakespeare's central theme is the difficulty of love, and he explored that theme through the motifs of disharmony, disparities between romantic partners, and the inequalities in the relationships of the main characters. And finally, it deals with how most of us have been guilty of being blinded by fairy dust in previous relationships. (That hit home. After talking through that theme, FX ordered two beers from room service.) Really, I concluded, the whole point of *Midsummer* could be summed up by the play's most famous line: *The course of true love never did run smooth.*

FX was an excellent student, listening, underlining passages, and asking good questions. His focus impressed me. In our student and married days, he was a let's-wing-it kind of actor, getting by on looks and energy. He learned his lines and had excellent diction and stage presence, of course, but the emotional work behind the characters wasn't always there. Apparently he'd matured. Maybe he really did become Washington, staying in character for weeks at a time as was reported on *Access Hollywood*. He was leaving in the morning for New York to meet with Taz Buchanan, and he wanted to be ready. He wanted Taz on his team. If all went well, the next time I'd see him would be in Ashland. At the end of our session, I tossed out the idea of a quick trip to Pasadena. He bit.

"It's one of those designer showcase houses. My mother—you remember her? Anne?—she's the chair of the benefit tonight. A last-minute replacement when the original chair Buffy Stevens went down with an extreme case of lockjaw. Anyway, it's a big deal in Pasadena and my whole family is showing up. Even my brother-in-law, Ted Seymour, the congressman. Maybe you've seen him on Bill Maher? I thought it would be fun to re-introduce you to everybody. I'm sure they'd love to see you again," I lied.

"I doubt that," FX answered, surely remembering the awful scene in our New York apartment when he walked in on Bumble packing up my stuff. I was too comatose to label boxes, but Bumble was in full fury. For years, I've tried to block out the image of her blotchy red face as she just kept repeating, "You suck, Francis!" over and over again. It was the most inarticulate Bumble has ever been. And I don't think FX was completely convinced that he did suck. He registered only slight annoyance as he changed from one black

T-shirt into another without a word and went back to rehearsal for an off-Broadway play. Now, years later, he was willing to face her and the rest of the family. "Just tell me what I'm supposed to do and I'll do it." He sat up straight and shook his head, running his fingers through his hair, like he was getting ready to go onstage in the next breath.

Showtime.

One of the oldest home-and-garden events in the country, the Pasadena Showcase House for the Arts could be described in one word: venerable. And there is nothing that Pasadenans appreciate more than venerable. The Rose Parade. A Wallace Neff house. The apricot chicken salad at Vivienne's. All venerable, all good. The Showcase House, as it was called, neatly fit into the same category as all of the above because of its enduring, impeccable taste and the millions that had been raised for music education.

Every year, the Showcase House was a massive undertaking in scale and ambition, executed by an army of well-suited female volunteers. First, a house large enough and spectacular enough to be worthy was identified. Then the committee got to work convincing the traffic-weary neighbors that months of trucks and tourists would be worth the inconvenience when their property values soared afterward. (Let's not even discuss the year that forty disgruntled neighbors on a certain street stormed the planning committee meeting and blocked the permitting process. Never before and never again, vowed the Showcase women.) After they secured the house, got permits in place, signed contracts with designers, and chose a color palette, the full-scale renovation of house and gardens took place, thanks to the generosity of local designers, contractors, and suppliers. When the remodeled house was unveiled to the public, a month of parties and public tours followed. Hundreds of volunteers who believed in the cause endured many hours on their feet in flat-soled shoes while they guarded the overly appointed Gentleman's Library or the whimsical Children's Tea Room.

Our exit from the Prius caused a mild stir among the crowd out in front, FX being so immediately recognizable and me being so vaguely familiar. The buzz drew the attention of Team Lancaster, who raised their eyebrows and dropped their jaws in unison, like a synchronized swim team out of water. I had certainly captured the element of surprise.

There was no red carpet, but my mother had commandeered the front hall of the 1926 Georgian Colonial house to stage a receiving line, as if she were a bride. My sisters Bumble and Sarah, the twins Honor and Hope (fully shod), and Bumble's lovely stepdaughter Maddie formed a phalanx of Lancasters around my mother. Congressman Ted Seymour (R-CA) anchored the end of the line. There he was, shaking hands and displaying his patented "I'm one of the good guys" smile. My father, never one to enjoy socializing with non-scientists, stood separately in quiet conversation with my other brother-in-law, who was fresh from work at the hospital.

Alone against the back wall stood a very attractive dark-haired guy in a blue suit who I assumed was one of Ted's aides. Mr. Blue Suit and I locked eyes for a second, and I suddenly felt wildly conspicuous, like a complete fraud arriving with a movie star. *Focus, Elizabeth.*

I executed the same head shake/shoulder set that FX had pulled in the car and started talking. "We're here. It looks fabulous, Mom! Look, I brought FX. Great news! I'm working with FX this summer in Ashland. He insisted on coming tonight to say hi to all of you. He really wants to support this fantastic cause!" I babbled like nobody's babbled before. I just kept talking until their collective blood pressures visibly lowered, then I slowed to a stop.

"Mom, you remember FX?"

"I was his mother-in-law, Elizabeth. I do recall him." Oh, Anne

Lancaster was bowed, but she was not broken. My mother offered FX her hand to shake, literally holding him at arm's length. Yet despite her outward coldness, there was a twinkle of merriment in her eye. This was a huge PR score for her. FX accepted it graciously, saying, "Mrs. Lancaster, you've done a wonderful job here for a wonderful cause. Thank you for welcoming me."

I had flashbacks of Cotillion circa 1989, me in a pink Gunne Sax atrocity and Timmy Van Eyke in a blue blazer two sizes too small shaking the bony hand of scary Mitsy Fairchild during the punch-and-cookie introduction portion of the evening.

I turned to my stone-faced father. "Dad?"

"Francis, what a surprise," my father said, reaching out to shake hands with equal parts dignity and disdain. Even FX looked nervous. I quickly ran through the other introductions, ending with Congressman Ted, who saw every new face as a potential supporter.

Ted gave FX a big smile. "I'm a big fan."

"As I am of yours," FX countered.

Lies are the glue that keep a family together.

Just then, the photographer from the local society newspaper *Look Out Pasadena!* stuck a camera into the proceedings. "Can I get a Lancaster family photo now that you're all here? Congressman Seymour? Dr. Lancaster, please?" The cute young thing in the jaunty newsboy chapeau tried to corral the group. "Wow, FX Fahey. I can't believe I'm meeting you. Your *Icarus* movies changed my life. After seeing the very first one when I was like eight, I knew I wanted to go to film school and blow people's minds."

And there you have it. Standing next to a member of Congress and a Nobel Prize winner, it was the actor who got the props. No irony was ever lost on my family. Bumble rolled her eyes and said, "Here he is, FX Fahey, agent of change." Then she whispered viciously in my ear, "Don't think I hadn't heard. Sarah told me you were wavering. I hope you know what you're doing. Oh, and I have something I need to ask you later. Find me."

"Okay, everybody look here please," shouted Newsboy Cap, snapping the fingers of one hand above her head, while with the other she held the camera to her eye. "Big smile, Lancaster family. Big smile."

POWER COUPLE #2

Oberon & Titania

FROM *A MIDSUMMER NIGHT'S DREAM*

HER: Queen of the Fairies and force to be reckoned with. Sassy, sexy, and proud. Uses her magic to get what she wants. Good dancer.

HIM: King of the Fairies, but he likes the ladies. One of the original players who enjoys the sport of the chase. Not above using a little black magic to win over a woman. Can be a jealous jerk, but that only makes him sexier. Suspiciously close relationship to Puck.

RELATIONSHIP HISTORY: Extremely turbulent. On again, off again, sometimes in the same scene. Custody battle over child/changeling. Epic fights that can upset the natural world, literally. Great make-up sex.

RELATIONSHIP LOW POINT: Oberon uses his magic to make Titania fall in love with a horse's ass. Really, a guy named Bottom wearing a donkey head.

WHY THEY WORK: Open marriage—very open. Use of performance-enhancing drugs. Barely clothed most of the time.

HIS HOTTEST LINE: "Ill met by moonlight, Proud Titania."

HER HOTTEST LINE: "What angel wakes me from my flowery bed?"

SHAKESPEAREAN COUPLE MOST LIKELY TO: Have a reality show.

WHO THEY REMIND YOU OF: That couple who lived down the hall from you sophomore year who had huge fights, broke up, and then got back together. Then another huge fight, breakup, and reconciliation. Or Carrie and Big.

CHEMISTRY FACTOR: 4 OUT OF 5

CHAPTER 5

Now that the Revelation by Fire portion of the evening was over, I was greatly enjoying the furtive glances and open stares from the other guests, so many of whom had doubted the "rumor" that I was once married to FX Fahey. I'd heard the whispers of disbelief more than once in my life when I was huddled in a bathroom stall at a bar/restaurant/reunion/wedding. My short marriage had become a sort of urban myth in Pasadena. But tonight, proof had arrived in a Prius, wearing a Dolce & Gabbana suit.

The crowd was the typical assortment of designers, money, and media, the sort of people who mixed easily in Pasadena. There was the old guard sporting their Bill Blass jackets over black or white pants, sipping wine and scanning for fellow country clubbers. The designers tended to be younger and hipper, but not so hip that they alienated their clients, who preferred Schumacher to steampunk. And the media was local, chummy, and in the bag for an event like the Showcase House.

Pierce DeVine was holding court near the deep blue pool; even though I could only see him from behind, I'd recognize the shape of his perfect head anywhere. When I dropped off the signed contract and the first of many checks, he told me he only committed to a guest bathroom in "the House" this year because, and I quote, "Those committee ladies will bleed a designer dry. Let somebody else do the kitchen for free." (Charity work really brings out the best in people.) Presumably, Pierce used his third eye to sense the presence of a movie star, because he turned, mid-conversation, to acknowledge us with a namaste gesture. I bowed my head in return, before realizing how ridiculous I must have looked.

I spotted several Divorced Dads in the crowd checking me out with new interest. These were the men my friends had set me up with because, as Shelly Bixby told me, "It's hard to find someone on the first go-round at your age." True, Shelly, but I was child-free, which I thought put me in a "more single" category than a man with two kids in grade school. Unfortunately, there weren't many men in Pasadena who'd had the good sense to divorce before they procreated like I did, so I made a few mistakes before I figured out that dating a divorced dad meant never getting to say, "I don't care about youth sports."

I caught the eye of one ex named Minot Stewart, or as I liked to call him, "the law firm of Minot Stewart." Minot was, in fact, a lawyer who was also very earnest and in way over his head with his two children on their every other week. His first wife left him for her trainer, which was so '90s it was almost too pathetic to believe. But he did have excellent manners and a healthy smile, which went a long way in my book. For the first few weeks, it looked like Minot might be one of the few Divorced Dads who could separate dating and parenting. We had a honeymoon period in which he barely mentioned travel-team tryouts or summer-camp plans. My first encounters with his daughters, Zoe and Chloe, were brief, fun, and enjoyable. Look at me, I thought—instant family!

But then Minot started treating me like a nanny, calling me from work on Friday to pick up his girls and get them to softball because he was "stuck on a phone call." Or asking me to buy gifts because the girls had to go to a birthday party and I would know what to get the birthday girl better than he would. I ended the relationship after one terrifying Saturday morning at a petting zoo with Zoe and Chloe while Minot "played golf with a client." (Really, if I wanted to be abandoned on a weekend morning for the golf course, I'd have to sign a prenup first.) I liked kids; I just didn't want to date them. When I broke it off, his first words were, "Does that mean you can't cover ballet practice on Thursday?"

But my loss was kindergarten teacher Suzy Badalian's gain. She swooped in and snagged Minot on the rebound, scoring a ring the next Christmas. A kindergarten teacher was the perfect choice to schlep his girls to ballet.

Now, happily married and self-satisfied, Suzy and Minot were trying really hard not look at FX and me as we weaved through the crowd. I busted them with a big wave in their direction.

My favorite reaction of the night was the neck-craning double take executed by Muffin O'Meara O'Malley, creator of four perfect children and a line of cashmere spa wear (Double O'M) that had just been sold into Neimans. Muffin had graciously set me up with not one but two of her banker husband's partners, mainly out of pity with a touch of politics. (Her husband wanted a face-to-face with Congressman Ted.) The setups had failed miserably, and the face-to-face had never happened, partly because I was too lazy to follow up with Ted and partly because I wanted to punish Muffin a little bit for taking the lead role in Pippin away from me in eleventh grade. We'd been mutually avoiding each other for months.

But tonight, Muffin was all graciousness and charm. After recovering from her initial reaction, she rushed over to greet me, bussing me pretentiously on both cheeks, then grabbing FX's right hand in a double-clutch pump shake. Without letting go, she informed us that she had just returned from London, where everyone was talking about the Washington movie. What one had to do with the other, I wasn't sure, but FX humbly accepted her praise, then exited to the bar with a gentle bow.

Muffin forced her death grip on me. "Oh, you bad girl. No wonder it didn't work out with George or Ramesh. You've been recycling, as the kids say." I was pretty sure the kids didn't say that, but I smiled conspiratorially. Arriving casually with my famous ex-husband was exactly the sort of personality rehab I needed in this town. I'd gone from Still Single to Still Happening in an instant.

"That's me, Elizabeth the Bad Girl. Who doesn't feel good about recycling? Excuse me, Muffin. I see that Bumble needs an intervention, and that's what sisters do for each other!" And with that I was off to rescue Bumble, who'd been cornered by one of the Showcase neighbors, who was a large donor to her husband's campaigns. Her previous career in PR had served her well in her relatively new role as the wife of a congressman. She did a lot of the Stand & Nod and the Smile & Laugh, as well as the Stare in Adoration, all performances she had perfected while representing celebrities. Currently, as Bumble stood listening to helmet-headed Adelaide Martin, she was performing the Agree & Move On, which was executed with lot of nodding and a steady stream of "Uh-hmmns."

When she and Ted were first married, about seven years ago, Bumble fashioned herself after Maria Shriver, the First Lady of California at the time. So many parallels, it was eerie, Bumble used to say. (Him a Republican; her a Democrat. Him a Republican; her with good hair.) But since Arnold and Maria's spectacular marital meltdown, she fashioned herself after Kate Middleton, which seemed a little grandiose. But what did I know about being the adoring spouse?

I was good at being the buffer sister, though. "Hello, Mrs. Martin. It's great to see you! Isn't the house wonderful? I think it's almost as big as yours, but not as stately! I hate to do this, but I have to steal Bumble away. My mother needs her. Please say hello to Betsy for me. Her Christmas card this year was beautiful. I've never seen white linen on children look so pressed!" I took Bumble by the elbow and led her out toward the gardens to hunt for FX, who had disappeared, and to find out why she had to talk to me.

"Thank you. She was going on and on about getting speed bumps put in on her street. Honestly, what does she think Ted does? Work at the Department of Public Works? The worst part of it is that because she's such a big donor, I'm actually going to have to put in a call about the speed bumps. Let's get a drink. I've talked to enough constituents tonight."

Bumble was working her way through the crowd with two white wines when I spotted FX on the veranda chatting up Candy McKenna. Do all famous people have some internal GPS that leads them to other famous people?

Truthfully, Candy was only very famous in zip codes 91101 to 91107. She was a disgraced Rose Queen who lost her favored-citizen status when she posed for *Playboy*'s Women of the Ivy League issue in the late '80s. An elephant never forgets and neither does a local, so Candy's personal comeback was never as complete as Vanessa Williams's, but her star was on the rise again. Years ago, she'd started a local gossip website called candysdish.com, a cleverly written look at the upper crust in Southern California with only a touch of snark. It started off serving, or skewering, the Pasadena community, but she soon wormed her way into Hollywood coverage, making the best use of her good looks, media savvy, and focus on celebrity charity events, as opposed to movie openings and awards shows. Now every big charity event got the candysdish treatment, complete with who was there, what they were wearing, and what was served for dinner, all wrapped in a big red feel-good bow. Somehow it humanized the celebs, making them seem just like other rich people, and they loved Candy for it.

No doubt, FX was laying the groundwork for the *Dire Necessity* Oscar campaign. I'd come to know Candy a bit through Bumble, and I liked her a lot. She was one of the few people in town who really didn't care what others thought of her.

Personally, my favorite section on candysdish.com was called "Why the Sour Face?" It was a delicious weekly roundup of socialites and their husbands caught bickering in public at yet another fundraiser. Each week, Candy and her secret army of cell phone cameras found couples locked in marital death glares. When I was feeling down and out about being single, I'd check "Why the Sour Face?" and gloat over a snapshot of Jennifer Lewis Tanner, my swim-team nemesis, berating her poor (but loaded, both in money and liquor) husband Tim Tanner at the Cloverfield auction after he bid ten thousand dollars for a shih tzu puppy that JLT clearly did not want. Those moments alone in front of my computer on a Saturday night convinced me that single is a very fine status.

Bumble had spotted FX with Candy, too. "He's in good hands. Or so I've heard about Candy," Bumble quipped as she slugged back some wine. "Watch him."

"This is a work relationship only. If he wants to be the fourth Mr. Candy McKenna, I have no problem with that. He does look good, doesn't he?"

"He's a movie star. That's his job. But yes, he looks good," she conceded. "I still don't think it's a good idea."

"It's your fault. I'm a victim here. You know how much a Pierce DeVine remodel costs. I had to take the work!"

Bumble laughed. "At least you're getting something out of it this time. More than I can say for your marriage. And, speaking of marriage...."

Here we go. The real reason Bumble wanted to talk to me.

"You know Ted and I have been trying to get pregnant and so far, no luck. Not that it's easy with him being on the other side of the country half the year."

I had to admit, being married to a congressman was not the slightest bit glamorous. Ted Seymour was a successful real estate developer who wandered into politics without much long-term planning. Good-looking, articulate, and a diplomat to the core, he stepped into a race for Congress when the chosen candidate admitted to hiring illegal immigrants for his cleaning-service empire. (Illegal immigrants cleaning bathrooms? What a shocker!) Enter Ted Seymour, fiscally conservative but socially liberal, just the kind of Republican that Californians liked. He was a single dad raising a young daughter when his campaign hired Bumble to run some fundraisers. She swears the last thing on her mind was any kind of relationship, but I'm pretty sure she gave the Seymour campaign a very low bid for her work to get in front of Ted. He was elected, and six months later, he and Bumble were married.

The honeymoon was short, very short. Bumble immediately became Ted's political surrogate and full-time fundraiser in Pasadena while he commuted back and forth to DC. But the biggest adjustment was becoming a stepmother to then ten-year-old Maddie. Ted could be gone for weeks at a time, and it was Bumble who held down the home front, stepping into the unfamiliar world of school volunteering, parent-teacher conferences, and weekend debate competitions. I give her a lot of credit. Lesser females would have crumbled under the microscope of Pasadena's competitive parenting posse, not to mention the bright lights of politics. Not Bumble. She just got Botox.

But I knew Bumble was lonely, and the stress of infertility was starting to take its toll. (The other day I caught her shoving a Ding Dong in her mouth at a gas station.) So where did I come into their infertility issues? I braced myself for the ask.

"I need you to take Maddie to Ashland with you this summer.

She won't go back to camp. She doesn't want to go on another one of those expensive fake mission programs to Guatemala. And God knows, her mother can't be bothered to forego her *very important* work in Reiki healing at that commune she lives in." Bumble was not a fan of Maddie's birth mother, a trust-fund hippie who bailed on the family when Maddie was a toddler and moved to Sun Valley. "You know I love Maddie, but I need her out of the house. This is it. I feel like it's our last shot at getting pregnant, and that means Summer Sexapalooza. Ted and I can't do that if Maddie's around."

Wow, I so did not want to picture Congressman Ted in a "Summer Sexapalooza." Now that I knew about their plan, I was glad I wasn't going to be around as a witness. Still, I wasn't sure I had the skills to entertain Maddie all summer. "You know I think Maddie's great. She smart and studious, a cool girl…."

"She could be your intern! She could help you do research for your book. Or help you backstage. Or do whatever interns do. Please, Elizabeth. We'll pay her expenses, even give her a salary that you could say was from you. She likes you and she loves the theater. And if you asked her, it wouldn't seem like it was my idea."

Bumble was pleading, honestly pleading. I did love Maddie. We always had fun when she spent the weekend when Bumble went off to Washington for a few days. She reminded me of me at seventeen: preferring books to boys and engaged in just enough intellectual snobbery to make her interesting but not standoffish. We'd bonded over Jane Austen novels and Zac Efron movies. Plus, her birth mother's behavior annoyed me beyond belief. How could you walk away from your daughter because you felt "suffocated"? Maybe I could use an intern.

"Okay, I'll ask her to come with me. But understand that I have work to do, so I can't watch her every minute. I can't babysit. And, if she doesn't want to come, I'm out. I'd be happy to have a willing intern, but not forced labor. Only if Maddie really wants to come. Understood?"

"Thank you, Elizabeth." Bumble hugged me. Then added, "Oh, and if you let Maddie fall for FX, I will kill you."

The real Bumble was back. "I can't help it if a teenage girl gets a crush on a movie star, okay? But, of course, I'll warn him and keep an eye on her. There will be a lot of attractive actors, so it's not just FX you have to worry about."

"Oh, that's not Maddie's thing. Really, she's too smart for that."

Well, she wasn't too smart to devour the *Twilight* books, because we both enjoyed those a few years ago. Bumble was boy crazy by age ten, so a girl like Maddie, who'd never been out with a boy, was a mystery to her. But not to me. I knew Maddie noticed boys, and when one finally noticed her, it would be her undoing.

Bumble took a quick look around the party. We were still alone by the koi pond. "I have one more favor to ask. Do you want a housesitter this summer?"

"I take it you have someone in mind…why, do you have a fertility goddess you want to stash at my place for the Sexapalooza?"

That cracked Bumble up. "No, although not a bad idea. Actually, Ted's chief of staff is moving here for the summer, during the congressional recess." She lowered her voice dramatically. "He's working on some stuff on the side for Ted. Some fact-finding. It would be great if he had a low-profile place to work out of. That's also free. Like your house."

"Is Ted involved in some scandal?" I was genuinely concerned now. Bumble usually wasn't so vague.

"No, no. Don't tell anyone, but he's considering a run for the governorship. So Rafa's going to do some temperature-taking, a little listening tour with movers and shakers here to see if Ted can build a coalition and make a run."

Relief, then curiosity. Being the tennis fan, my ears shot up at the name Rafa. For one crazy moment, I pictured Rafael Nadal sleeping in my bed with nothing on but a headband. The thought gave me great pleasure. Bumble's strange expression pulled me back from the brink. I recovered, "Governor Ted? And First Lady Bumble. Wow, that's really something. That's huge."

"I know. But Ted actually cares and thinks he could make a difference. And so do I," she said. "And I really want to be a First Lady."

"You would be a great First Lady. To the Governor's Manor born." I had no doubt about Bumble, but I wanted to flush out a few more details about the housesitter. "So who's Rafa?"

I was pretty sure he was the guy I'd had some disturbing eye contact with on my way into the party. I didn't want to let on that I'd noticed Mr. Blue Suit, or Bumble would have a field day.

Instead, she filled in the blanks with her Wikipedia-like recall, "He was here with Ted earlier, but they left for another event. Let me see, what can I tell you? Late thirties. Very smart, policy-savvy, good social skills. From the Antelope Valley here in California, fifth-generation farming family, they grow plants or trees or something. Ag not really his thing, so Rafa went to Georgetown, poli sci. Worked for both state and national candidates before he and Ted connected at a conference last year. Good match. Rafa gets California, which is not easy to do."

I had to ask, "Will his whole family be living in my house?"

"He's single, no time for relationships, but he's constantly fighting off the advances of ambitious young women who want to work on the Hill. Or so he claims. I'm not sure he fights them all off."

An ambitious Republican go-getter with an active social life? Rafa and I had nothing in common. Still, it was Bumble, and I couldn't refuse. "You know, for someone who didn't want me to go to Ashland, you're certainly capitalizing on my absence."

"Farmer's son. Your garden will never look better," Bumble promised, as she went off to find Maddie and head home.

Just then, FX and Candy circled around to our part of the grotto. Clearly, the two of them had enjoyed themselves, as they were talking and laughing easily. *Dear God, don't let Candy have heard us talking about Ted's political aspirations.* Not to worry, as Candy unwrapped her arm from FX's and announced, "Well, Elizabeth, I can see why you married him, and I can guess why you divorced him. How very sophisticated to work together again after all these years. I work with one of my exes, but he's a gay real estate agent, so it's not quite the same." Candy gave the international sign for kisses to all, turning FX back over to my custody. "He's all yours. Again. Keep me in the loop with the Shakespeare thing."

FX turned to me and made a slight bow. "Have I fulfilled all your requirements for the evening? Or do I need to make one more turn about the grounds to satisfy the locals?"

"We're done here. Let's go home." I blushed. "I mean, you go to your home and I'll go to mine."

"I figured, Elizabeth," he said, taking my arm and leading the way to our waiting chauffeur-driven Prius. "That wasn't too bad, was it?"

No, it wasn't.

Elizabethean Fashion Dos & Don'ts for the Modern Woman

DO: Neck Ruffle
DON'T: Petticoats

Neck ruffles can hide everything from aging to hickeys. Petticoats, however, only make your hips look bigger. And no one, except Keira Knightley, needs her hips to look bigger.

DO: Oversized Sleeves with Pockets
DON'T: Chain Girdle

Yes please (!) to tucking your cell phone or tablet right into your sleeve. How handy. But no thanks to weighty under-garments that will only hold you up in airport security.

DO: Embroidery
DON'T: Fur

Stitchery over sable. Think gold and lush for just the right touch of luxe, not soft and furry, because that's just asking for trouble from PETA.

CHAPTER 6

"I'm Rafa."

And I am standing at my front door in my bathrobe and it's nearly noon, I thought, but chose not to say it out loud. My body reacted with third-degree panic, but my face must have registered nothing, because Mr. Blue Suit, in yet another fantastic blue suit, felt the need to amend his earlier statement. "I work for Ted. Bumble said I should check out the place to see if it works for the campaign. She said she'd call ahead?"

Well, she didn't. Or maybe she had, but I'd turned my phone off to work on my book proposal. I'd lost track of time (and fashion sense) while outlining chapter ideas. Here's one now! "Chenille Isn't Sexy: Why Shakespeare's Romantic Heroines Never Wear Bathrobes." Remember when Ophelia showed up in that nightgown? That didn't end well. I stammered, "I didn't get that call. I was working and I turned the phone off. Please come in. I'm Elizabeth."

I crossed my arms tightly against my chest, like a tween in a training bra, in a desperate attempt to keep the two sides of my robe together. My sleepwear underneath wasn't much better: a US Open T-shirt and granny panties. Sure, the FedEx guy was used to seeing me like this, but not my brother-in-law's chief of staff. I let go long enough to grab a belt off a raincoat in the front hall. A winning accessory choice. Bathrobe secured, I turned to face my guest.

Rafa Moreno appeared to be a Very Busy Man, as evidenced by the constant buzzing of his Droid, but he slowed down enough to take in my living room, which I appreciated. And then I noticed the large supply of drugstore items I'd left on the coffee table, because I was too lazy to walk them fifteen feet to my bathroom the night before. Now they lay there in plain sight, creating a sort of feminine product buffet, complete with a centerpiece showcasing a canister of hair removal cream. I considered darting to the other side of the room to block the sight of the spread with my body but thought that would only call attention to my sloth. And my unwanted body hair.

Rafa graciously pretended not to notice. "Bumble calls you Elizabeth the Professor. I saw you arrive last night with FX Fahey. You guys were married, right?"

That seemed like an obvious question for a guy who clearly knew the answer, but he said it like FX and I might have played on the same softball team after work, so I tried to copy his tone. I covered by clearing my breakfast dishes into the kitchen and shouting over my shoulder. "Yup, we were. A long time ago. Working with him now. He's doing a play and I'm a creative consultant."

"Sounds interesting," he said, though his own disinterest was evident in his tone of voice. He was surveying the real estate, assessing the square footage. "This will work. It's nice of you to donate it to Ted's campaign."

Donate it to the campaign? "Well, Ted is a good man, and my sister literally doesn't take no for an answer," I responded, because, clearly, trying to explain that I hadn't quite agreed a hundred percent to this arrangement seemed like a waste of time. Classic Bumble. Rafa thought he was checking me out, not vice versa. *Dear Bumble, thank you for sending me the attractive housesitter that I wasn't really sure I wanted. I'm sure everything will work out great, even though it freaks me out that a stranger will have access to my underwear drawer. Especially one who looks so good in a blue suit. Love, your sister Elizabeth.* "Why don't you look around to see if the place suits the campaign's needs, and I'm going to get out of my bathrobe."

Oh my God.

"That came out...."

Rafa put his hand up. "No need. I'll go look around your garden. You can give me an official tour when you're dressed. In actual clothes." Then he smiled for the first time, and it was unnerving.

"Good plan," I whispered.

"Your garden is amazing." I found Rafa wandering around the backyard with a cup of coffee that he'd helped himself to. I wasn't sure how I felt about that, but I let it go. "Must be a lot of work."

Three years earlier, before Urban Homesteading became a regular blog at the *New York Times*, I tore up half the backyard and created a starter vegetable garden. At the time I was involved with yet another closeted gay colleague, Mark. (Seriously, the man was in his thirties. Wouldn't he know by now?) I needed some place to put my pent-up sexual frustration that didn't involve romance novels and nachos, so I started mulching. That first summer, I experimented with a few dozen tomato vines and some basil. The plants flourished, I coped, and, by August, Mark came out to me over a caprese salad. I really wasn't that surprised about him, and the tomatoes were delicious, so the relationship wasn't a complete loss. Now the garden was a multiple-bed extravaganza with a wide variety of edibles, including an entire row of rainbow chard. I was on the verge of getting chickens.

"I spend a lot of time out here. My grandmother was the great gardener. I'm just trying to maintain her vision but add my own twist. My goal is to be completely self-sustaining in two years. If I could only figure out how to grow Oreos. Do you garden?"

Now I was the one asking a question I obviously knew the answer to. Despite his heritage, he had the pallor of a man who spent sixteen hours a day at the office and the other eight thinking about the office. "First circle" was the term Bumble had used to describe Rafa's relationship with Ted. I didn't think first circles were allowed hobbies. Or exposure to sunlight.

"I grew up on a farm, so I like tending things. But my job doesn't allow me time to get dirty. In that way. But maybe this summer I can get back to the land." Not likely in that suit, I thought. He changed the subject. "I assume you have WiFi here? And my cell reception seems good."

"In the main house, yes. But not in the guest house...."

"Great, I'll set up in the main house," he informed me. Not exactly what I had envisioned. "Anything else I need to know about? Ghosts? Spies? Nosy neighbors?"

"Is that why you won't be working out of Ted's field office? Nosy neighbors?"

"We want to keep this as quiet as possible for as long as possible. The election's still twenty months off. Other items I need to know about?"

Clearly, he was use to working off an agenda. "I don't have a dishwasher."

"I don't really generate any dishes. I mainly eat out of Styrofoam containers. Don't tell the environmentalists that." Rafa was distracted by my thriving artichoke plants, which were ready to be harvested. I only had half a dozen plants, but they made a big statement. "My grandmother grew artichokes, too," he said. "I'm so used to seeing them on a plate with butter, I'd forgotten how much the plants look like science fiction. I wonder who the first guy was to pick one of these and try to eat it."

"The Greeks," I blurted out like a contestant on *Jeopardy*. I immediately felt idiotic, but that didn't stop me. "The first written references to artichokes come from Greek mythology."

He clearly didn't expect an answer to his semi-rhetorical question, so I carried on, circling the plant as I told him the story. "According to Aegean legend, the first artichoke to be picked was actually a young girl named Cynara. She lived on an island that Zeus and Poseidon visited. Cynara was completely unafraid of the gods, so Zeus took the opportunity to seduce her, good guy that he was. He was so pleased with Cynara, he made her a goddess and took her to Olympia. But Cynara got homesick and ditched Zeus for a few days to visit her homeland. Zeus was furious at the affront, so he hurled her back to earth and turned her into an artichoke."

"Now that's a bad breakup," Rafa said. He was touching the artichokes but examining me.

I felt a giant wave of self-consciousness wash over me, just like when I spotted him at the party. *What was it about this guy?* To cover my discomfort, I explained, "There's a vague artichoke reference in *Hamlet.* Shakespeare uses the phrase 'heart of heart' to describe the depth of his feelings for his dear friend Horatio, who is ruled by reason, not passion, a quality Hamlet admires to his core."

"Heart of heart," Rafa repeated slowly, as if he truly understood the phrase for the first time. His face lit up. I'd seen that look before with my students, when I'd touched something deep inside their intellect. But it had been a long time since I'd seen it in a man's face. "Free reading in your spare time?"

"I wrote a paper on it once."

"The Importance of Artichokes in Shakespeare's *Hamlet*?"

"Pretty much."

"That's vital work you do, Professor," Rafa mocked. Then his voice softened. "I'll never eat an artichoke the same way again. And I'm pretty sure we'll use that heart of heart bit in a campaign speech. It's good."

"Another donation." We both laughed.

His Droid went off, but he didn't look down to acknowledge it. "Sorry I have to rush, but we're flying back to Washington this afternoon. Can I see the rest of the place, so I'll know what I need in terms of office supplies and tech? Then I'll get out of your hair."

Speaking of hair, Rafa had good hair. A thick, full head of black hair. "Sure. It has three bedrooms, including the master. I'd prefer if the master wasn't 'donated to the campaign.' But the guest room is available, and you can use the third bedroom as your office. That's what I do."

"Got it, your bedroom off-limits. Any other restricted areas?"

I bet that line worked on interns. "The air conditioning is a little quirky. Good news is that the adobe walls keep the house cool even on hot days. The stove has its own personality—it's an old O'Keefe & Merritt—but it sounds like you won't be turning it on, so no worries. The yard guy comes on Monday and the trash guy comes on Friday."

"Anybody else show up around here?" Rafa said from underneath the desk in my office, where he was checking out the outlet situation.

"The meter reader shows up once a month. Other than that, it's just me." I tried not to sound too pathetic. Or defensive. Or eager.

Rafa stood up and wiped his hands on a handkerchief he produced from his pocket. Who carries a handkerchief these days? Then he dipped into his coat one more time, "Here's my card with all my contact information. Can I get yours in case I have any other questions? I'll confirm my arrival date with you and Bumble, of course."

I looked down: Rafael Moreno. Chief of Staff. Giant Congressional seal. And I had nothing. So I scribbled my e-mail address and cell number on a Post-it and made a mental note to get actual cards before I headed to Ashland. "Don't hesitate to call." Whoa, definitely too eager. "Anything for the campaign."

I texted Bumble: Don't think chief of staff interested in watering my plants.

She replied: Metaphor?

I answered: No, literally.

The phone chimed with a text from an unfamiliar number. I tapped the screen: Rafa here. Do you have cable?

I replied: Yes. C-Span?

He responded: Wimbledon.

I saved his number to my contact list.

Another chime. It was FX from New York: Having Indian at that place on Essex Street. Reminds me of you. Want something?

I replied: We have great Indian here in Pasadena.

RIGHTEOUS ROLE MODEL

Juliet Capulet

FROM *ROMEO & JULIET*

WHO SHE IS: She's Juliet, *the* Juliet. Innocent, obedient teenage daughter of the Capulets who takes one look at Romeo Montague, sworn enemy of her family, and that is that. Goodbye arranged fiancé Paris. Goodbye controlling mother. Hello womanhood.

WHAT TO STEAL FROM JULIET:

- Determined, strong, sober-minded personality
- Loves to read
- Great fashion sense
- Totally fakes out her parents and her nurse
- Matures with grace and wit

WHAT TO SKIP: Definitely the suicide. And really, stabbing yourself in the heart? That is brutal.

DEFINING MOMENT: She walks the walk. After begging Romeo to deny thy father and refuse thy name, she does just that and leaves all that she knows to follow her heart.

HER BEST RELATIONSHIP ADVICE: "Well, do not swear: Although I joy in thee, I have to joy of this contract to-night; It is too rash, too unadvised; too sudden; Too like the lightening, which doth cease to be Ere one can say, 'It lightens'."

WHAT SHE MEANS: Romeo, stop right there. This is too much, too soon. (Oh, if she had only paid a little more attention to her own advice.)

WHO JULIET WOULD HANG OUT WITH AT THE COFFEEHOUSE: Emma Watson.

CHAPTER 7

Maddie stood in the doorway of Smiths Coffee, searching for my table and the iced mocha latte I'd ordered for her. Tucked into a table for two in the back of the warehouse-like space, I'd been watching the door and waved her over enthusiastically. With her short, dark bob and hipster-dorky glasses on top of the distinctive plaid skirt and blazer from the Eastmont School for Girls, Maddie almost looked like a character from a CW show. Almost, because she lacked the sophistication needed to pull off her look with irony. She had been wearing the same uniform skirt to school since she was five. She felt so cursed with dark hair in a sea of blond ponytails that she simply cut it off. And she wore glasses because she needed them, not because they made her look like Zooey Deschanel. She was a work in progress but she was years from completion.

Even though she was nowhere near her adult self, Maddie already had an impressive resume that included a half dozen AP classes, a GPA of over 4.0, the mastery of a sport and/or musical instrument, and the standard travel-abroad experience that typically blossomed into a fully funded 501(c)3. At school she excelled in languages and the arts, so her schedule was packed with classes like AP Studio Art, a concept that struck me as a crime against creativity. After a family safari/humanitarian mission to Kenya, she started an organization that supplied sanitary napkins to schoolgirls in East Africa so they could continue with their education after they reached puberty. It was called the Big Red Tent and she'd received several national commendations for her work, though I suspected the Congressman might have had something to do with that. On the athletic front, Maddie had zero skills, but she was the manager and token white girl on the school's all-Asian table tennis team, a nationally ranked powerhouse. To top it all off, she played the flute. *The flute!*

But in the high-stakes world of trophy teens, Maddie was just another super-smart, super-talented supergirl. Girls like Maddie were a dime a dozen, according to every parent who ever said the words "college" and "admissions" in the same sentence. (Believe me, as a college professor at a community college, I'd heard the same story a million times about the brilliant kid who got in nowhere and ended up in my class. Thanks, Mom and Dad! Insults all around.) As a congressman's daughter, Maddie would be an excellent candidate at many fine colleges by her senior year, but she had her heart set on Swarthmore. She followed the acceptance rate like others follow the stock market. She put so much pressure on herself that sometimes I wondered if she might implode. Or develop an eating disorder and simply fade away. But Maddie continued to thrive, despite her stunning success.

Sometimes I felt sorry for high school boys. How could they compete with this whole new brand of girls? The Alpharellas, I'd heard them called by the proud parents who pretended to be at the mercy of daughters who combined the traits of academic and social Alpha Girls with the personal grooming standards of Cinderella. The poor boys in my classes were outmatched in almost every area except one: confidence. Apparently, confidence paid off in the end, because men were still running the world and making more cents on the dollar. How was that possible? I was rooting for the girls of Maddie's generation, but I feared they'd be too burnt out from achieving by the time they reached their twenties to muster the energy to upset the status quo.

"Hi, Elizabeth!" Maddie dropped her ninety-pound backpack and plopped into the well-worn club chair next to me. "I love your scarf! Is that H&M?"

Good eye. "Yeah. I was out to lunch the other day and spilled something down the front of my shirt right before class. So I bought this to cover up the damage."

"So funny. It looks great. Thanks for this," she said holding up her drink. "I wish we had a coffee bar at school."

Well, in truth, the Eastmont School for Girls did have a sushi chef and a forty-seven-ingredient salad station, so her wish for a coffee bar was not completely unreasonable. "From what I can see, your generation needs less coffee and more sleep. My students are exhausted but wired most of the time. It's not a good combo. What's happening at school?"

"I'm in the middle of AP tests, so it's been really brutal. I have sooooo much work to do. Did you take all these tests?" Maddie often used me as a cultural historian, which delighted me but also made me wonder for the millionth time why her mother had left her. It's like she was trying to create a high school yearbook for her MIA mom. Did your parents let you go to a lot of concerts? *Only to see the Philharmonic at the Hollywood Bowl.* Did so many kids smoke weed in your day? *Yes, but it wasn't as strong as it is these days, so nobody cared.* Did you really wear those high-waisted jeans? *No, those were for moms. We were the first generation of leggings-wearers, with slouchy white socks and Keds. Super-hot.* I loved my role. "You are the standardized-test generation. We didn't have a million AP classes, only a couple, and some people took the class without even taking the test. I feel sorry for you all, having to be judged all the time, having your intellects poked and probed and labeled. It's crazy."

"Don't let my father hear you say that. There's nothing he loves more than a standardized test!" Maddie was right. Congressman Ted was pro-testing, both publicly and privately. The papers referred to his stance as No Test Left Behind. On the home front, Maddie had already taken the SATs three times, starting in her freshman year.

"So, I wanted to ask you something. I don't know what your plans are for the summer, but you may have heard that I'm going to Ashland to work on a production of…."

"*Midsummer Night's Dream* with FX Fahey. Yes, I think I've heard, Elizabeth." Maddie was on top of things.

"So I was wondering if you might want to come with me to Oregon. To work for me as my assistant. I'll need some help on the production and I'm working on a book…."

"Oh my God, oh my God, oh my God. YES! I can't believe this. Thank you. I'll do anything. Get coffee. Make copies. Scrub floors. Anything!" Maddie was beside herself, and I had suddenly become World's Coolest Aunt, as if that title was in jeopardy. "Oh, wait, did you ask my dad yet? He might want me to do one of those summer school sessions at Stanford. I so don't want to go back there."

That's why I loved Maddie, because Stanford didn't impress her. I laid down the law in my best Professor Lancaster, Academic Advisor tone of voice. "I did. It's all cleared with your father. You'll live with me, and there's even a salary involved. But I want to be clear, this is a real job. It's work, not camp. I'm not your babysitter."

"I get it. I'm so excited. Best summer job ever. Oh my gosh, this experience will make the best college essay! I will work so hard. Thank you. Wait until I tell Emma!" Maddie really seemed to understand, because she was already texting her people. Then she added, "And FX Fahey is so cute!"

Oh boy.

The message read: I am here. Where are you?

It was either the existential question of all time delivered via text or my father was wandering around the PCC campus looking for me. I guessed the latter and responded: In my office. Will meet you in sculpture garden in 5.

My mind was racing. *What was my father doing on my turf?* The text was slightly alarming, but it did serve to jolt me into action. I had been daydreaming at my desk, more focused on what to pack for Ashland than grading my students' final papers. At this point in the semester, my students were barely hanging on, and I was even more burnt trying to get them to the finish line. *King Lear* was the final play on the syllabus, and it always freaked me out a little. The powerful father, the three daughters vying for his attention, the ensuing battles. It was all a little too close to the Lancaster family teen years, so the interruption from my father at this particular moment was eerie. I gathered my folders and headed out the door, happy to escape yet another paper entitled, *"King Lear* and the Origins of Tragic Irony." *Really? Ya think you're the first to think that one up?* I wanted to scream. That kind of attitude was my clue that the school year needed to come to an end.

My father had been on campus only a few times, even though we worked less than a mile apart. I'd occasionally invite him to a president's reception or trustees' cocktail party if I'd been summoned to attend. We didn't have too many of those in the community college system, but when we did, I realized the advantages of arriving with a Nobel winner. You could walk straight up to the president and shake hands, and then leave early because you'd brought such a distinguished guest. It was an excellent partygoing strategy, and my father was happy to oblige because afterward we always hit Señor Pescado for fish tacos.

But today's visit was so unexpected it made me worry. Was he sick? Was my mother sick? Oh my God, did Roger Federer die?

I hustled over to the Boone Sculpture Garden to find out. Though the PCC campus lacked the romance and history of Caltech, it was bright and inviting in its own way, a jewel in the California community college system. Current budget issues aside, the campus featured new buildings, well-maintained gardens, and athletic facilities that rivaled those of any private college. The school was well supported by a foundation that made sure the campus befitted the impressive list of alumni and the aesthetic standards of Pasadena. It was a pleasure to stroll the grounds on any given day, but especially on a beautiful April afternoon like today. My office was a short walk from the sculpture garden, and I spotted my father immediately, wandering the outer perimeter of the Jody Pinto–designed water feature.

He waved me over, pointing to the massive water channel and sweeping his hand outward to invoke the whole plaza. "The water creates the effect of a galaxy spinning on its axis. All the forms seem to rotate around the center of the plaza. This is a special spot." He didn't look well.

"It is. It's also a great place to have lunch." I laughed, reminded of the mantra with which my father approached life: Physics is everything and everything is physics. Charming now as he stood mesmerized by the massive public art installation, not so charming when he tried to teach me how to drive, yelling phrases like "gyroscopic force" and "threshold of motion" instead of "Turn!" and "Stop!"

"This is a special spot, Elizabeth," he repeated, as if he was working up to something bigger.

"Yes." Again I agreed but was pretty sure the next sentence out of his mouth was going to include the words "brain tumor" and "three months to live."

Much to my surprise, he offered some unsolicited advice. "But maybe you do need more of a challenge. In your career pursuits."

Relief then anger rushed over my being. Oh, I see, he wasn't dying, but my career was. I sighed, *"Et tu, Brute."*

"Now hear me out. I'm not like your mother, but I don't understand this nonsense this summer. Why are you running off to Oregon with that actor if you're satisfied with your work? It's a sign that something is off." I was taken aback at his surprising display of emotional awareness. He'd never acknowledged my emotional equilibrium before. (There's no crying in physics!) If I wasn't so annoyed, I might have been touched.

"Nothing's off. I just need to get away." *Mainly from these kinds of conversations.* "The work sounds fun and challenging, that's all. I'm not pining away for my ex-husband, if that's what everyone is concerned about. It's a change of scene, and I need the money to remodel my kitchen. It's a smart work move, not a step backward."

I was stomping around the plaza a bit, behavior not befitting a grown woman. And that indeed was my problem: Outside my family, I was capable; inside my family, I was thirteen. "I don't understand why this is such a big deal."

"Your mother and I are worried about you."

"Both of you are worried?" I was skeptical that worry was the main motivator here. My father never, ever worried; he believed in the Theory of Everything, so for him, things happened whether you worried or not. And my mother wasn't a big fan of worrying either; she was a doer, not a thinker.

"'Well, I'm worried. I don't trust that man. Is he really being honest with you? Your mother, on the other hand, is enjoying spreading the news," he admitted, not making eye contact. Richard Lancaster was not a big fan of the heart-to-heart (kinetic friction!), but I could tell he was really trying to have a meaningful conversation. He must really not trust FX. His instincts were worth something.

I backed off. "There's nothing to worry about, Dad. It's a couple of months and then I'll be back, hopefully recharged and ready to remodel. Maybe even with a book deal. See, all good. But I won't be back with my ex-husband. I promise you."

He looked relieved and satisfied, as if he had to hear me say out loud that I had no interest in FX so he could really believe it. With newfound confidence, he took in the scene around him. Maya Kim, a student from last semester, walked by and waved. I returned the gesture. My father noted the exchange. "You know, you're a much better teacher than I am."

Okay, now I was slightly astonished. "Really? Then where's my Nobel?"

"That's for research, not for teaching. I hate teaching. It's a necessary evil so I can continue my work."

That's not the reality I remembered. "Your students love you. I grew up with all those adoring grad students hanging around the house, drinking Mom's coffee. I saw the way they looked at you, like you were Jesus with a laptop."

He laughed. "My students don't adore me, they fear me. And they should. I have no patience for fools, and most eighteen-year-olds are fools."

"Some, not all," I countered.

"See, that's what makes you a better teacher. Every couple of years, a kid comes along with real talent, someone who deserves my time. But most of them? They're smart and they end up with PhDs, but then they go into managing hedge funds or writing computer models for the oil industry, not advancing physics. But you believe in your students and their promise."

I was touched. And then I felt a little foolish. I really did think every kid deserved a shot. So many of my students had done amazing things to get this far: escaped extreme poverty, learned English from cartoons, worked two jobs to support their families and pay for college. They embodied the work ethic of yesteryear, not the expectations of the entitled generation. True, not every student was a poster child for the American Dream, but a lot were. "Is that a weakness?"

"No! Have you seen your ratings on rottenprofessors.com?" I let out a big belly laugh. The image of my father checking out the evil but all-powerful professor-ranking site was too much. "You have four out of five stars! And three chilies for hotness. I only have two stars and no chilies."

Now he was killing me. "That's because you have like ninety percent men in your classes. I'm sure the few female students you have think you're hot. They just don't rate statistically. You're at least two chilies." And then, because it seemed impolite to ignore his efforts and because it had been on my mind, I asked, "Do you really think I should put together a resume and send it to your friend at Redfield?"

"Nah. Not unless you really want to. But tell your mother you did and then we're both off the hook."

FX had taken to texting me at all hours of the day and night with little bits of information and inspiration: Heard Ashland has great farmer's market. Or: Theseus is asshole. Don't remember hating him this much in college. Even quotes from the play that tickled his fancy: Joy gentle friends. Joy and Fresh love accompany your hearts.

The texts were little pick-me-ups and a way to stay close but not too close, as I finished up the last few weeks of school and prepared for the summer. I'd spend a few moments composing witty replies, then get back to grading papers or doing research.

But on this particular Wednesday, FX texted me with a simple statement: Taz is in. Then he followed up separately with a message that seemed less than manly: !!!!!!!

I'll be honest, of all the aspects of my gig with FX, working with noted director and creative genius Taz Buchanan was the most terrifying. Advising a movie star ex-husband was nothing compared to monitoring the man *Time* magazine called "The Visionaries' Visionary." (Guess they needed to sell some magazines that week to the TED crowd.) Taz Buchanan had pushed theatrical productions to the level of grand opera and turned small, dark stories into movie mega-musicals. No Taz Buchanan production was ever just on the surface level. He dug deep. He dug sideways. He turned things up on end and over again. His take on *Death of a Salesman*, set against the fall of Lehman Brothers, was currently burning up the boards in the West End, thanks in part to the brilliant casting of Jon Bon Jovi as Willie Loman. He had an innate understanding of the material, the ability to see the contemporary in the classic, and a rocking sense of theater. Love it or hate it, a Taz Buchanan production was always an event.

There's no telling what Taz might do to *Midsummer* to put his personal stamp on it. And it was my job to make sure that his personal stamp didn't become *Coriolanus, Part Deux* and ruin FX's reputation. I considered Googling "How to tame a wild director."

Instead, I texted FX back: !!!!!

QUIZ

Which Shakespearean Bad Boy Is for You?

ARE YOU AN URBAN GO-GETTER? You work hard, you play hard, and lately, you've been finding that old reliable boyfriend a little soft. You don't have a lot of time between your high-pressured job, your parcours workouts, and *The Bachelorette*. You're just looking for someone exciting you can squeeze in every so often.

YOU NEED A GUY WHO: Puts the booty in booty call.

MEET: Bertram, the cad from *All's Well That Ends Well*. He's rich, he's hot, and he's totally above you. Plus, he's married. But that doesn't stop him from stepping out on his wife, so if you can put up with his attitude, give him a call. Like Tiger Woods before rehab.

ARE YOU A NAVEL-GAZING BROOKLYN BOHO? If only you had a hit TV show and a wardrobe of unflattering Peter Pan–collared dresses like Lena Dunham! You're so close to full-fledged self-absorption, with your Chinese character tats and low-paying job in publishing.

YOU NEED A GUY WHO: Makes you feel worse about your body than you already do but will also be the heartbreaking subject of your bestselling memoir in twenty years.

MEET: Prince Hal. Someday he'll become the honorable Henry V, but now Prince Hal is a spoiled rich kid who parties hard and loves a good prank—just like a Kennedy! He's the kind of guy who might take an interest in the intellectual girl in the corner, if only to win a bet with his drinking buddies. And you can bet he'll never call back! But think of the advance on your book: *My Night with Prince Hal.*

ARE YOU A SUBURBAN SORORITY SISTER? Five years from now, you'll be walking down the aisle in a big white dress with ten bridesmaids and a wicked hangover. Until then, you're going to have some fun, fun, fun, especially on football weekends!

YOU NEED A GUY WHO: You can't take home to Daddy.

MEET: Falstaff. Yes, that Falstaff, the pleasure seeker, the lover of wine, women, and song. He's way too old for you, it will never last, and besides, he's a liar, a thief, and a cheat, but he epitomizes the lovable rogue. Think Vince Vaughn circa 2005. See? Kind of appealing, right?

ARE YOU A BOOKWORM BETTY? You were honored to be voted Most Likely to Become a Librarian, and your membership in the Jane Austen Society means the world to you. It's just that you haven't had a real date since prom, unless you count that hookup at the Renaissance Faire three years ago.

YOU NEED A GUY: With a large…vocabulary. That's right, a large vocabulary.

MEET: Mercutio, Romeo's homey. Funny, scene-stealer, life of the party. And believe me, he gets invited to all the best parties. Possible drug issues, maybe bipolar, but always a good time. Today's version: Lil Wayne.

CHAPTER 8

Congressman and Mrs. Seymour's backyard had appeared in the July 2011 issue of *House Beautiful*. The article featured the happy couple hosting their annual Fourth of July bash, complete with red, white, and blue outfits and "freedom-tinis." (Really, if it was an "annual" party, then apparently I'd been left off the invitation list for years.) Bumble had secured the story, hired a food stylist, and art-directed the guest list to represent a Noah's Ark of Ted's supporters: two gays, two Hispanics, two Asians, two African-Americans, two Armenians, and Bumble and Ted. The feature, initially a coup for Bumble, became a headache for Ted.

Two conservative radio-talk-show hosts, Ron and Ben, made a fuss over the Pennsylvania bluestone used around the pool instead of California-mined slate, and they continued to beat that issue into the ground for weeks. Liberal newspaper editorials pounced on the enormous grill area, which was positioned as a "let them eat cake" offense, as if Ted should run a soup kitchen out of his backyard. And the outdoor fireplace, slipped in just before they were banned for air-pollution reasons, had drawn the ire of environmentalists. Bumble was furious. "The guy is a self-made man, a real estate genius. Local boy makes good. Really started from zero, not like that fake self-made Donald Trump whose dad gave him zillions. That's why they elected him! Of course he used high-quality materials! And those Brown Jordan chairs were designed right here in Pasadena! Why didn't anyone mention that?"

The whole incident had made Ted incredibly cynical about any press coverage, and he certainly wasn't going to open up his home and his life to any further scrutiny if he didn't have to. Bumble had confided to me that it was the one big stumbling block in terms of running for governor. There were so many congresspeople in California that the media spotlight was on Ted only every once in a while. But there was only one governor, and he wasn't thrilled about being a target for every pundit with a microphone or blog—not after Slategate.

But on this night, the yard looked perfectly lovely, and no one objected to the built-in wine cooler or the excessive use of pink and white balloons. Using printed invitations and the promise of paella, Bumble had gathered the family and a few friends to say goodbye to Maddie and me before our Ashland adventure. In typical Lancaster fashion, Bumble refused to stage any sort of potluck affair. Where was the control in that?

As somebody who routinely hosted student and faculty get-togethers at my house, where invariably some poetry teacher in wearable art insisted on bringing Trader Joe's hummus or two-day-old grocery-store veggie trays, I admired Bumble's stance against random contributions of food. I also appreciated that I could just show up in my new shift dress and relax after days of getting ready for my trip. I was wiped out from the extreme cleaning jag I went on before my housesitter set up camp. I think I injured my rotator cuff vacuuming.

As soon as I arrived, Anne Lancaster was on the move. Wearing a pink and green Lily Pulitzer tunic, because dressing to match the invitation was her generational cross to bear, my mother cornered me in between the rosemary urns and the iceberg rose hedge. She quickly confirmed that my father and I had, ahem, discussed the matter. She made it sound like we were hatching a scam to import exotic animals from Costa Rica instead of sending off a resume to a small liberal arts college. I said we, ahem, had, which was true, but I left it at that, as my father and I had agreed.

Then she informed me of her plans to come to Ashland to see the play when it opened. She was bringing along Dependable Jane and Funseeker Mary Pat, otherwise known as the Girls. The trio had started the Faculty Wives Club at Caltech, now called the more politically correct Caltech Women's Union, when they were young, lonely newlyweds married to brilliant scientists. Their enviable bond had lasted almost forty years. Dependable Jane could sell real estate in her sleep, which was helpful because her husband, a geologist, liked the ponies at Santa Anita a little too much. Funseeker Mary Pat, now a widow whose husband had been a chemical engineer, was Pasadena's caterer emeritus. Her recent retirement had left the party scene devoid of mashed potato bars and salmon mousse terrines. The trio wanted to spend a girls' weekend in Ashland seeing great theater, soaking up the artsy atmosphere, and consuming crumbles made from local berries for breakfast. Maybe, my mother suggested, I could even arrange a backstage tour and a lunch with the cast.

It had never crossed my mind that my mother, or any of my family, would follow me to Ashland. But of course she wouldn't miss an opportunity to take her moment, even if it was really my moment. Honestly, as immature as it sounds, I hoped that if I didn't directly respond, her plans would evaporate. So I deflected any further questioning. "Talk to my assistant. She's doing my calendar." Yup, I threw Maddie under the bus and exited to the bar. I was beginning to understand the benefits of having an assistant.

Maddie had invited a few friends, all of whom were named

Emma. Maddie and the Emmas were huddled by the pool, texting and laughing at each other's texts. All the girls were wearing bikinis and tiny shorts, but it was clear they had no intention of actually swimming. The late-May pool temperature and their general self-consciousness would prevent them from diving in. But ever since Maddie had signed on for the Ashland trip, she seemed to be walking with a little swagger. It was nice to see her come out of her shell. I only hoped she didn't come too far out of her shell on my watch.

I staked out a position on the patio, within striking distance of both the tapas and the sangria. I knew I should mingle with Bumble's friends, mostly parents of the Emmas, who stood on the far side of the lawn. But those Brown Jordan chairs from the classic Summit collection were so cozy, I couldn't bear the thought of walking across the lawn and engaging in small talk. I knew they'd be yakking nonstop about college admissions, as the parents of rising seniors. (Unless, of course, one of the Emmas was bleeding from the head, at which point they might stop, toss her a tourniquet, and then resume talking about SAT prep.) I was saved from pretending to care as Sarah plopped down next to me, positioning herself with a clear view of the pool to watch her girls. Younger and impervious to public opinion, Hope and Honor jumped into the pool with no hesitation. Sarah noted, "They feel no cold. How is that possible?"

"Kids never get cold. I think the act of 'bringing a little shawl in case it gets chilly' is some sort of dividing line between youth and not youth. I don't go anywhere without a fake pashmina. I freeze in my classroom while my students are barely dressed," I said, pouring Sarah a glass of Bumble's white wine sangria, hesitating a moment while handing it to her. "Are you on call?"

"No, free as a bird all weekend! But Steven is, so he can drive home. I may have two glasses of sangria!" Sarah lifted her glass in a toast. "To escaping! So—are you ready?"

It was a loaded question, of course. My bags were packed, the car was serviced, and all female-related products, battery operated and otherwise, had been removed from my bedroom, just in case my houseguest breached the perimeter. Plus I'd purchased a generous supply of Target sundresses and secured an excellent haircut and fresh highlights from my stylist, Begonia, at Joseph Josephs Salon. So in theory, I was ready. But did I really know what I was walking into? Definitely not.

"I guess so. It'll be great, right? And if it isn't, it'll make great material for my book. How perfect that a *relationship expert* like myself should enter into a completely ill-advised relationship with her ex-husband. I can do a whole chapter on why not to work with your ex. I'll call it Why Exes Aren't Sexy or…."

"I hope you come up with better chapter titles than that!" Bumble interrupted, sneaking up on us with bacon-wrapped figs. She passed the platter of tapas and joined the conversation. "How about The Shaming of the Shrew? Or A Midsummer Night's Merde Storm!"

That made us all laugh. It might have been the French or the sangria, but nobody could crack us up more than we cracked each other up. And once we were on a roll, watch out. So Sarah added, "As You Liked It…But Not So Much Anymore."

I tossed out, "All's Well That Ends…in a Divorce and a Decade of Resentment."

"The Merry Wives of Windsor…Weren't Married to FX Fahey." Bumble snorted, most unattractively. By now I was having trouble breathing. Sarah wasn't faring any better, choking on her fig and her laughter. Nothing bonded my sisters like mocking my potentially humiliating situation.

Then a different voice joined in. "Somebody's having fun. What are you playing?"

We all turned to see Rafa Moreno, in a close-fitting white button-down and tan linen pants, holding a bottle of beer in one hand and files in the other. His hair had lost its perfectly groomed quality and his clothes were slightly wrinkled, as if he'd been sporting and gaming in the open air like some sort of minor Royal. His gray complexion had turned a sun-kissed olive, and his green eyes appeared to have been highlighted with liquid gold. What a difference a few rounds of golf (or a quick game of polo?) in the California sunshine could make. I was really regretting that open-mouthed guffawing with my sisters. How long had he been standing there? I tried to recover my dignity. "Just batting around some potential campaign slogans for Ted. How about 'Sey-mour, Pay Less'?"

"I'll make you a deal. You stick to teaching, I'll stick to politics," Rafa replied, reaching for the tapas platter and popping one of those bacon-wrapped figs into his mouth. Then he directed his gaze at Sarah, who was clearly wondering about our mystery guest's identity, judging by her wide eyes and slack jaw. He was smooth. "Hi, I'm Rafa Moreno. I work for Ted. You must be Sarah, taking the night off from curing cancer. Honor to meet you."

Sarah was charmed. "Well, this is an emergency of sorts. Our little sister needs some help. We really were brainstorming, just not political slogans."

Bumble couldn't resist, "Yes, Elizabeth is writing a self-help book on contemporary relationships. Based, of course, on the romantic ideals established four hundred years ago by a guy named William Shakespeare." I was as red as the roasted-beets-with-goat-cheese skewers that Bumble offered to our new guest. She continued because she had the floor. "Of course, lately, Elizabeth's own personal experience in this area has been restricted to singles' night at Whole Foods."

I took the bait. "There are a lot of single men there. They're not straight single men, but they're single."

"Moving on from artichokes, I see," Rafa said as he turned to me, and I made a mental note: Remove those Anaïs Nin books from the home bookshelves stat. This man must not know my secrets.

Artichokes? Bumble and Sarah looked at me suspiciously, so I covered flawlessly. "Yes, I've completed my Shakespearean produce research, so now I'm moving onto people. There's a lot of Shakespeare going on all around me."

'Really? Like what?" Rafa asked.

"Well, for instance, after some careful analysis, I posit that Bumble and Ted are remarkably similar to the Macbeths." This got a rise out of Bumble, so I continued. "They had some hot moments before things started to get, you know, bloody. They worked as a team of equals, the wife was a valued advisor in the husband's work, and they liked to socialize with the peasants, I mean, the people. Together, they amassed a lot of power, and that created a very sexy, intense relationship. Just like you and Ted, Bumble!" The image struck everyone's delight: Bumble and Ted and their witches' brew of politics, publicity, and power.

Rafa jumped in. "Then what happened?"

"Lady Macbeth's ambition outgrew her husband's. Their communication devolved into manipulation. Passion gave way to paranoia. And they started murdering people."

"That's never a political strategy I recommend."

Sarah piped up, "I'd keep your eye on Bumble, Rafa. If she suggests knocking off the Democratic challenger, you may have a situation on your hands."

"Or as my man Will would say, *'Their hands and faces were all badged with blood.'* Not a good photo op."

Bumble was not amused. "We are not the Macbeths."

It was rare that I got the best of her. "You are so going in the book. I'll just call you the Clintons! But you'll know it's you."

Rafa finished his beer. "Would you mind keeping that theory to yourself for, say, eighteen months or so? The attack ads could be pretty rough." He was obviously ready to hit the road, and I felt surprisingly disappointed. "I'm off. Headed home to Acton. My niece's Fiesta de Quince is this weekend and for once I'm actually around to play the good uncle."

"Is that like a *quinceañera*?" I asked, wanting to extend the conversation.

"Yes, but the Argentine version. Less pink, more dancing. I have to learn some kind of minuet tonight."

"Your family must miss you," Sarah said. "Do you see them much?"

"Well, my mother's learned to use Skype, so you never know when they're going to drop in," Rafa said, but clearly he didn't mind too much. "I'll be back Monday and, I think, moving into your house that day, Elizabeth. Great meeting you, Sarah. Thanks for the hospitality, Bumble."

Bumble had moved on from Lady Macbeth to Lady of the Manor. "Wait! I don't have a gift for your niece. Do you think she wants a Congressional Christmas Ornament, circa 2009? I have a stash of those. Let me grab one!" Again, there was no saying no to Bumble. Even Rafa knew that.

The delay gave me an opening. "Hey, I have an extra set of house keys in my car. I was going to give them to Bumble tonight to pass along, but I may as well turn them over to you now," I said, hoping that my legs didn't give out under the weight of his gaze.

Please let me get to the car without tripping.

The small white Porta Viaggio bag, once home to a spectacular roasted eggplant panini, now held a set of keys, a big bunch of basil, the first of my Early Girls, and the last of my artichokes. They were all intended for Bumble, but I felt the fruits of my labor could be used for a higher purpose. I handed over the bag to Rafa. "The keys are in here, plus some things from my garden. If you're going home, take the artichokes to your grandmother. If she's still alive, that is." Ah, a lovely gesture made awkward by the specter of death.

"She is and she'll love these. Thank you." Oh, he had wonderful manners. "And again, thanks for letting me stay in your house."

"I'll leave a few pages of notes in the kitchen. Local restaurants, instructions for, you know, stuff." The small-talk portion of the evening was not going well, so I tried a different tactic. "What kind of farm does your family own? Beef?"

"I think beef farms are called ranches," he managed to say without completely cutting me down to size.

"That is true." *Beef farm?* I shouldn't be allowed to talk to grown men. I should stick to students and actors, period. "Does your family own a cattle ranch? You said your family is Argentine. Your people are known for their beef, aren't they?"

"They are. But the story is that when my great-great-great-grandfather moved here in the 1880s, he worked on a ranch for a week and hated the stench, so he found a little plot of land, filed for it under the Homestead Act, and started a honey farm. He was a beekeeper. And we still keep bees. But over the years, we expanded and now we grow lilacs in the spring and pears in the fall."

That was no beef farm; that was Marie Antoinette's playground! I was enchanted. "You grow lilacs and pears and honey. It must smell delicious!"

"It does. You should visit sometime during lilac season. You can smell the blossoms as soon as you drive into town." Was he actually inviting me to a weekend in Lilacville? I bet he'd look amazing in a lilac dress shirt. "They have bus tours you can pick up from the Glendale Galleria."

Apparently not. "Maybe someday. You know, I've planted lilacs three years in a row at my house, but they never make it. I think it gets too warm at night here."

"Maybe. They do prefer nights that get below freezing and days with warm sun. But lilacs are also very temperamental. Even if the environment is right, they still may not thrive. They need to be in just the right place. But they're worth the trouble. They're much more ambrosial than cattle." Rafa smiled, showing off his large vocabulary. "Dulce Viento."

"'Sweet wind'?" I was putting my limited Spanish to work. I spent twelve years studying French at the Eastmont School for Girls, because, really, who speaks Spanish in Southern California?

"Yes, Sweet Wind. Dulce Viento. That's the name of my family's farm." Rafa was leaning against a modest rental car, but it might as well have been a white steed. His Droid bravado was gone, replaced by humility highlighted by perfect teeth. Sweet Mother of God. I was pretty much ready to throw in the towel on theater, teaching, and good sushi and head to the homestead when Bumble came barreling out of the house with a dramatically wrapped re-gift. "Wait, don't leave without a token of Congressional power! Plus I threw in fifty bucks—that's enough, right?"

The moment was over. Bumble thrust the package into his hands and headed back into the house to be the hostess with the mostest. The chief of staff responded to his boss's wife's back. "That's very generous. Anna will love this. Thanks, Bumble."

Yes, teens do love collectible Christmas items in May, I thought, but I held my tongue and followed Rafa's all-business example. Clearly he wanted to get on the road. "Let me know if you have any questions about the house. Otherwise, mi casa es su casa. Good luck this summer."

Just then my phone buzzed. It was a text from FX. I tried not to look, but it was like a siren song, and I took my eyes off Rafa for a second. I glanced down to read the words: Wait till you hear Taz's concept. Mind-blowing. See u Monday.

Mind-blowing?

I looked up from my phone to see Mr. Manners waiting for me to finish being distracted. "Everything okay?"

"FX. Text. Apparently, the production's going to be mind-blowing." There was no explaining.

Rafa wrapped up the conversation neatly. "Sounds important, so I'll say goodbye. I see you're busy. Best of luck on your work, too."

And then, like a sweet wind, he was gone.

The Macbeths

FROM THE SCOTTISH PLAY

HER: Loving, supportive wife with unfortunate ambitious streak. Wants to stand by her man, as long as he carries out the murder she plans and becomes king of Scotland. Known for her meticulous attention to detail. Wracked with guilt.

HIM: A brave soldier and powerful man prone to self-doubt and vulnerable to prophecies from witches. Goes to great lengths to make the Missus happy. Wife accuses him of being "too full of the milk of human kindness," but that changes.

RELATIONSHIP HISTORY
Literature's original power couple. A happy, lusty marriage that gets way off track when one atrocity leads to another in their desire to rule Scotland. In the end, a lot of people die, including both of them.

CHEMISTRY FACTOR: 4 OUT OF 5

BEST MOMENT: Lady Macbeth calls on the evil spirits to "unsex" her so she can commit murder like a guy. Haven't we all called on the evil spirits for unsexing at least once?

WORST MOMENT: Lady Macbeth trash-talking her man when he refuses to commit murder. Emasculation and manipulation is never pretty, and in this case it really gets ugly.

WHY THEY WORK: She holds the sexual power and he holds the knife.

TURN-ONS: Joint alienation, partnership in crime.

TURN-OFFS: Bloody hands, Banquo's ghost.

SHAKESPEAREAN COUPLE MOST LIKELY TO: Hold office.

WHO THEY REMIND YOU OF: The Reagans, the Clintons, the Eminems, the Jolie-Pitts.

CHAPTER 9

Ashland, Oregon, a picture-perfect town in the heart of the Rogue River Valley, was once an important railroad juncture in the late nineteenth and early twentieth centuries. Situated halfway between Portland and San Francisco, Ashland thrived on the rail trade, taking particular advantage of the orchard fruits from the valley. The wealth and power of the Southern Pacific brought with it rapid expansion, political clout, and an abundance of Victorian architecture and stately hotels. Nature also smiled on the little town at the foot of the Siskiyou mountains, blessing it with a natural spring that the Women's Civic Improvement Club developed into a lush hundred-acre public park drawing health seekers from all over. With their good fortune, Ashland's citizens aimed higher, developing a sophisticated small town with its own college and a commitment to the arts. The final jewel in Ashland's crown debuted in 1935, when college professor Angus Bowmer established a theater festival that would become the world-renowned Oregon Shakespeare Festival.

Now a high-end resort area and a haven for retirees, Ashland remains a hub of sorts, except instead of shipping magnates and timber barons, it's home to theater junkies, actors of all shapes and sizes, students from the local college, organic farmers, and those who enjoy wearing fleece year-round. Real estate costs have risen exponentially with each new wave of Californians and baby boomers. Locals and transplants alike revel in their reputation for independence and quirky politics, evidenced by the fact that the unofficial mascot is the Spotted Owl, the poster bird for endangered species everywhere that first came to fame here more than twenty years ago. The eclectic population, the natural beauty, and the abundance of artisanal coffee and craft beer made Ashland the perfect spot to spend the summer.

Maddie and I would be living in a painfully charming rental cottage on Seventh Street in the painfully charming Railroad District. Located right in the heart of Ashland, the neighborhood featured street after street of once-modest cottages built for the railroad workers between 1900 and 1910, each now worth about half a million bucks. There appeared to be some city ordinance that required at least one three-story Victorian B&B on every block. The place was lousy with accommodations called the Black Swan or Anne Hathaway's B&B, complete with mandatory white wicker furniture and flowering baskets on the front porch.

I wish I could claim credit for having found the perfect sage-and-purple-trimmed two-bedroom house with a porch in the front and a hot tub in back, but it wasn't me. It was Angie, an assistant to FX's business manager, who handled all the arrangements. (The scope of the FX Fahey Industrial Complex was coming into focus. It takes a village, and many assistants, to service a movie star.) In the short time I'd spent working with Angie via e-mail, it was clear that she was both proficient and oblivious. Proficient at researching, negotiating, securing, and documenting the huge number of details it takes to relocate multiple people; oblivious to the cost that said relocation requires. When she sent me the links to three possible houses, I saw that all three cottages were for sale, not seasonal rentals. When I told Angie this, she just said, "Everything's negotiable."

Apparently Angie was right, because a week later, she sent me the keys to my first-choice place, the house with the remodeled kitchen, arched doorways, and claw-foot tub. She assured me that she'd get new beds and linens brought in, and the owner would take up the awful green carpet in the bathrooms because, she said, Hollywood "doesn't do carpet in the bathrooms."

"Is linoleum okay?" she asked.

I hadn't even balked at the carpet.

Angie threw in a cleaning service every week and offered to have someone come in to do our laundry on Tuesdays and Fridays. She also provided information about a grocery delivery service, an in-house masseuse, and a nearby yoga studio and said she'd arranged for billing to go directly to her. I said no to the laundry, the grocery delivery, and the masseuse, because that all seemed a little too much. But yes to yoga, because I had a feeling I was going to need a little stress relief. Angie sent along the keys to our Ashland dream house as well as a "bible of information" (her words) about all things Ashland and all things FX.

My guess is that she had no idea that I'd been married to FX, and she clearly thought I'd be doing a lot of his personal bidding this summer. In addition to a four-page list of his preferred *everything*, from face soap (Dove Unscented, the same soap since college, I noted) to iced beverages (double-shot latte with one-percent milk and a half squirt of vanilla syrup) to white undershirts (TJ Second Skin). The bible also included a list of women with whom he had slept who were not to be mentioned to the press *(Carla Bruni!)* and another list of women he was interested in sleeping with, should the occasion arise *(Stockard Channing?)*. I wasn't sure what disturbed me more: absorbing the lengthy columns of names or the fact that "Elizabeth Lancaster" wasn't included on either list. I tossed the bible into a closet until I could decide the best course of action, burning it or tearing it to shreds, one page at a time.

But that first morning in Ashland, the needs and desires of FX Fahey were far from the top of my mind. The kitchen of our little cottage was flooded with morning light, and I had my first chance to get a good look at our home away from home for the next ten weeks. It was clean, bright, and creamy yellow, like the website promised. The kitchen was stocked with the essentials: coffee, milk, English muffins. I brewed some coffee, changed into some socially acceptable yoga pants, a fleece pullover, and my Uggs, and headed out to the front porch.

Maddie and I had pulled in late the night before after a grueling 700-mile drive from Southern California to Southern Oregon. Maddie talked nonstop for ten hours. I'd brought a few books on tape that I thought would help pass the time, but she was her own book on tape. I now knew the last names of all the Emmas and where they were spending the summer. I found out why she stopped taking flute from Mr. Tom. (Yes, he did touch her thigh, which, as she reminded me, "is not a part of my body involved in playing the flute *at all!*") I was fully versed in the rules of table tennis and the political drama that played out when one of the top players got a B in math and was benched by her parents. And she told me about the mean girl in her class she suspected of attempting to trap her in some sort of scandal so she could post on YouTube to discredit Congressman Ted. By the time we reached the Oregon border, I was pretty sure that a) Maddie would run out of things to say by July Fourth, and b) Maddie needed to get out of Pasadena as much as I did.

Maybe it was the cool, clean morning air or the sound of the train whistle in the background, but I felt a shot of renewed energy. I'd spent the last five summers grinding it out in the heat and smog of Southern California, teaching a few torturous remedial writing classes, moving dirt, and catching up on back issues of *Sunset* and *Cottage Living*. Basically, I'd done nothing in the moving-forward department, except the garden. Even just thinking about my life made me realize how static my status quo had been for a long while.

Now I felt ready for something new, even if it meant reconnecting with something old, like an ex-husband. Over the last week, I had pieced together a to-do list of personal improvements I wanted to tackle this summer. Top three items: the play, the book, and my desire to upgrade my wardrobe by adding more color and less black. Add to that mastering the art of omelet making and I was a walking *Glamour* article, if anyone still read *Glamour*.

"I can do this," I said to no one, in a most atypical personal pep talk. "It's the Summer of Me."

To my surprise, somebody answered, in the form of a cold nose rubbing against my hand. *What the hell?* The sensation scared me to death, as if Oregon might be home to marauding packs of wild coyotes. I let out a pathetic scream, cut short when I saw it was just a mid-size fluffy brown dog. Well, sort of fluffy anyway. The dog dodged behind a chair, proving that yes, they really are more scared of us than we are of them.

Ashamed of my overreaction, I tried my best dog-lover patois, even though I wasn't that experienced talking to dogs. "Here, puppy. That's okay. Come here." He/she came toward me timidly, head down but tail wagging slowly. "Who are you? What's your name? Are you a boy or a girl?"

Thanks to my complete lack of canine knowledge, I assumed the stray was a boy because he was light brown, and that's a boy color. He had no collar or tags and a look in his eyes that said he'd been on his own for a while. His fur was matted and he was whimpering slightly, as if he was incredibly relieved to make contact with another living being. Once I started petting him, his tail went nuts. He gave me a grateful look. I was smitten.

"Are you lost? Do you live around here?" For the first time, I understood why so many cartoons feature talking dogs. Who wouldn't love their dog to speak up just once? They're no help when you need them to answer a few simple questions. I walked down the porch steps with Fido at my heels and looked both ways down Seventh Street, expecting to see an owner looking for his dog. Or maybe the dog would head home for breakfast. Oregon was kind of a lawless place. Maybe dogs didn't need to be on leashes here. Maybe they walked themselves? But there was no one on the street except a teenager on a skateboard headed in the other direction. I noticed a lost-pet sign on the telephone pole and called to my new friend, "Come on. Let's go see if this is you."

But the flyer was for a missing ferret. *A ferret?* There really are wild marauding animals around here, I thought. I needed to protect this dog from that ferret. Then I thought about what my sister Sarah, the Advice Whisperer, had said to me: Get a dog. A dog would distract my mother from my career. A dog would distract me from dreams about FX. A dog would be an excellent prop at social events where everybody else had a spouse. Could this be the first challenge in my Summer of Me vow to say, "Yes!" more than "No"? Perhaps. But for now, I didn't want to get too attached, because a dog this cute must have a family. "Come on, let's go inside and get you some water."

Maybe water was his cue—just then, he lifted his leg on a bush. Yup, I had a new man in my life. A fluffy brown man.

Maddie burst through the door, ready for the day. "Oh, who's this little guy?"

Without thinking, I answered, "Puck."

By the end of the day, I'd unpacked all my clothes and set up my office in the front room with my computer, a bust of William S, and two whiteboards, one for *Midsummer* and one for my book. I secured groceries for several days and a supply of scented candles to last the summer, because it seemed like the thing to do in Ashland.

Maddie and I managed to give Puck a bath with the hose, buy a matching plaid leash and collar, and make a dramatic Lost Dog sign, featuring before and after photos of our new roommate. We called the animal shelter to see if anyone was looking for a brown dog, but the volunteer said it had been slow the last few days, only a few lost cats and, of course, the ferret. No lost dogs at all. I tasked Maddie with walking around town to hang up the signs, because it seemed like the right thing to do. Neither of us was all that enthusiastic about returning Puck to his rightful owner, least of all Puck, who was really enjoying his new hemp-filled pet bed and chew bone.

I was settling in with a glass of iced tea and my notes on *Midsummer* when a text from FX came in: Here in Ashland. Dinner tonight with Taz? 7 at my place. The address followed. *Oh, God, here we go.*

⊗

Maddie shook her head as I modeled my outfit for dinner with Taz and FX. With conviction, she handed me a pair of jeans and a blouse. "Not that, these."

I reassessed my black sheath dress. "Too job interview-y?"

"I've never been on a job interview, so I don't know. But just not cool."

She was right. Nobody looked cool in a sheath dress. I took her choices then confessed, "Why am I so nervous?"

"Because FX is so cute?" I knew Maddie was dying to ask me more about him, like she did about everything else. What was our first kiss like? How did I know I was in love? Was he, you know, good in bed? (Romantic and perfect; Love at first sight; Pretty good but not great, though I didn't know that at 22. According to his bible, he's had a lot of experience since then.) Bumble must have set down some ground rules, because Maddie hadn't asked a single thing about him on the drive up. That warning and the nondisclosure agreement we both had to sign had obviously silenced her.

"No, that's not it. He's like an old shoe to me. A really cute old shoe," I acknowledged, even though that wasn't completely accurate.

"But Taz...."

"You got this, Elizabeth." Maddie sounded like the table tennis team manager she was. *Yeah, I got this.*

I changed into the jeans and the filmy floral blouse I'd bought at a boutique in Pasadena in support of my decision to wear more color. It was the sort of piece that other women could pull off with ease, looking like they'd just come from the beach in 1973. But I worried that I looked like I was in costume for a revival of *Godspell.* "What do you think?"

"Very cool."

At least I looked cool on the outside, even if my insides were a hot churning mess.

FAKE THE SHAKE

6 Classy Ways to Throw Down an Insult

1. "Thou art as loathsome as a toad."
FROM: *Troilus and Cressida*
WHEN TO USE: Excellent all-purpose exit line for almost any offending situation, romantic or otherwise.

2. "I do desire we may be better strangers."
FROM: *As You Like It*
WHEN TO USE: Understated line to kiss off any unwanted attention. Especially good in a bar when approached by drunken bro who slurs the words, "Hey baby, wanna see my Sigma Phi?"

3. "Thou art a boil, a plague sore, an embossed carbuncle in my corrupted blood!"
FROM: *King Lear* (He said this to his daughter Regan. Totally harsh.)
WHEN TO USE: Even if you only get out the words "embossed carbuncle," this one is worth knowing. Same situation as #2 if Frat Boy doesn't get your first line.

4. "Methinks thou art a general offence and every man should beat thee."
FROM: *All's Well That Ends Well*
WHEN TO USE: When the guy you're talking to is clearly checking out a woman behind you. Works well in group settings when you have physical backup.

5. "Thou art unfit for any place but hell."
FROM: *Richard III*
WHEN TO USE: He's cheating and you're leaving. Say it and keep walking.

6. "You starvelling, you eel-skin, you dried neat's-tongue, you bull's-pizzle, you stock-fish—O for breath to utter what is like thee!—you tailor's-yard, you sheath, you bow-case, you vile standing tuck!"
FROM: *Henry IV, Part 1*
WHEN TO USE: Right before you say the line above from *Richard III*. Really lay into that last bit about the "vile standing tuck," whatever that means.

CHAPTER 10

"I took the whole place for the summer. Isn't it great?" FX threw his arm in a giant circle, implying that all within sight belonged to him: the two small cottages, the lovely spa, the tea garden, and the rock-lined private hot springs. Tucked into a corner of the Railroad District, the Chozu Bath & Tea Garden was now FXHQ for the duration of our stay. Top-notch assistant Angie had mumbled something about finding FX a place "with a staff and without any chintz"—not easy to do in Ashland. (The chintz part, not the staff part.) But in the Anything's Negotiable spirit, she'd found FX the only Japanese-inspired hideaway in Southern Oregon and made it his for ten weeks. The arrangements included a masseuse and an in-house sushi chef to serve him as needed. "I had to buy out some of the guests who had already booked in, but wait until you soak in the hot-spring tubs. Perfect ratio of salt. Like the Amanpuri Phuket."

Just what I needed. I was already a wreck and now he'd reminded me how out of my comfort zone I was. This was Hollywood in

Ashland; I was Pasadena in Ashland. I tried to blend in.

"Next time, I'll bring my suit."

"Or not," FX winked, and unbelievably, I blushed. Here was a man I'd been naked with for most of the latter half of the '90s and I blushed at the thought of even skinny-dipping with him. Skinny-dipping! *Get a grip, Elizabeth.* FX, used to blushing girls, barely registered my color. "Wine, beer, or tea?"

Definitely wine.

"So can I get a hint about what Taz is thinking?" I was hoping for a preview before Taz showed up so I could be prepared for whatever creative grenade the Australian might toss. On the short walk over from my house to FX's compound, I'd worked up a sweat thinking about all the dodgy *Midsummer*s that Taz might pitch: Zombie *Midsummer*. All-male *Midsummer*. *Midsummer* in Vegas. FX had been tight-lipped until now, and that scared me a little. "What's so mind-blowing?"

A voice boomed out. "Mind-blowing? I assume you're talking about me." From behind a changing-room door, the unmistakable Taz Buchanan appeared. He certainly hadn't overdressed for the meeting: He was wearing a sarong and not much else, even though the weather was cool. My first thought: So glad I'm not wearing that sheath dress.

Taz came in for the double kiss. He was medium height, well built, and not so much handsome as fierce looking. His chest was still slightly damp, and he smelled of salt and lavender from the spa. "You must be Lizzie. You've done a marvelous job getting this lad up to speed. All those years doing action movies, wasn't sure FX could handle this much plot and dialogue. Are you ready to make magic?"

I took a big swig of wine and braced myself. "You bet." *You bet? Was I freaking Canadian?*

FX stepped in, much to my relief. "Put a shirt on, Taz, and let Elizabeth catch her breath. I don't think she's seen that many men in skirts in Pasadena."

Taz roared, the kind of laughter you read about in books but rarely ever hear in person. Though his real name was Arthur Buchanan and he wasn't from Tasmania, his zeal for life landed him the nickname Taz at a Sydney prep school (where he shocked school officials by performing Hamlet's famed soliloquy in drag). Thirty seconds into our relationship, I saw why female stars fell for him, producers courted him, and actors revered him. He was like a giant magnet of energy. According to a *Vanity Fair* profile, he used his charm to pull people into his projects and then hammered everyone on set during the production to get the best out of them. And he only slept four hours a night, dabbled in veganism, and played Midnight Oil albums at least once a day.

It's not easy to upstage FX Fahey, but Taz Buchanan was a close, close second. Tan and robust, he looked like he spent his summers surfing at Bondi Beach. To go with the sarong, he threw on a fitted Lacoste shirt and a black beanie to cover his famously bald head. His blue eyes were, well, spectacular. I'm really going to enjoy working with him, I thought.

"There. Fully dressed, milady." Taz gave a little bow.

So I'd already been identified as the prude.

"Thank you." Yes, I should have come up with something more clever than that, but I didn't have that "instant rapport" gene that so many Hollywood types possessed. I'd watched Bumble do it—immediately assimilate to her surroundings with false intimacy. The inside jokes from the get-go. The nicknames on day one. The complete ease with complete strangers simply because they, too, were in the business. Maybe because I wasn't in the business, I tended to wait to get to know a person before I pretended to know a person. But I tried my best to play the part. "I was just working on some CliffsNotes for our boy there."

"Thanks, Liz. Make sure you put in the phonetic spellings for any really tricky words." Taz continued to mock FX, much to my pleasure.

"Will do."

FX piped up. "Good thing you're both here to back me up. I'd be standing onstage shell-shocked without you."

A slight, dark-haired woman dressed in black appeared with a tray of sushi, some exotic-looking rolls, and miso soup. She set them down soundlessly on the teak table and didn't make eye contact with any of us. I wondered if that was in FX's contract rider, negotiated of course by Angie: "Staff is not to speak until addressed, or make eye contact with Mr. Fahey or any of his guests during the term of agreement." Was FX really that kind of diva? But just then he said, "Thanks, Ming. Looks wonderful. So, should we get on with it?" *Oh, good. FX hadn't gone totally diva.*

"That's my cue," Taz said, taking a healthy swig of beer and going into director mode. "All right, Professor. I hear you're a tough audience, but humor me for a bit. Imagine this. A big party in a bucolic setting, youth versus the establishment, magical forces at work, a traveling band of merry pranksters, the 'love the one you're with' ethos...."

Taz had me so far. Pretty much all the essential elements of *Midsummer*, but in that Australian accent, they sounded new and fresh. I couldn't help but smile.

He paused dramatically and then announced, "It's hot. It's sexy. It's young. I'm talking about *A Midsummer Night's Dream*...at Woodstock 1969."

Whoa.

"Can ya dig it?" FX added lightly, but his expression was serious. This was his career, and it was my only job to make sure he didn't get humiliated again. I recognized the flicker of doubt. Either "*A Midsummer Night's Dream* at Woodstock 1969" was an off-the-charts concept that worked beautifully or it was a hokey disaster. At this point, he wasn't quite sure which. Neither was I.

I bought some time, grilling Taz on a few of the details to make sure I really understood his vision. I'd developed this method over my years of teaching—it's how to poke holes in a student's thesis statement without coming right out and saying that it doesn't work. "So, take me through this. The big party in a bucolic setting...."

"That's the main event," Taz said. "The wedding of Theseus and Hippolyta. They've got four days of partying before the ceremony."

"Youth versus the establishment?"

"Young lovers Hermia and Lysander escaping the wishes of the king to be with each other instead of being forced into an arranged marriage."

"Magical forces?"

"Fairy dust, aka LSD, or pot—take your pick."

"Got it. And I take it the Merry Pranksters are the traveling players, the Rude Mechanicals?"

"Yeah, as Deadheads."

"Love the one you're with?"

"Never a stranger passion than Titania the Fairy Queen falling for Bottom the Ass," Taz concluded with a satisfied grin.

"Well?" FX stared at me. "What do you think?"

This was my money moment. I could have dug in my heels and asked to hear more justification for the modern dress, not being a fan of most contemporary interpretations of Shakespeare. I could have asked a million practical questions about the production or the casting. I could have zeroed in on how FX might benefit from this concept as opposed to a traditional production. Maybe it was the wine or the tea lights in the trees, but I decided to go with my gut. "It's brilliant. In every way. Fun, sexy, summery. Woodstock is exactly the sort of setting Shakespeare himself would have exploited for his own use. In fact, it's the same sort of woodsy, magical setting he exploited in *Midsummer*. Wonderful. I love it."

Taz nodded in appreciation, but the set of his jaw told me he already knew that it worked. Had he just been humoring me? Did Taz resent that I was a gatekeeper?

I let those worries go, because FX smiled a huge smile of relief.

He stood up and circled the table, coming behind me to give me a hug. His arms wrapped around me completely. His body was warm against my shoulders, and I felt his breath against my neck. I relaxed back into his grasp. Clearly, I had validated his instincts, which is always a good feeling. But more than that, there was a flicker of our connection from years ago. We were on the same page. That was a good feeling, too.

"Sushi?" FX asked, and we settled into discussing the details of the production. Taz described his vision of a stage filled with music, color, and good love. A balance between the known world and the psychedelic, the locals and the hippies. The young lovers would awaken in the woods after a night of mayhem to the strains of the famous Jimi Hendrix version of the national anthem. If the production was half as dynamic as Taz's description, it would be a sensation, one of the hottest tickets of the summer anywhere, let alone in Ashland.

From an interpretation standpoint, it was right on point. But I had to ask a practical question. "I know this isn't my area, but how are you going to pull all this off? It's only a few weeks until you open."

FX impressed me with his answer. He was not just a star but a producer on the play, and it showed. "This is a repertory company, so the actors are used to juggling multiple shows on really tight rehearsal schedules. Many of them have done *Midsummer* before somewhere, in some capacity. So staging and blocking should go really quickly. Lines are no issue.

"And our big leap is to do most of the magic with a theater-of-the-mind aesthetic. Complicated sets are out. No time, no money. Costumes will be very simple and easy. We've got our designer scouring thrift stores now.

"Imagine Theseus, King of Athens, in a Nehru jacket," FX said.

"Or a dashiki?" I suggested.

"No, that's Oberon. But exactly." Taz took over the explaining.

"The lighting and the music will be key. It's where we'll make the 'theater' happen. My people are working on the music rights like 24/7, so the whole show will be soundtracked to the Woodstock soundtrack. Whatever we can clear, we'll use. And my lighting director is the best. We're also using big-screen projections for a rock-concert feel."

FX refilled my glass and said, "The festival's director is completely behind this. Gus Grant is new, so he wants to bring some new energy, new concepts to Ashland. The ticketing is going to be done by a daily lottery, with people lining up to get wristbands. They hope that will bring younger audiences here. Hey, normally, they wouldn't let a guy like me show up and do one play and call it a day. I'd have to be in two or three productions and earn my repertory stripes. But I know Gus from way back. He's happy to have me." FX's face registered self-consciousness. "Or, I should say, us." Taz didn't look comforted.

"To *Midsummer!*" I toasted, hoping to cover the slight.

"To *Midsummer!*" the boys replied.

I looked up past my raised glass and saw that there were actually stars in the night sky, something we don't really have in Southern California. They surprised me for a second. I had to recalibrate my brain, recalling where I was and what was happening. It was a delightful realization that I'd have many more conversations like this over the next few weeks. Then I got another surprise.

"So Liz, how long are you staying. Few days?" It was Taz, and it appeared to be a genuine question. I was dumbstruck.

FX answered for me, because apparently my mouth was no longer functional. "Elizabeth's here all summer. She's writing a book about Shakespeare and contemporary relationships." His eyes pleaded with me to play along. "Ashland's the perfect place for that, right?"

I summoned the fewest words I could get away with at the moment. "You bet."

"What exactly does Taz think I'm doing here?" I tried to keep the negativity out of my voice, because I was acutely aware that FX was both my idiot ex-husband and my boss.

"It doesn't matter what Taz thinks. You work for me. Can you slow down?"

I slowed my race walk to a stomp to allow FX to catch up with me. We were on our way back to my cottage. I thought my head might explode. "I'm not that comfortable with vague job descriptions and undefined relationships. Ever. I need to know the plan. The whole plan. And where I fit in."

"I respect that. But Taz is Taz, and I have to respect him as well."

"What?" I stopped stomping long enough to call FX out on his human-resources mumbo jumbo.

"Here's the deal. If Taz knew that I was more concerned about my reputation than his artistic vision, he'd never have agreed to work on this. Taz is all about Taz, and you gotta get on board the whole way. No questions asked. He doesn't tolerate, you know, the risk-averse." FX was clearly struggling to not look like a complete wimp. "I told him you were helping me with the text and the lines, as a Shakespearean scholar."

"But not that I was your ex-wife here to make sure you didn't humiliate yourself prior to an Oscar campaign?"

"Right." At least he was being honest with me now. I flashed back to the conversation I'd had with my father near the fountain. He thought FX wasn't being honest. How had he known?

"So now what's the plan? I just stick around, show up at rehearsal and insinuate myself into the production? Keeping one eye on Taz and the other on details like making sure you don't look like a fop in a Nehru jacket?"

"Yes!" FX was thrilled that I'd come up with the exact right wording to complete my job description. "Nice use of the word fop!"

"I was kidding."

'Well, I'm not."

I took a deep breath and started walking again, slower this time, more resolved to my predicament. There was nothing I could do. "I wish you had told me."

"Then you wouldn't have come," he said. That was true. I would have stayed home with my beets and my kale and my crappy kitchen. But I'd already cashed the first paycheck and, back in Pasadena, Pierce DeVine had pulled the permits, so I'd just have to play along.

"Tell me what to do."

FX casually put his arm over my shoulder. "You just said it. Watch rehearsals. Keep a low profile. Give me your notes. That's all. And don't worry, everyone will just assume you're there because we're sleeping together. You won't have to explain much."

Really? Would the cast and crew actually think I was the follow-up to a Brazilian supermodel? My green tea regimen must be working. Much to my chagrin, I was tickled by the thought and oddly comforted. He may have worked the old bait and switch on me, but apparently I still had it going on. "Fine."

We arrived in front of my cottage, and the screen door opened. Maddie stepped out on the front porch and waved. Puck headed down the stairs and trotted out to the sidewalk, circling me like I was his long-lost BFF, even though we'd been acquainted for less than twenty-four hours.

"Who's that?" FX asked quietly, pointing to Maddie.

Now I had an omission to confess. Oh well, mine seemed insignificant in comparison. "My assistant Maddie. Thanks for approving her via Angie. She's also my seventeen-year-old niece. So do not even look in her direction or my sister Bumble will beat you."

"Say no more. And who's this?" FX leaned down and rubbed Puck's belly.

"My assistant's assistant. Puck. He's on your payroll, too."

FX stood up and looked straight into my eyes. For one second, I thought he might kiss me, but instead he gave me a light punch on the shoulder, brother-style. "We're quite a team. Goodnight, Lizzie."

When the phone rang about fifteen minutes later, I was already in bed enjoying several Anthropologie catalogs I'd packed for just this purpose. I loved spending my last few waking minutes in a fantasy world of home products and flowing skirts, especially tonight, when the situation with Taz looked so grim. I couldn't even bear to mention anything to Maddie, who was chomping at the bit to meet the Great Oz. I'd exchanged a few pleasantries, thanked her for the tip on the sheath dress, and headed to my room with Puck, who must have really disliked his former owners, because he'd certainly made himself at home at Sage Cottage over the last sixteen hours.

I picked up without looking at the number, assuming it was FX. "Yes, dahlink," I said, using an extravagant Zsa Zsa Gabor accent.

Silence, then a voice that was definitely not FX's responded. "I am wearing your bathrobe, but still it feels a little soon for 'darling.'"

Oh, no. "Rafa? My mistake. I thought you were…never mind." My face was suddenly flushed and I felt the urge to put on lipstick. How did my hair look? "Is everything okay?"

"Sorry to call so late." He sounded genuinely sorry. "You're obviously expecting someone else, so I'll be quick."

No, nobody else, I wanted to shout. *Who else would call after 10 p.m.?* I haven't gotten a call after 10 p.m. *in years!* Except for that one creepy student in 2011 and why bother Rafa with that? Instead of responding, I managed a sad little gurgling sound, which he politely ignored.

"I'm trying to do my laundry," he said.

"Is this a first for you?" I was trying to get a handle on the conversation, so I overcompensated with sarcasm. If only my brain would stop picturing him in my house in my robe. Any robe. Or no robe. "Do you need me to talk you through separating the colors and the whites?"

Rafa was up for the challenge. "Hey, I know how to do laundry. Although, I admit, I've been a fluff 'n' fold guy for about the last decade."

I pictured him walking out of a DC dry cleaners with an armful of blue suits and stacks of crisp white shirts and ironed Brooks Brothers boxers. "Fair enough. You're a busy man. You're entitled to fluff 'n' fold. What's the problem?"

"I can't seem to get the water to go into the machine. All the right buttons are pushed, but the water refuses to cooperate."

I laughed. "Apparently you didn't get to page ten of the manual I left in the kitchen: Helpful Hints for Living in an Old House."

"I only made it to page eight before the wax candles burned out."

"You have to turn on the master water first, then you can run the washer. In the back of the washer, to the left, look for a green handle. Turn it a half turn and then wait like ten seconds. Then the water will fill when you push 'on.'"

"That's convenient," he replied, obviously not amused by my inefficient system and slightly embarrassed that he didn't figure out this simple system himself. "Can I ask why you just can't leave the handle in that position all the time?"

"Oh you can." I paused for dramatic effect. "But then you wouldn't be able to run the shower. Laundry or shower, take your pick." Please pick shower. Please pick shower.

I could hear him straining as he reached behind the washer. "I could put on my dirty clothes and wear them into the shower."

My face flushed again. "That's another way to save time and resources."

"Got it. Thanks. Anything I need to know about the dryer? Is it connected to the TV or the coffeemaker?"

"The dryer is an independent. I think that's what your people say. But don't overload it and don't mind the loud noises during the final minute. It's possessed by a cat in heat. Seriously." It's true. Almost weekly, I was startled by the high-pitched wailing that the dryer let out. "But feel free to dry your clothes and brew coffee at the same time."

"Next time I'll consult the manual before calling."

"I don't mind." Really. There was a pause and I had to quell the urge to ask him about his day. Or tell him about mine. But it was 10:30 and the guy was doing laundry. He didn't want to hear about my life; he wanted to wash some white T-shirts, have a beer, and go to bed. "Call any time."

Rafa paused. "Thanks, Elizabeth. I'll let you get back to whatever you were doing. Oh, and I'm not really wearing your robe."

"I know. I am. Good night." Sweet prince.

FAKE THE SHAKE
Love vs. Lust

Need some help figuring out if it's the real deal or just a fleeting passion
that's going to flame out after a few weeks? Let the Bard
be your guide. Read his words and see which ones best describe
your relationship.

LOVE:
"My bounty is as boundless
    as the sea,
My love as deep;
    the more I give to thee,
The more I have,
    for both are infinite."
— *Romeo & Juliet*

LUST:
"Eternity was in our lips and eyes,
Bliss in our brows' bent;
    none our parts so poor
But was a race of heaven."
— *Antony & Cleopatra*

LOVE:
"Doubt thou the stars are fire;
Doubt that the sun doth move;
Doubt truth to be a liar;
But never doubt I love."
— *Hamlet*

LUST:
"Love is a spirit all compact of fire."
— *Venus & Adonis*

LOVE:
"I would not wish any companion
    in the world but you."
— The *Tempest*

LUST:
"I'll make my heaven
    in a lady's lap."
— *Henry VI, Part 3*

**OR, IN ONE SIMPLE
COMPARE & CONTRAST:**
"Love comforteth like
    sunshine after rain,
But Lust's effect is
    tempest after sun;
Love's gentle spring
    doth always fresh remain,
Lust's winter comes
    ere summer half be done;
Love surfeits not,
    Lust like a glutton dies;
Love is all truth,
    Lust full of forged lies."
— *Venus & Adonis*

CHAPTER 11

I had two choices: I could wallow in the disappointment that I wouldn't be a co-creator of a groundbreaking production of *Midsummer* or I could suck it up and perpetuate the traditional Lancaster method of denial: just pretend it wasn't happening. After the third text from Bumble asking how we were doing and a call from my mother about my fictitious Redfield resume, I chose the Suck It Up and Deny method. If my family knew that my much-ballyhooed creative consultant role had been reduced to Professional Fake Girlfriend with Strong but Privately Held Opinions, I'd be humiliated. I needed to create a diversion and fortunately, I had two: my book and my new dog.

Please don't let Puck's owners turn up.

As far as my book went, the only drawback was the actual writing. I learned very quickly that a pithy one-page query letter is not nearly as difficult to write as a forty-page nonfiction-book proposal. Let's just say it didn't exactly expand itself. I was pretty much going to have to research, outline, and write the whole book before I could reduce it to a sharp proposal. This is where my lack of any actual relationship expertise was really a drawback. Not to mention my lack of actual relationships.

FX had texted me that the first read-through was at two and he'd like me to "slip in the back." (Always a good feeling to know you're wanted.) That meant I had the whole morning to kill working on my book. Fortunately, I had one tiny idea, and I hoped it would lead to something vaguely resembling *Bridget Jones* meets *Downton Abbey*. Otherwise I'd have a whole lot of Shakespeare and not much romance.

But first, I needed to convince Maddie that the book was my top priority. I didn't want her communicating to Bumble and the rest of Pasadena that I'd been banned from the *Midsummer* set. She needed to think that my book *All's Fair* was now, as they say in Hollywood, in "first position," and *Midsummer* was so under control that it barely needed my attention. I was an awful aunt and mentor.

I called a staff meeting and Maddie and Puck attended. "As my new editorial assistant, I need you to go out and get every women's magazine on the stands. And any publication that features photos of couples, celebrity or not. I'm putting together an inspiration board for *All's Fair*. It's like Pinterest but with real paper. We need to put in a lot of time on the book."

Maddie totally fell for it. "I have so many ideas on how I can help. I can do the real Pinterest board and Facebook, blog, Instagram, and Twitter. Plus, you know, research."

"Good. I have the Shakespeare covered. I need a little help with pop culture." My one tiny idea stemmed from the conversation at our going-away party. Comparing Bumble and Ted to the Macbeths had gotten me thinking. There was something in the idea that contemporary couples could be Shakespearean archetypes. I wasn't quite sure where that would go, but it was better than dwelling on sixteenth-century couples, so I filled Maddie in on the project basics, adding, "Here's my big concept: I'm positioning myself as a relationship commentator, not a relationship expert. See the difference?"

"Sort of. Are you a commentator because you haven't really had any relationships in a while? Except that thing with FX? I mean, that's what Bumble says. That you're scared." From the look of discomfort on her face, Maddie knew invoking the name Bumble was a miscalculation the second it came out of her lip-glossed mouth.

Breathe. It's not Maddie's fault. *Dear Bumble, thanks for confiding in your teen stepdaughter that I have relationship issues. It makes me feel so much closer to Maddie, knowing that we've both had the same number of boyfriends in the last year: zero. Plus we share the maturity level of a college freshman. Please let me take care of Maddie for you as you enjoy all that sex! Love, your sister, Elizabeth.* I wanted to be snarky, but I still had to win Maddie over completely, so I said, "Okay, that 'thing with FX' was an actual marriage, so yes, it took me a while to get over. And I have had other relationships. I'm not scared. I just haven't been lucky enough to meet someone as great as, say, your dad."

"I'm sorry, Elizabeth."

"No need to apologize. I'm just trying to explain my point of view, not justify my relationship history. The good news is I won't be giving advice in the book."

"That seems smart. That's what Bumble would say. And Nana Anne!" Maddie blurted out.

Oh good, my sister *and* my mother had been chatting openly about my love life. Unfortunately, they did have a point. But just because I hadn't really been with anyone since the law firm of Minot Stewart, it doesn't mean I'd forgotten what it was like to be in a relationship. *Count to ten, Elizabeth.* "Just get the magazines and we'll have some fun this morning working on my outline ideas. This afternoon, we have a read-through for *Midsummer*. It's a closed rehearsal, but I think I can sneak you in through the back door."

I was shameless, using Maddie as both shield and sword. As penance for my deeds, I suggested she look for a good bakery nearby and buy us a treat.

I set to work creating an inspiration wall in the living room. I wrote the names of Shakespearean couples on colorful notecards and taped them to the wall, starting with the obvious, like Romeo and Juliet, and working my way down the list to such lesser-known figures as Troilus and Cressida. In between, I added such crowd faves as Katherine and Petruchio and Sebastian and Viola, and then a similar number of downer couples like Othello and Desdemona. They'd provide the framework for the romantic archetypes. I included quotes and key words. *Who ever loved that loved not at first sight? The very instant that I saw you, did my heart fly to your service. Love is a spirit all compact of fire.* I admit, some quotes made me hot. I slapped a photo of Bumble and Ted right next to the Macbeths and stood back to admire my handiwork.

I figured if I could move the cards around for several hours, then I could successfully claim to have "worked on my book all morning," even if I did nothing else. That was only two more hours, if I knocked off for lunch at 11:30. I taped slowly.

Maddie burst through the front door, flush with the success of her first latte run of the summer. "Found a great coffee place right down the street on Fourth. They roast their own beans. You'll love it. And I bought us one cinnamon chocolate croissant to split at Deux Chats bakery. Your skinny latte, boss."

A buttery pastry and a nonfat latte. Girl's gotta cut back somewhere.

Maddie studied the wall while I burned my mouth on the scalding latte. "Oh, Rosalind and Orlando. From *As You Like It.* I like them. They seem like a fun couple, like Posh and Becks."

"Really? Rosalind and Orlando seem like David and Victoria Beckham. How?"

"Love at first sight. Rosalind is a noble, like Posh. And didn't she check out Orlando while he was wrestling? That's kind of like soccer. They just had a lot of chemistry right off the bat."

"I don't think being a Spice Girl makes you a noble, but Rosalind did spend most of *As You Like It* in men's clothing, and Victoria Beckham is a little mannish, isn't she?" It wasn't epic, but it was a start. "Is there a picture of them in *US Weekly*?"

Of course there was. Posh and Becks went up on the wall next to the names Rosalind and Orlando, and we were off.

I'd never really experienced a creative lightbulb moment before. I'd always been more of a plugger and a plodder. Whether it was a middle school paper or my doctoral thesis, I took a slow and steady approach, with my most insightful writing coming after weeks, if not months, of careful work. But at that moment, with my mouth burned to bits, I swear a lightbulb went off. My tiny idea was going to work. "Okay, Maddie, go through all those magazines and rip out the photos of any celebrity couples. Or any couples at all. Or anyone that anybody might know—politicians, writers, journalists, athletes. We're onto something."

By lunchtime, the wall was filled with photos, quotes, and even more notecards. I was starting to see the book. The characters that I'd read about and lectured about for so long became contemporary role models for what to do and what not to do in a relationship. And almost every memorable Shakespearean character seemed to have a well-known pop doppelganger. I made lists of Guys Your Mother Will Love, Guys Your Father Will Love, and In-laws to Avoid at All Costs. (Hello, Lady Capulet.) I created a montage of Shakespearean Bad Girls, Good Girls, and Just Plain Nuts Girls and their modern counterparts. (Funny how there was a different phase of Lindsay Lohan to fit all three categories.) Finally, I made a list of Renaissance Relationship Red Flags, including: Talks to Ghosts; Always at Battle;

and Has Weird Thing for Sister. (I'm looking at you, Laertes.)

We were giddy with ideas. Even Puck could feel the excitement and raced around the living room chasing his tail. When I heard a knock on the door, I looked at my phone and was surprised to see it was past noon. Puck padded to the door with me.

It was FX, looking for a lunch date. He was in his trademark black T-shirt and jeans with a lightweight suede jacket thrown on. His skin was damp and flushed, and his hair was still wet, like he'd just jumped out of his own personal hot spring. He pulled a tube of lip balm out of his pocket and swiped it on his perfect lips. "Wanna go to lunch and then head over to the read-through? Together?"

I couldn't miss his meaning. He wasn't going to make me actually sneak in the back. I could walk through the front door with him. The star. "Sounds great."

I introduced him to a suddenly self-conscious Maddie, who couldn't stop smiling while looking at her feet. FX welcomed her to "the team," which only made her blush deeper. He bent down to pet Puck, and it occurred to me that the dog was the only one in the room who wasn't impressed by FX.

"Whatcha doing?" he asked after noticing our huge inspiration board. He almost seemed a tad jealous that he'd been left out.

"Brainstorming for my book," I announced with a Vanna White hand gesture. "We are on fire. That William S is quite the relationship guru."

FX took in the scene. He smiled as he put the photos and the concept together in his mind. Then he studied the notecards, reading one aloud: "Best Shakespearean pickup lines. Elizabethan version: *Come woo me, woo me. For I am in a holiday humor and likely to consent.* Today's version: *I'm totally drunk. Wanna hook up?*" He snorted with laughter. "This is great, Lizzie!"

A shot of pleasure went through me. It was only one line, but it represented the whole concept. "Thanks. Will you blurb it? My agent wants to know."

"Of course. How about this? 'The best book on modern relation-ships ever. I wish I'd read it before I married the author.'"

It was my turn to laugh, but it came out more of a wistful sigh. Our eyes met for a second or more. He smiled his weekend-box-office-winning smile, and I reciprocated the best I could. Then I remembered Maddie was in the room. Her eyes were wide with wonder, as if she was discovering a great truth for the first time. FX wasn't a movie star to me. He was the boy who broke my heart. Now it was my turn for self-consciousness. I lightened enough to say, "That's a perfect blurb. It's going right on the cover of my proposal. FX Fahey says...."

"Pretty much guarantees a bestseller. I am publishing gold. Do I get any sort of writing credit for the blurb?"

"No. But I'll send you a free copy of the book."

"Deal. Okay, let's go to lunch. I'm starving. I've been working out all morning. Angie found this beast of a trainer here who is, like, a smoke jumper in his spare time. He has me flipping tires and moving barrels and crap. Have you ever done that kind of workout?"

Of course I hadn't. "I'm an English professor. I garden and play tennis. I don't move truck tires."

"But you could. One day, you're coming with me. Maddie, you in on the tires? Is that your thing?" FX pointed at the stunned seventeen-year-old. She couldn't believe FX had said her name out loud.

"I manage the table tennis team," she responded.

"Now that's some heavy lifting," he teased. "How much do those balls weigh? Half an ounce? Are you coming to lunch with us?"

Surely this was the best day of her young life thus far. She looked at me for guidance. "Umm...."

"Yes, of course. Come. Let's get all our stuff. We'll go straight to the theater after lunch, right?" It occurred to me that I could use Maddie at lunch. My stomach had been a little warm and gooey when I spent time alone with FX. Having a chaperone would take any edge off our conversation.

"Okay, sure. But, I have to tell you something...." She looked really worried.

Oh no, less than seventy-two hours into our big adventure and something had gone horribly wrong. Had she talked to a reporter? Given the barista FX's cell number? Had Puck's parents called?

"I'm a vegetarian," she confessed.

Relief.

"Thank God. I thought the *National Enquirer* was going to be outside. Since when are you a vegetarian?" I asked, recalling her scarfing down an In-N-Out Burger on the drive up.

"Since yesterday. You know, since my dad gets a lot of support from Big Ag, I have to eat meat at home. But starting yesterday, I'm a vegetarian. I'll tell him when I get home in August. I'm working up to it, but I thought you should know."

"Thank you. FX, do you have any issues with vegetarians?" I asked with mock seriousness.

"Some of my best friends are vegetarians."

At the brew pub we tucked into a booth and ordered a round of iced teas and various meals, with and without meat. FX considered a beer but decided against it. There was too much at stake with the first read-through to arrive with the local Caldera IPA on his breath. He had to impress his director and the cast of seasoned actors.

I sensed his nerves by the way he was talking nonstop about being on set with live tigers in his last film. Apparently he'd played a dirty cop at a rendezvous gone wrong at the Bronx Zoo. He held up his hands about a foot apart, "Have you ever stood this close to a tiger?"

He genuinely waited for an answer

Again, Maddie and I shook our heads. What does he think we

do all day? "FX, English teacher, high school senior. No tigers in our daily lives."

As he went on about choreographing the tiger chase scene, I could see that Maddie was entranced. Once she got over her initial shyness, she returned to the savvy congressman's daughter that she was. Her life in Southern California included fundraisers, ribbon cuttings, and various backstage meet-and-greets with her father's supporters, who were occasionally famous. She had hung with the Schwarzenegger kids and appeared on behalf of her father at rallies. At school, her classmates were the daughters of Academy Award–winning screenwriters and sitcom actors. Emma #3's dad had been in a seminal '80s rock band that had once toured with Squeeze. Maddie could handle a movie star.

It occurred to me that if things had worked out differently, FX would have been her uncle. And I was relieved to see that's exactly the way he was treating her, like she was his high school niece. I could honestly report to Bumble that she had nothing to worry about when it came to Maddie. Except, of course, an iron deficiency from the lack of meat, but I didn't feel that was my department.

Just then, a duo of college girls in Oregon State T-shirts approached the table. They stood about ten feet away at first, as if we weren't going to notice their staring and gawking. FX tensed, then breathed deeply and turned to the young women, "Hi, can I help you?" Something he had obviously said a zillion times.

"We love you!" the girls shrieked, in fine Tri Delt form. "Can we take a picture with you?"

FX graciously posed for photos, signed several autographs, and thanked the girls for their support. He was lovely and charming and clearly over this part of his life. By the time the disturbance was over, half the restaurant seemed headed our way for their own Facebook trophies. FX signaled the waiter, giving him the international hand motion for "Check, please." We were only about halfway through our meals, but I couldn't blame him.

I thought about shoving down the other half of my BLT but decided to take advantage of the weight-loss opportunity. No wonder celebrities were so skinny—they never got to finish a meal.

"Does that get old?" I asked FX as he paid the bill.

"Part of the job. I hear it gets worse when they stop asking."

Maddie rolled her eyes as we headed out the door. "That never would have happened in Pasadena." That's true. We might not boast as many movie stars as Brentwood or Beverly Hills, but Pasadenans were sophisticated enough to let a guy eat his turkey sandwich in peace.

FX smiled as he slipped on his Ray-Bans. "I think I'll be safe with these on. Next time, I'll wear a baseball hat. Let's walk."

POWER COUPLE #4

Henry & Katherine

FROM HENRY V

HER: Princess and political pawn. The daughter of the king of France, married off to keep the peace with England. Gentle, feminine, a girly girl. More wily in the ways of men than she lets on. Speaks very little English, or pretends not to understand, to gain a romantic advantage. Totally plays the King of England.

HIM: Reformed bad boy, now king of England. Focused, disciplined, leader of men. Once he sets his mind to a task, he will stop at nothing to accomplish it. Brilliant orator, inspiring speaker, and one of the great flirters in the entire Shakespearean canon.

MEET CUTE: In a palace near the battlefield, with their countries at war, surrounded by translators and advisors. And then a treaty is signed.

WHY THEY WORK: It's bigger than the both of them: He is England and she is France.

BEST LINE MAYBE EVER: "You have witchcraft in your lips, Kate."

RELATIONSHIP MOTTO: "Customs curtsy to great kings. We are the makers of manners, Kate."

SHAKESPEAREAN COUPLE MOST LIKELY TO: Appear on the cover of *People* a record number of times.

WHO THEY REMIND YOU OF: The Duke and Duchess of Cambridge, if Will had to conquer France before he could marry Kate, and Kate had to learn a foreign language. Or Beyonce and Jay-Z.

CHEMISTRY FACTOR: 4.5 OUT OF 5

CHAPTER 12

The heart of the Oregon Shakespeare Festival lies in the bustling theater complex that sits a short but steep hike up from East Main Street. Comprising multiple theaters, rehearsal spaces, scenery and costume workshops, and offices, this is where all the action happens during festival season. From the faithfully re-created outdoor Elizabethan stage, to the elegant Angus Bowmer theater, to the intimate new black-box space, the three-block beehive was bursting with creative energy and theater adoration even this early in the season. The courtyard in between the theaters was the hub for ticket selling, pre-play lectures, musical performances, and glorious banners. It was also the spot to line up before a play and to gather to discuss the work after the curtain came down. The beloved, verdant Lithia Park provided a cooling background even on the hottest summer days. It was Ashland's Times Square, Central Park, and Lincoln Center combined, minus the car horns and taxicabs but with the lovely Tudor Guild Gift Shop, staffed by lovely Tudor

Guild volunteers, who were there for all of your Shakespeare-themed cocktail-napkin needs.

I'd been here a half dozen times before as a theatergoer with students and friends, but never like this, on the inside of a production. As we climbed the pitch up Pioneer Street, I felt my pulse racing. This is why I came to Ashland, to feel this sense of excitement and purpose.

I was so happy to be among my people that I almost forgot I wasn't really wanted. FX took my hand and squeezed it. "Here we are!"

Well, at least one person wanted me here.

We ducked into the New Theater, which, according to the press guide that Angie had included in our welcome packet, had recently been renamed the Thomas Theater, thanks to the generosity of a group of donors, none of whom were named Thomas. The new name hadn't caught on yet, but the festival was trying. The rehearsal space for *Midsummer* was inside the complex, and FX knew where we were headed. The security person at the door nodded as we produced IDs, noting that only FX was on the list, but he waved us all through when FX said, "They're with me." I should take him to LAX with me.

We stood in the wide hallway, pausing before heading into the room where the cast and production team would be waiting. FX looked more nervous than I'd seen him look since we started this grand experiment back in April. He took a deep breath. "Back onstage, Lizzie. Can you believe it?"

"I can," I said. "You'll be great. You know that, right? This is going to be epic."

"It will, won't it?" he said, but he didn't look like he believed it.

I tried to assuage his fears. "Do you want to create a safe sign? Like an SOS?"

He shook his head, but I went on. "Just in case you feel like something is going awry and you want a gut check." Yes, it was a little foolish, but I was getting paid to look out for his broader interests, and besides, I needed a little job security. That kitchen wasn't going to remodel itself. And I was not losing that prep sink just because some Aussie director didn't want to share the spotlight. The least I could do was make myself available, even if I had to pretend to be invisible. "Believe me, if things are going really badly, I'll call 911. But short of that, you might need me."

"Well...."

"If you're concerned, flash me a peace sign." I demonstrated. "I'll take notes and talk to you about it after."

"Okay, that's a good plan. But it's going to be great, right?"

"It's gonna be great."

It was going to be great, if the three-hour read-through was any indication. From the moment we stepped through the door, it felt like we'd entered another world. A world of magical words and wonderful actors and big, big thinkers. I was afraid to use the bathroom because I didn't want to miss a second of the rehearsal.

Taz dominated the afternoon, but the actors held up their end in terms of electricity. Because of the short timeline and the last-minute nature of the production, the casting had been done by the OSF casting director, not Taz and FX. But it was clear that the actors were seasoned and lovely to look at, with skin of every color. For some reason, they also smelled really good, like they'd all gone out together in the lavender fields, rolled around, and headed into the read-through. I hoped the perfumed air was symbolic of the love and harmony to come.

Maddie and I slipped into a dark corner, kept our heads down, and observed the proceedings like they, in and of themselves, were a piece of theater. It took me right back to my high school productions. I could pick out the diva, the ingénue, the bit players, and the leads.

There was the guy who'd been desperate for attention at sixteen and was still desperate for attention at thirty-six. The players might have been more polished and professional, but the dynamics were the same.

Taz and his crew were already deep in conversation as the actors wandered in. I guessed his choreographer, Phoebe, was the woman in all black with the wide headband and dreadlocks. The lighting designer, I think Taz had called him Jason, was a tall, thin man with a short beard and neatly cuffed jeans, like Carson Cressly with half the sass. Lulu, his stage manager, was a short, stocky woman with a buzz cut, a tight white T-shirt, and Dickies, and she'd clearly break heads if anyone missed a cue. The sound designer, a young guy in a Radiohead T-shirt, hung on every word Taz delivered. The costume designer, Zadie, a striking woman with a long gray ponytail, exuded energy and color, perfect for the show. Off to the side, a young intern, about the same age as Maddie, juggled two cell phones and a clipboard. He looked absolutely terrified. This was a formidable team and obviously one that did not need a community college English professor to advise them on how to mount a production of any sort. What was FX thinking? What was I thinking?

I noticed the actors sneaking quick glances at FX as he waded his way through the crowd, introducing himself and shaking hands. The youngish foursome, laughing a little too loudly, must be playing the young lovers. The actor playing Puck was easy to spot, spry and slightly green, as if he'd had a little too much to drink last night. A gaggle of character actors stood in a circle telling stories; they were probably the ones who'd been cast as the Deadheads/Rude Mechanicals. One was even wearing a tie-dyed T-shirt in solidarity. These were professionals who had dozens of plays, Shakespeare and otherwise, on their resumes. Belonging to a well-established repertory company like OSF allowed them the sorts of perks most actors never achieved: steady paychecks, regular work, and artistic satisfaction. But FX was a rich movie star and *People*'s Sexiest Man on Earth 2008, and those were credits that ninety-nine-point-nine percent of working actors would never earn.

Right away, FX found the actress who'd play Titania to his Oberon. Her name was Sabrina Cooke, and according to her bio on the website, which I'd memorized that morning over coffee, she had studied at UNC and Juilliard, been a member of the company for ten years, and had a recurring role on *Law & Order: SVU*, among other TV parts. This summer, in addition to her *Midsummer* role, Sabrina was Katherine, Queen of France, in *Henry V*, and she was also playing Cinderella in the production of a new high-concept musical called *Medea/Macbeth/Cinderella*.

Oh good, I thought, she not only can act but sing and dance while doing both light comedy and heavy drama. A real no-talent.

Sabrina was striking in that "Nicole Kidman is my Personal Jesus" kind of way, with skin that had never been sunburned, an emerald green scarf, and deep auburn hair that looked like it cost a small fortune to maintain. Where did she find a colorist that good in this neck of the woods, I wondered, as I watched her toss her locks back and forth. Even from a distance, I could tell FX was charmed. I felt a little sick to my stomach.

The scene took me right back to New York City in 1998, when FX had debuted in *Cymbeline*, his first gig out of college. He'd won a small but noticeable part in the Public Theater's production with Liev Schreiber, that summer's offering for Shakespeare in the Park. I toiled away as a production intern, which meant mountains of copying, sorting, filing, and occasionally handing out free tickets on street corners. Meanwhile, FX got his first taste of New York applause, great reviews, and willing cast mates. As I watched him now, my face burning, I couldn't help but wonder how many Sabrinas there had been in our short marriage. Well, besides the one I knew about.

Better not to think about it. Denial was my Personal Jesus.

Fortunately, just as I was about to spiral downward into what Bumble would call "a pity party for one," Taz started off the rehearsal with a rousing speech that outlined his vision for the play and the schedule over the next two weeks leading up to opening night. Then he introduced FX, who got a small round of applause. He humbly thanked the company for welcoming him into their midst under special circumstances. "I know you're all performing at least three roles this season, six nights a week, with barely a day off. I'd like to get at least some credit for doing two roles in one play a couple of days a week. First round on me after we open."

A short cheer went up from the other actors. FX glanced at me and I gave him the thumbs up. Not our safe sign, but I thought he'd understand the meaning.

Once the read-through started, Taz exerted his control. He was more of a conductor than director. He stood in the front of the room, his ripped arms highlighted by his body-hugging white shirt, commanding the actors to speak. Occasionally he grabbed the actors and led them through simple blocking while they did their speeches, like a dance partner. Sometimes he'd stop actors mid-scene to praise and skip ahead. "Good, good. No need to read further. Let's move on. Next...." Or give them an instruction and have them try it again. At the tops of scenes, he'd point to his technical crew, as if he held a baton in right hand, and they chimed in with what the lighting would look like, what the costumes might suggest, what music would be in the background to give the actors a sense of what they were working with. There was laughter and romance from the words on the page, but there was also pressure and high expectations from Taz. By the time the last line was delivered, the vibe in the room was a collective shout. Taz was dripping in sweat.

I was blown away.

After thanking everyone for their hard work, Taz sent the actors off for the night. Many of them had to be onstage in a few hours, as the season was already in full swing, including productions of *Henry V, The Tempest, Our Town*, and two new plays by young playwrights. "Good work. Lulu's posted the call sheet for the next week. Get your sleep and eat your Wheaties, because this show is going to rock 'n' roll." For the first time all day, Taz looked in my direction. He gave me a subdued head lift and eyebrow raise. I reciprocated with a brief smile.

That guy didn't like me.

"So?" FX asked after the rest of the cast had left.

"That was something else. Everyone is so good. That was a first read-through and the pace and chemistry was crazy good."

"I know. Just…wow. I haven't felt like this in years. Remember *Cymbeline?*" *Yeah, I did.* I hesitated, and FX quickly amended his question. "The electricity onstage? It felt like that."

Taz wandered over and skipped the pleasantries. "FX, are you staying? Lots to go over. We're ordering dinner. Maybe your intern can help our intern Dylan here."

My jaw dropped. Confirmed. Taz really didn't like me. No way I was helping the shiny-faced teen in black jeans get dinner for Lulu, et al. Then FX piped up, "Yeah, I'll stay. Maddie, are you busy? Can you help the other intern get food for us?"

Oh, Taz meant Maddie. I felt a huge wave of relief and then realized that Maddie was going to get to listen in on production details and I was being sent home. I jumped in to save face. "Great idea. I have to run home to walk the dog. This was fantastic to watch, Taz. Thanks for letting me observe. So much to take home to my students. Maddie, you'll stay, right?"

"I'd love to." Her enthusiasm for fetching food made me suspicious until I saw her mooning at intern Dylan. Of course, she was excited about being near a movie star and a famous director, but clearly she was more thrilled to be near another soul who loved theater, wore glasses, and was cute. Maddie turned to me, "You sure, Elizabeth?"

"Of course, you're here to learn. And one of the most important things you can learn how to do in your career is order meals. I think you have a leg up on Dylan, because I know Bumble doesn't cook. But don't walk home alone. Text me if you need me to come get you."

Oh God, I sounded like a soccer mom. FX laughed. "It's Ashland. I think the last crime committed here was in 1982 and involved lawn gnomes."

"Hey, we have a missing ferret on our street. You don't know what happened to that ferret."

"I'll make sure she gets home safely," Dylan said with a shy smile.

3 Guys
Your Mom Will Love

COUNT PARIS FROM *ROMEO & JULIET*

The guy Juliet was supposed to marry if her parents had had their way before Romeo had his. Stiff and formal, an awkward dancer, and a really bad kisser. Often portrayed as overbearing and presumptuous, but methinks he's just trying to win Juliet with trumped-up courage and faith in the future.
Who He Reminds Us of: Matthew Crawley.
Why Moms Love Him: Rich, polite, and no threat to daughter's virginity.
Major Drawback: Lacks passion.

DUKE ORSINO FROM *TWELFTH NIGHT*

The perfect gentleman: handsome, brave, virtuous, and rich. Tends to romantic melancholy (*"If music be the food of love, play on"*) but not so melancholic that he's a downer. Quickly switches affections from the unattainable Olivia to the former pageboy Viola, but that's okay because he's got a poet's soul and an investment banker's net worth.
Who He Reminds Us of: James Franco with more money.
Why Moms Love Him: Enjoys the arts. Willing to accompany the in-laws to the symphony and write large checks to arts charities.
Major Drawback: Enough with the Renaissance Man thing.

WESTMORELAND FROM *HENRY IV, PARTS 1 & 2,* AND *HENRY V*

Stand-up guy, loyal servant to the king, honorable soldier. Has tremendous influence with those in power. Sparked the famous St. Crispin's Day speech in *Henry V*, wondering what all those guys in England were doing lying in bed instead of standing up on the battlefield at Agincourt.
Who He Reminds Us of: General Petreus, pre-scandal.
Why Moms Love Him: Wears impressive medals to society events. Has great access to the king. Improves overall status of family by reputation.
Major Drawback: Not home much.

CHAPTER 13

Now I understood why dogs have been so valued across the span of history: Nobody was ever as happy to see me as Puck was when I arrived home. I was dejected and bitter; he was ecstatic and nonjudgmental. He'd been holed up in the crate we bought the first day he arrived and was clearly ready for company, food, and a little walk. His tail wagged like crazy as he slipped in and out and around my legs. Frankly, his unjustified but unbridled love was exactly what I needed. I hugged him with abandon.

Well, this is really working out, I thought as I let Puck out the back door and opened a can of dog food. I'm home alone with a stray dog while my niece has already worked her way into the inner circle. Then it dawned on me that having Maddie on the inside would be incredibly helpful. I couldn't sit through every rehearsal. Taz's disdain made that clear. But Maddie could. Everybody loves somebody who's willing to go for sandwiches. At least now I'd have some eyes and ears in the room.

Of course, I'd have to come clean with Maddie and give her the scoop on FX's concerns and my situation vis-à-vis Taz. After watching her handle herself over the past week, I was pretty sure she could keep my status as an outsider a secret from everyone in Pasadena. It wasn't quite the same as being in the room, but having her there was as close as I was going to get. I let Puck back in the house. He looked up at me hopefully, and I rewarded him with dinner. It was nice to be needed.

One trip to the Ashland Food Co-op and I felt like a new person. Puck and I made the six-block walk together with our reusable shopping bags. First, I was relieved to see that no one had ripped a tag with my phone number off the bottom of the lost-dog poster Maddie had hung up on the community board next to the flyer with the headline "Global Peace through Inner Peace." (The healer promised to align your chakras, enhance harmonic resonance, and donate all fees to support women in war zones. Win, win, win.) I was beginning to think that Puck had arrived through a spiritual portal and intended to hasten my own chakra alignment. Every time I saw his tail wag, I felt my own personal harmonic resonance.

I tied him outside to a post, next to the water bowl the co-op provided, and dashed into the store. I went for the basics: local produce, a sampling of soft cheeses courtesy of the goats of the Rogue River Valley, and a few prepared foods, including quinoa nut loaf. Nut loaf!

Back in my tidy yellow kitchen, I was reheating the co-op's local summer squash with bagna cauda and fried capers. Normally I wasn't a fan of prepared foods, being slightly suspicious of food-borne illnesses. But Ashland was so clean, and a bagna cauda—a "hot bath" of olive oil, anchovies, and garlic—struck me as exactly the sort of thing that a single girl with dog could eat without worrying about breath issues. And who can say no to fried capers?

June in Oregon meant long days and lovely evenings, like this one, with its pinkish sunset glow on the mountains, moderate temperature, and night-blooming jasmine just beginning to burst. Now that it appeared the rehearsal period would be, umm, less intense than I'd anticipated, and my evenings might be free, I'd make plans to take in the other OSF shows already up. But there'd be time enough to get tickets and immerse myself in culture later. After the stress of the day, I was happy to jump into my cozy clothes, pour a glass of wine, and study the Food Co-op event calendar. (Yes! A mixer at the end of the month!)

My cell phone rang and Rafa's name popped up on the screen. More questions about laundry! I took a deep breath, waited another ring, and answered, trying to simulate a "just picking this up and not knowing who's on the other end" quality in my voice. "Hello. This is Elizabeth."

"Hey, it's Rafa. Sorry to bother you. Is this a bad time?"

"No, I'm just cooking dinner." *Too domestic?* Too domestic.

Or maybe not. Surprisingly Rafa responded, "Me, too. It's just that I can't turn on the stove. I keep turning the knobs and nothing happens. And I checked your manual. Nothing in there at all about the stove."

I defended myself. "I thought you weren't ever going to turn on my old stove."

"Yeah, well, that was before I discovered that no restaurant in Pasadena delivers, except Dominos. You live one mile from civilization, but restaurants act like it's Timbuktu."

The shock in his voice made me laugh. "That's true. It's not New York or DC. There aren't sesame noodles a phone call away." I relaxed into the conversation. "You can go pick up food. You're in California. We drive."

I could tell he was wandering around the kitchen, getting out pots and putting away dishes.

"Here's the thing, I don't really feel like getting in my car at the end of the day and standing in line somewhere. Why engage with people when I can just stay here?"

A chill ran through me. That's exactly the sort of thing I say. Once I'm home in my casita, I never feel like leaving. "Then you're going to have to learn to turn on my stove. Do you want me to talk you through it?" I pictured him in his gleaming white shirt approaching my 1952 four-burner-plus-griddle O'Keefe & Merritt range like it was a bucking bronco. But this was no bronco—it needed a gentle touch. "Approach with caution," I said.

"Can I just ask, what's the deal? Why can't I just turn the knobs and see the flames, like every other stove in America?" Oh, Mr. Type A was a little impatient.

"It has a double pilot system. That's what my grandmother always told me. One pilot is lit all the time, so you don't smell gas. But to fire up the burners, you need to hand light the second pilot. Not exactly professional grade."

"Or really that safe."

"That's true. And don't get me started on the fact that the oven doesn't hold heat. Do not attempt Christmas cookies; you'll be disappointed. When I re-do the kitchen, the stove goes. Somebody will want it to restore, but I need to move on. Our relationship is too unstable." Maybe I should write a relationship book about appliances instead of Shakespeare? I was definitely more skilled at working with inanimate objects. But I kept that to myself as I gave the instructions. "Okay, find the long-handled lighter in the drawer on the left next to the stove. Grab it and take a big step back."

"That sounds ominous." It was. I didn't want singed eyebrows or other disfiguring accidents on my conscience.

I guided Rafa through the procedure, carefully describing the secret opening of the mysterious second pilot. He managed just fine, thanking me for the excellent verbal directions. He sounded as if he was about to sign off, but I wasn't quite ready to say goodbye. "So what's for dinner?"

He balked a second, then admitted, "I picked some of your tomatoes and the basil. I'm making a simple uncooked sauce for pasta. And one of your eggplants looked ready, so I thought I'd sauté it up in some olive oil. Want to see the eggplant? It's a beauty."

I thought he was kidding, about his cooking skills and my vegetables, so I played along. "Oh, yeah, what a gorgeous eggplant! And is that Kraft Mac & Cheese for dessert?"

Rafa wasn't kidding. "You don't believe me? I'll show you the eggplant and my skills. I never said I couldn't cook, I said I didn't cook. Big difference. What's your Skype handle?"

Total panic shot through me on every level. First of all, I had the lamest Skype name of all times, created during an academic conference when it seemed charming and quaint. And second, I was wearing a very unflattering mock turtleneck and a scrunchie from the mid-'90s that was not for public consumption. But I didn't want the guy to think I was intimidated by a little video chatting. "Okay, give me five minutes while I..." *Apply lipstick. Throw on camisole and V-neck sweater. Switch to white wine to prevent teeth staining. Secure flattering lighting in kitchen. Ditch scrunchie for good.* "... log onto my laptop. I do need to check out your eggplant. I mean, my eggplant."

Then I confessed my Skype name: Elizabeth.The.First.

"That is huge." I was, of course, talking about the eggplant, but I could have been talking about any aspect of the evening: I was video chatting with an attractive single man, who was in his trademark white dress shirt but had rolled up the sleeves to expose some fine-looking forearms. I sprayed on a shot of Coco perfume, an oldie but goodie, for my own sort of *courage liquide*, as the French would say. And I used dry shampoo for the first time in twenty years and it worked like crazy. My hair looked fantastic. Mental note: Get more Pssssst. But even in stop-motion Skype, I could tell Rafa had a curious look on his face, so I tried to make it clear I was talking about eggplant. "The eggplant. It's so purple and ripe. You've been there less than a week and already the vegetables are growing bigger for you than for me. What's your secret?"

"I sing to them at night when the moon is full," he said in a fake Euro accent, as he picked up my large knife and prepared to slice the eggplant. He had positioned his laptop on the counter, allowing me a wide-angle shot of the kitchen, his haul from my garden, and his workstation. I wish I had a slightly closer view of him, but I took what I could get. "Actually, I wander around the garden talking on my cell phone to potential supporters. I think the plants think I'm talking to them. They like the attention. Did you have any final thoughts for the eggplant before it meets its demise?"

"Just make it quick. I don't want him to feel any pain." And Rafa did just that, proving he had some knife skills to go along with those forearms. He salted the slices to draw out the water and fired up the olive oil and garlic. I liked watching him cook in my kitchen. Really. "How's your work going?"

"It's early, but I think your brother-in-law is going to be the next governor of California. A lot of influential people on both sides of the aisle respect him. That's a good sign." He blotted the eggplant slices with a paper towel and laid them in the pan to brown. I could hear the sizzle. He opened a bottle of red wine, no fear of teeth staining, and looked into the screen again. "How are things there?"

I almost punted with a pat answer but decided to take advantage of a political strategist as long as I had one on the line. I figured if Rafa could manage a ravenous press, a hostile environment in Washington, and my sister Bumble, he could help me manage Taz. So, emboldened by distance and Viognier, I asked, "In politics, when you have to win over somebody, what do you do?"

"Identify what you have to offer them first." He didn't ask for details, just went straight for results. I appreciated that, but I didn't quite understand his point.

"What do you mean?"

"I'm assuming you want to win them over because you need something from them, like an agreement or information or access. You're not trying to win them over because you want to be liked or get votes to be prom queen, right?" He expertly turned the eggplant slices in the pan and moved on to testing his pasta while I thought about his question. He stared into the screen, waiting for my answer.

Well, yes, I did want to be liked and I would have enjoyed being prom queen, but those weren't my immediate needs. Rafa was right. I needed access to do my job. "So, you're suggesting I figure out what I have to offer before I can get what I need out of the, let's call him, unwilling, party?"

"Yes. What can you provide that nobody else can? So the unwilling party wants to work with you. Trust is a two-way street, and sometimes you have to be the one in the crosswalk first."

"Wow, listen to you, Mr. Political Pundit!" *What did I have to offer Taz?* Not much, frankly. Except a good relationship with FX and a seventeen-year-old niece willing to run errands. That was a start, I guess. I could head into the crosswalk with that.

Rafa was plating his dinner like a *Top Chef* winner: a mound of spaghetti topped with fresh tomato sauce and a side of sautéed eggplant finished with a drizzle of olive oil, a handful of Parmesan, and a touch of fresh parsley. "Is that my parsley?"

Rafa nodded. "Do you mind?"

"Of course not. It's there to be eaten."

He sat down on the stool, with his wine and his full plate, taking a bite. "I wish you could taste everything. Delicious."

Believe me, Rafa, so do I. *So do I.* I was just about to dish up my sad little serving of summer squash when I heard footsteps on the front porch. Puck let out a couple of barks and Maddie burst through the door, laughing as if she'd just heard a really great joke. FX followed behind, announcing loudly for everyone in a half-mile radius to hear. "Hi honey, we're home. Dinner smells good!"

Time to say goodbye to my digital dinner date before FX and Maddie caught me. "I have company. I have to...."

"Of course. Thanks for lighting my fire," he said, knowing how goofy it sounded but eliciting a laugh from me anyway.

"You're welcome. Thanks for the advice."

"Anytime. I mean it." And by the look in his eyes, I'd say he really did mean it.

I was closing my laptop when FX and Maddie found me in the kitchen. Maddie was glowing, her eyes shining, as if the last few hours had changed her life. Clearly being in that creative hot pot meant she could never go back to her little life in Pasadena. I'd felt like that before.

"Guess what?" she asked dramatically.

"What?" I responded, playing along.

"FX is going to be naked!"

"What?" I turned to FX for confirmation that this was a hilarious practical joke the two of them were playing on prim Aunt Elizabeth to make her squirm.

But his sheepish grin told me otherwise. "Yup. Full frontal."

Relationship Red Flags

THEN	NOW
Always at War	Always Playing World of Warcraft
Beheads Rivals	Bad Bedhead
Primogeniture Rage	Facebook Envy
Bloodthirsty	Enjoys Vampire Lifestyle
Cross-dressing	Meggings
Easily Manipulated	Enjoys Manicures
Talks to Spirits	Talks to Fake Girlfriends
Eavesdrops behind Curtains	Installs GPS Tracker
Slanderous Tongue	Pierced Face
Oedipus Complex	Oedipus Complex

CHAPTER 14

"Really? Totally naked?"

FX and I had moved to the front porch of Sage Cottage to discuss the matter without Maddie listening. I did manage to warn her under my breath as we walked outside, "Don't put this on Facebook. Remember that nondisclosure agreement we signed." I was deadly serious and she could tell. She nodded and went upstairs with Puck. Daughter of a congressman—she can keep her mouth shut.

Now I was turning my attention to the other child in my care. I started softly, so I didn't force him into a corner defending his position. But as an advocate of the Bard, I had a difficult time dialing back my disdain. "Please explain. Because at first hearing, it sounds so…unnecessary. Although of course I don't want to be accused of pre-judging a creative genius like Taz Buchanan."

FX sat back into the dark all-weather wicker furniture like he hadn't a care in the world, but I sensed a simmering panic underneath his cool demeanor. *Full frontal onstage! Get the Xanax, stat!* Still, he remained calm as he elaborated, because after all, he was an actor. "You know in Act 4, Scene 1, when all the young lovers are running around the forest in a spell thanks to Puck? Then they fall for all the wrong people. That scene? Then Oberon wakes up Titania after she's been drugged and has mistakenly fallen in love with an ass."

"Yes, I know," I said curtly. I believe I was the one who interpreted the play for him, not vice versa. I made the international sign for "let's go" by rolling my hands, hoping he would dispense with Remedial Theater 101.

"Right, of course you do. Oberon has that line near the end, 'Sound music! Come, queen, and take hands with me. Rock the ground whereon these sleepers be.' That line?"

"Yup." Again, I get it. *I'm familiar with the play.*

"Well, Taz thinks we should really rock the ground. Like rock the ground. So after we exit on Titania's line, there's a break. He's adding a musical interlude. And he thinks Oberon should seduce Titania onstage. With a dance thing." Oh, he was so nervous, so unsure of this whole idea that he was practically sweating now.

"Like a dance thing? Like a striptease?"

FX nodded.

I needed a moment to collect myself, not wanting to respond too soon, because my instinct was too blurt out, *Holy cow!* Midsummer Night's Dream *is a middle school staple! Ya think getting busy with the fairy queen onstage is going to solidify your support for an Oscar? More likely it will secure you a place in the Creepy Guy Hall of Fame.* "Is there anything else I need to know? Any other details that might impact my opinion of this interpretation?"

FX reached for something, anything. "The music is great. It's Sly and the Family Stone's 'M'Lady.' They actually played that at Woodstock. You know that one?" He did a few bars and some mouth guitar, but it really didn't matter. The song choice was not going to influence my opinion.

I leaned forward, using my Professor Lancaster voice. "FX, you know this is a very risky idea, don't you? Being naked onstage for no apparent reason except shock value could really backfire."

"Well, everybody else is going to be naked."

Oh my God, no wonder Taz didn't want me at the production meeting. Professor Lancaster having a conniption in front of everyone. "What do you mean everyone else is going to be naked?"

He took a deep breath, clearly hoping I would follow suit before my head exploded. "The idea is that the night in the forest is one long Woodstockian dream sequence-slash-drug trip. And he's thinking that, naturally, the young lovers—Hippolyta, Demetrius, Helena, and Lysander—will slowly lose items of clothing as they cavort through the woods. Getting less and less dressed until eventually, bam, they're discovered the next morning by the King and Dad, in the buff. Like busted college kids."

That actually made me howl. See, I'm not a total prude. "Okay, that is hilarious! Funny, fun, implied in the text. I love that idea," I said, genuinely delighted by the image in my head of young hippies playing a kind of spell-induced strip poker. Then I got serious. "But you're a famous movie star who wants to be taken seriously as an actor. You're talking about a trumped-up scene whose sole purpose is to get you naked. It's not in the play, it's not implicit in the lines. It's not necessary. Trust me, keep your clothes on."

"You really think it's that bad of an idea?"

"Yes, career suicide. It's one thing if you're Daniel Radcliffe and you're trying to make everyone forget you've played a boy wizard for ten years, so you take your clothes off in *Equus*. But you don't need to take your clothes off in front of an audience of Bus Tour Bettys." Just then, the image of my mother, Dependable Jane, and Funseeker Mary Pat in the front row rushed to mind. The horror, the horror if they saw my ex-husband *au natural*! Imagine the lunch afterward with the cast! The shocking e-mails and texts that would be sent back to Pasadena, to the Showcase Sustainers and Caltech wives. The hanging teases I'd have to endure for the rest of my life. That's not an inside joke I wanted to share with my mother.

FX tried to reassure me. "Actually, only I'm going to strip. Titania will stay clothed. It's supposed to be this sexy offering of myself to, you know, *milady*."

Even worse. "You're FX Fahey. You're plenty sexy fully dressed." I blurted out the deep dark truth before I could overthink the implications.

"Really?" He closed the distance between us and looked down into my eyes expectantly. He breathed in deeply again and I remembered the perfume I'd put on earlier. Did he recognize the scent? I stepped back.

Eyes on the prize. Eyes on the prize. A dishwasher at long last. "Don't. This is what you're paying me for. Don't confuse good judgment with…longing." I paused and squared my shoulders. FX looked disappointed, so I conceded, "But yes, you are plenty sexy fully dressed."

We stood quietly for a moment, letting the statement and the situation sink in. Had I been too harsh? What did I really know about acting? Nothing, really. Doing scenes in class wasn't anything like what real actors did. I'd never lost myself in a character, so maybe, in context, this scene would work. It could be the bold gesture that would single out FX as a fearless performer. But it just felt cheesy and more male-stripper-at-a-birthday-bash than brave. So I asked, "Does it strike you as the right choice in that moment?"

FX didn't hesitate. "Have you seen the guy playing Lysander? He's ripped! I don't want to be compared to him." Of course. This was more about his abs than his art.

Well, at least we were both on the same page, even if it was for different reasons. But something about how it all went down was bothering me. I didn't trust that Taz. "So let me get this straight. Did Taz just drop this bombshell on you today?"

"Yeah. I mean, he's been hinting at some form of skin, making the whole production really hot. But I didn't think he meant *this*."

It was almost like Taz was practicing some kind of directorial hazing, testing the mettle of his actors in a sinister way. I knew FX didn't want to look weak in the director's eyes. "Well, can you play along and then a few days before opening, tell him you just can't do it? It's just not working for you?"

"We have this press conference on Monday, announcing the show and the special ticket sales and the unusual nature of the production. So I don't really want this announced to the public if I have no intention of going through with it." Tick-tock, the clock was running. I wasn't Bumble but I could hear her voice in my head: This could be a PR fiasco. It had the potential to be *Coriolanus 2: The Undoing of FX Fahey* before the show even opened.

"What are we going to do?" he asked.

Didn't he mean *I?* "You can't just say no? I mean, at this point, Taz won't bail, will he? Or have your agent call him. Hank can tell him you don't want to do nudity."

FX cocked his head and shrugged his shoulders, but not in a puppy-dog way, more in a pit-bull way. "I'd rather it didn't come from me. Or Hank. I'd rather it came from you, so it seems like more of an artistic decision, not a personal decision I'm making for the benefit of my career. Just convince Taz like you convinced me. It's not authentic to the text. End of story."

Ah yes, it was time for the FX Fahey Industrial Complex to spring into action. If I wanted that Caesarstone countertop, I was going to have to get him out of this.

Back inside, I contemplated my situation and reheated my squash for the third time. The fried capers looked more like limp capers, but I was starving so it would have to do. While the oven did its thing, I checked in on Maddie. She was tucked into bed, fully engrossed in multiple electronic devices when I knocked and entered. She glanced up from her laptop to greet me. I explained my earlier panic. "Sorry,

I didn't mean to lecture you about the nondisclosure agreement. It's just really important to FX that this play goes off well. I know you won't say anything."

"I won't. I like FX. And I kinda get it, you know, having to be careful about revealing what goes on behind the scenes." Of course, she was talking about her own mini-fishbowl-life in Pasadena.

Her phone buzzed. "One of the Emmas?" I asked.

"No, it's Dylan. The other intern who's working for Taz?" Of course, the pale hipster in the glasses who was also sent to fetch dinner. "He's cool. He grew up in Klamath Falls, doesn't that sound magical? He's in college here in Ashland at Southern Oregon. You know what he's majoring in?"

I shook my head, but I was pretty sure I knew the answer: fresh-faced, sheltered high school girls from California. But maybe I was being too protective.

"History with a minor in Shakespeare Studies, how cool is that? Have you ever heard of that minor?"

"No. That sounds fantastic." Goodbye, Swarthmore, hello Southern Oregon. Her father would have a field day with that educational trade. On the downside, Maddie was a goner. But on the upside, I had an inside source. "Like a dream. Makes me want to be an undergrad all over again. So are you going to rehearsal tomorrow? With FX and everybody?"

She hesitated, "If it's okay with you. I think Taz thinks I'm working for FX. And FX seems to kind of think that, too. But I know you wanted me to put together a list of Shakespearean breakup lines, so I can do that before the ten o'clock call time."

I feigned understanding when I really felt elation. "Don't worry about the book for now. This is an incredible opportunity to see a show come together in a really short time. Do what you need to do to be helpful to FX and the production. Once the show's up and running, we'll have plenty of time to work on the book stuff."

The phone buzzed again. Apparently, Mr. Minoring in

Shakespeare was getting impatient. "Maddie, do you tell people right off the bat that your dad is a congressman?"

"Not usually. I used to in the beginning because I thought it was awesome. But then people would say things like, 'All politicians are crooks.' Or 'Republicans are facists.' It really upsets me when people say stuff like that. So now I wait to see if it's even worth it. You have to pick your moments."

So true.

I was supposed to be the Shakespearean scholar, so I asked myself: What would Iago do?

I sat on a stool at the kitchen counter, eating my dried-out dinner and contemplating my next move. I had to think like Othello's villain if I was to outwit Taz. Unfortunately, I didn't have an Iago bone in my body. My only thought was to go to Taz and beg for mercy, which didn't exactly fall in the master manipulator category. I thought about calling my sister Sarah for advice, but it was too late to call a doctor and not have the reason be life-threatening. She barely got to sleep as it was without me interrupting her for my petty problems. And I thought about calling Bumble but feared the resulting Pandora's box of recriminations. And forget calling my parents. The fake Redfield resume was gnawing away at the piece of my soul still affected by Guilt Generated by my Mother, and my father simply didn't operate on this plane. I looked at Puck and he wagged his tail. He believed in me.

Just then, my phone beeped; it was my dad. His text said: Did you watch Wimbledon tune-up. New American kid looks good.

I texted back: Missed him. Will check out tomorrow.

When another ping sounded, I expected another tennis-related text. But it was from Rafa: Thanks for dinner "date."

His quotation marks, not mine. Oh well. The day wasn't a total washout.

RIGHTEOUS ROLE MODEL

Regan & Goneril

FROM *KING LEAR*

WHO THEY ARE: The two baddest sisters in all of literature: scheming she-wolves who lie, cheat, and plot their way through life. The game is on after their father, King Lear, sets up a no-win competition called "Who loves Daddy the most?" These wicked daughters declare their filial love to secure their half of his kingdom, then humiliate dear ol' dad. Also included in their relationship bag o' tricks: philandering, emasculating, and murdering. In the end, they both die horrible deaths.

WHY THEY ARE RIGHTEOUS: They are utterly shameless. And in a world in which we are constantly exposed to manufactured shamelessness—like those fake housewives or those fake sisters from Calabasas—Regan and Goneril are the real deal, driven by their desire for power and ambitious for their own sake. They are females who are unafraid of being feared. You have to appreciate their commitment.

WHAT TO STEAL FROM THEM:

⚜ Their extreme self-love. Low self-esteem is not an issue for the Lear girls.

⚜ Their support of each other. Until they don't and both end up dead.

⚜ A No Guts, No Glory attitude. And by guts, I mean actual guts on the ground.

⚜ Their intolerance of houseguests. No knights for multiple nights, Dad.

WHAT TO SKIP: Going after your married sister's hot boyfriend is never a good idea. Neither is poisoning her.

WHO THEY REMIND YOU OF: Cinderella's tormentors, Drizella and Anastasia, on steroids.

WHERE THE MODERN-DAY SISTERS WOULD HAVE WORKED: Lehman Brothers.

CHAPTER 15

Operation Seeds of Doubt was in motion. Hiking through Lithia Park with Puck, I thought some more about Rafa's advice and what exactly I had to offer that no one else could provide: history. I had a history with FX, and I could use that to my advantage. I didn't have to convince Taz to change his mind on the gratuitous nude scene; I just had to plant seeds of doubt so he would question his own judgment. About an hour into our trek, I had two additional realizations: Puck doesn't like pugs (a bad puppyhood memory, no doubt), and you can get a lot of thinking done while walking a dog. By the time we passed the duck pond, the swimming hole, and finally the playground, I'd formulated my line of attack. Puck was exhausted, but I was ready to jump into the crosswalk, as Rafa had said. I should have gotten a dog years ago; I could have accomplished so much more by now.

I was lying in wait at Paddy's, an Irish pub just off Main Street. A text from my asset Maddie had tipped me off that the production team and some of the cast were headed over for a beer or two after a long day of rehearsal. I embraced a "no time like the present" attitude and got thirsty. My plan was to strike up a conversation with Taz about the added elements of the play, tossing out my concern casually, as if we were just two people talking at a pub. I was hoping to get in a little one-on-one time with him before the karaoke started, then head home on the off chance that Rafa needed my assistance. The more I thought about my plan, the more I realized that my de-maturation process was still going on. Sitting there, in my blue jeans and peasant blouse with a completely pre-scripted conversation in my head, I was in high school again. Except now I could legally drink.

The pub was lively, filled with theatergoers, local college kids, and gray-haired ceramists all taking advantage of the happy-hour pints. Four outdoorsy types in their twenties, sporting baseball caps and Keens, were throwing darts after a day of leading tourists down the Rogue River. What looked to be a few actors were playing backgammon at a corner table. I'd seen several alarming flyers at the Food Co-op about the death of Ashland thanks to the intolerance of the recently arrived baby boomers and the rising real estate prices that were choking out "real" Ashlanders. But despite those accusations and the rancor over a recent city ordinance outlawing public drumming, the mix of locals and tourists, new money and old hippies had clearly reached a happy détente at Paddy's. There was Celtic music in the background and laughter and conversation in the foreground. I nursed my pint of Ten Barrel IPA and soaked in the atmosphere.

In Pasadena, I was usually on high alert at bars, as if any moment a former Eastmont classmate was going to bust me for being "still divorced." Or some former neighbor of my parents, now a downsized condo dweller, might insist that I join them and their cronies for a "lovely evening" at Symphony in the Park. But here, anonymous in Ashland, I felt at home.

I almost forgot why I'd come to Paddy's in the first place until Taz walked in.

"So, did FX tell you about the booty call scene with Oberon and Titania?"

Taz was well into his third beer by now, and happy hour had long since ended. (I believe the term is "hollow leg.") Unfortunately, it had taken me this long to position myself next to him at the bar. The group that piled in from rehearsal originally numbered seven or eight but had slowly dwindled. FX, camouflaged in a Mariners' cap, had wandered over to the darts board with his attentive co-star, Sabrina, leaving me stuck with stage manager Lulu. She made several passes at me, which I pretended not to understand. (Actually, Lulu, I look nothing like Tegan *or* Sara, but I appreciate their music.) My patience had paid off, because now I was shoulder to shoulder with Taz. He opened up the conversation with a challenging edge in his voice. It was all I could have hoped for in the moment.

"He did." And then, in a risky move, I tried to pull off a look that implied that I was concerned but reluctant to say anything—risky because unlike half the patrons in Paddy's, I wasn't an actor. The director stared back quizzically. I must have sold it, so I continued as planned. "There are a million reasons why that's not my cup of tea. But I'm sure you know what's right for the production."

"What's one reason?"

"You've already pegged me as a stickler when it comes to interpretation. I'm not a big fan of adding scenes to the original work. Certain plays can take editing, for sure. But I can't think of a single instance where a new scene has enhanced the dramatic arc of a play, not when it comes to Shakespeare's work. Sorry."

Taz was amused that I dared question him. I think after all the beer he was beginning to warm up to me. "Don't be sorry, Lizzie.

You're entitled to have strong opinions. I disagree with you, but you're entitled."

"Give me some credit. I like what you're doing with the young lovers. Their wild night sounds perfectly in keeping with the play's themes."

"Thank you." He lifted his glass in a toast, but I couldn't really reciprocate, as mine was empty. So I signaled to the bartender and ordered another beer I had no intention of drinking.

I lowered my voice and leaned in. "You know what surprises me most? FX. I guess he's more comfortable with that sort of thing now. Certainly wasn't when we were together."

Now Taz was really interested. "What do you mean?"

"You know we were married, right?" My beer arrived and I took a little sip, just to give that information some time to sink in.

He looked surprised. "No, I didn't know you were married. I mean, FX said you were an ex. I thought he meant an ex-girlfriend."

"Oh, much more than that. Ex-wife. I was Mrs. Fahey. So I know him pretty well." I stepped back, taking in all of Taz for effect. My eyes drifted below his belt buckle, and I nodded my head in what some might call "a knowing fashion." I hoped my meaning was clear, because I was so far out of my comfort zone that I couldn't possibly be more specific. He appeared to get my drift, so I went in for the kill with a whisper. "I'm surprised he'd want to, um, go public with his private parts. He must really, really trust you."

I felt my face burn with shame as I simultaneously smeared FX and saved him. Please let this work. Or I was going to be the one exposed.

"What do you mean?"

I shrugged my shoulders and said sweetly. "Maybe he's had surgery. Or therapy. But obviously the issues he had when we were married are no longer there. Although, I don't know? Do they have testicle replacement surgery?"

Taz went white as I lifted my glass to my lips. *Money! Just call me the Gardener, because I'm planting the seeds.* The look on Taz's face told me that he wasn't ready to go there with his production. Exploited nudity was once thing; freak of nature another. FX was safe and so was my built-in microwave. As Iago would say, *but for my sport and profit,* I think I'll drink this beer after all.

From across the bar, FX caught my eye. He'd obviously been keeping one eye on the dartboard and one eye on Taz and me. He flashed me a peace sign, our safe signal. Do I tell him a half-truth or reveal that I outed him (falsely) as half man? I opted for the half-truth.

I texted him: I think you'll be able to keep your clothes on.

After reading it, he blew me a kiss. And then blew me off to resume his game with Sabrina.

Maddie texted me as I walked home, triumphant: With Dylan. Home by?

I panicked. Home by what? I didn't know. Was this simply a curfew question or the opportunity for me to pass along a life lesson? My only experience with young romance was *Romeo & Juliet* and FX & Elizabeth, and neither ended well. How about "Home before you commit to a double suicide pact"? Or "Home before you fall in love with a guy over Shakespeare and lose your head and heart"? Maybe, more succinctly, "Home before you marry him"?

I called Bumble. I'd been avoiding actual conversation with her to spare myself any further details on her summer project. But she'd managed to send texts that crossed the Too Much Information barrier, the least cringeworthy being: Think we made that baby today. Twice! Twins? *Ugh.*

But on the topic of Maddie, Dylan, and curfew, I needed her input. "Hey. Is this a bad time? No details, please. Just a simple yes or no."

Bumble laughed, "It's fine. Ted's out and I'm home alone. With my feet up on the wall."

"Seriously, I don't want to know about your baby-making voodoo. But I do have a question about Maddie." Bumble was already aware of Dylan, as I'd sent her a few photos in an e-mail with the subject line, "Hermione meets her Ron." I explained the current dilemma. "She swears they're just friends. But they look really friendly. And he is in college. Is there stuff I need to tell her?"

"Like birds and bees stuff? God no. Her 'get in touch with your sexuality' mother gave her a copy of *Our Bodies, Ourselves* when she was like eight. She probably knows more about sex than you do," Bumble said, not without a hint of truth. "Seriously, that woman calls her when there's a full moon and asks about her hormone levels and if she's drinking her purity tea or whatever. Never once has she asked Maddie about Algebra 2 or her SATs, only tides-of-the-moon sort of things."

No wonder Maddie drank specific teas on specific nights! When she bought five different kids of tea, she informed me it was for balance. She never said hormonal balance. Maybe I should try her tea regimen? "Okay, so my role is to monitor from afar and make sure she's home by midnight?"

"Say 11:30. Midnight sounds dangerous. She's a sensible girl, like you." I'm pretty sure that was a compliment. "Oh, and I think you were wrong about Rafa."

My mind did a quick inventory of the statements I might have made to Bumble about Rafa. I hadn't let on about anything more than the most perfunctory conversations with him, so I was stumped. "What do you mean?"

"I think he does want to water your plants."

"Huh?"

"Ted and I stopped by there the other day and we found him in your garden, all sweaty and dirty in a T-shirt and shorts. He was weeding. Like he cared."

I didn't respond immediately, distracted by the mental image of a sweaty and dirty Rafa. And other parts of my body. (I definitely needed to get a hormonal-tea recommendation tonight.) Then I recovered. "That's nice of him. Well, I have to answer Maddie. Talk soon."

"Thanks, Elizabeth."

I texted Maddie: 11:30. No drams of poison.

She replied: K. Huh?

Call? Not call? Call? Not call? I sat at my kitchen table, contemplating the blue Skype bubble on my laptop. Did I have the kind of relationship with Rafa in which I could ring him up even if we didn't have a household situation to discuss? Maybe not, but I wanted to let him know that his strategy had worked. Plus I'd just refreshed my concealer.

I clicked on "dial" and then felt foolish. Don't answer, I prayed, but then I heard the familiar high-pitched whoop, signaling a received call. Too late. Rafa's face came into view. He was sitting in my living room, obviously working even though it was well past nine. There was a stack of files and papers on the desk in front of him. In the background I saw a whiteboard with names and cards, but I couldn't make out the words. He looked pleased to see me. "Hey."

"Hey. Hi. Hello." Oh brother, let's see how many more greeting variations I can come up with. "I wanted to check in and see how… all the appliances were getting along."

"They seem to be getting along just fine. How are your appliances?"

"My appliances are good, too." Could the concealer possibly be concealing my awkwardness? "Um, I thought you might want to know that I employed your strategy. I identified what I had to offer and offered it up to the unwilling party. I plunged right into that crosswalk."

Rafa relaxed back against the couch and crossed him arms, "Good for you. Did the unwilling party bite?"

"He did. I think I got him."

"I bet you did. Men have a hard time saying no to smart women. You've got our numbers."

The compliment surprised me. "Oh no, we don't. It only looks that way." Rafa was obviously busy, and I didn't see any cooking together in our immediate future, so I let him off the hook. "I can tell you're in the middle of something, so I'll let you go."

But Rafa kept going with chief-of-staff talk. "Well, it appears that we may have to go public with Ted's interest a little sooner than we wanted. There were some rumblings and speculation in the press today about the possibility. And some of it is not favorable. We're getting bombarded with interview requests. So I'm trying to figure out a timeline and our staffing needs before a meeting tomorrow morning. It could be go time."

The visual of sweaty, dirty Rafa was replaced with a snapshot of Rafa working alone in a pin-clean apartment done in tasteful muted colors but devoid of personality because he'd never had so much as a weekend off to pick up some accent pillows. I challenged him, "Is this what your life is like? The last guy up at night, the first guy up in the morning?"

"Pretty much." He laughed. "Ninety-nine percent of the time, I love it. Okay, ninety-five percent of the time. The other five percent I wish I had a more normal life."

"What does 'more normal' mean?" I was curious about his definition because I'd had the same thought so many times about what I'd be doing at a single precise moment if I were Sarah and I had twins to feed dinner, or if I were Bumble and I had nightly fundraisers to attend on behalf of a spouse. What would my life be like if it was more than just me? What would it be like if it was more normal?

"A family, a wife, a lawn to mow. You know, that sort of thing. I wonder sometimes if I don't have those things because I have this job. Or if I have this job because I don't have those things."

"It's probably a little of both, don't you think?" Thank you, Dr. Lancaster, amateur analyst.

Rafa nodded. "Yeah. It doesn't help that everyone I meet in Washington is a lot like me. Dedicated to the job and not that available for a lot more than...." He paused to think about exactly what to say.

I pushed because I was curious about what he might be looking for. And, after all, I was writing a relationship book, so this conversation could also be called research. "More than what?"

"Let's just say that the people I'm surrounded by came to DC to make a difference and get ahead. And not necessarily in that order. They have short attention spans when it comes to interpersonal relationships." Rafa looked sheepish as he concluded, "Me included."

Ah, work hard, play hard, and leave before breakfast. That whole scenario was totally not my issue. I'm sure Bumble and Sarah could each offer up a short lecture on what exactly my issues were, but they had nothing to do with not enough time or interest. According to my sisters, my singledom centered around a lack of self-confidence and sex appeal. (I think black turtlenecks can be very alluring in the right circumstance, but Bumble disagrees.) Honestly, I've never done any emotional digging on my own. That's what gardening is for. So I tried to buck up Rafa on his self-assessment. "So the relationship thing isn't working out. But you're making a difference, right?"

"Yup," he sighed. "One press conference at a time."

"Good luck."

"I'll check in tomorrow." With that, Rafa clicked off, but something in me clicked on. We had moved beyond appliances.

Rosalind & Orlando

FROM *AS YOU LIKE IT*

HER: One of Shakespeare's most delightful leading ladies. Independent, fun, charming, and not afraid to go into exile dressed like a man. Has much to say about the foolishness of love, but can't help falling in love anyway.

HIM: Forest-dwelling little brother. A gentleman despite the lack of formal education. Noble, loyal, and brave when he needs to be. No match for Rosalind intellectually, but handsome enough to compensate.

BRILLIANT RELATIONSHIP MOVE: Rosalind dresses as a man to instruct Orlando on how to woo a woman, proving you can, in fact, have your cake and eat it, too.

WHY THEY WORK: She's smart and he's adorable.

HIS BEST ADVICE: "Live a little; comfort a little; cheer thyself a little."

HER BEST ADVICE: "Men are April when they woo, December when they wed: maids are May when they are maids, but the sky changes when they are wives."

SHAKESPEAREAN COUPLE MOST LIKELY TO: Co-host a morning talk show.

WHO THEY REMIND YOU OF: Kelly Ripa and Michael Strahan.

CHEMISTRY FACTOR: 3.5 OUT OF 5

CHAPTER 16

The address may have been Ashland, but the opening night felt like pure Broadway. The June air was crisp and cool, a perfect night for outdoor theater, and those lucky enough to have scored tickets in the daily lottery were dressed in layers as advised by the OSF website. A film crew from *Access Hollywood* waited outside the theater and, no doubt, reviewers from the *Los Angeles Times*, the *New York Times*, and *People* were inside. The crowd was abuzz in anticipation of the production that Taz Buchanan had described at the press conference as an "in-your-face, out-of-body mind-blower." (Oh, Taz, that's a lot of body parts for one phrase.) But there was no doubt that the thirty-years-younger-than-the-average crowd was ready to party Elizabethan style, probably titillated even further by the show's No One Under 18 warning. Though the details had been kept vague, clearly the feeling in the crowd was that this *Midsummer* would indeed include sex, drugs, and rock 'n' roll. Some of the audience members seemed to be dressed in costume, sporting Grateful Dead

T-shirts and Indian-print skirts. Then again, that could just be what college kids still wore in Southern Oregon. It was exciting to be a tiny part of it, even if only from my house seat in the last row, view partially obstructed.

Maddie texted me from backstage: I'm SO nervous. Why?????? She was on duty in the bowels of the theater, where the actors readied themselves in a locker room–style dressing area and waited in a run-down green room equipped with a closed-circuit TV to monitor the progress onstage several floors above. No star treatment at OSF for FX or any of the actors. It was opening night and the energy in those claustrophobic spaces must be tangible. I was excited for her and a little jealous. She had become an integral part of the production team and FX's personal assistant, handling everything from his social media needs to his green tea demands. I texted her back: Me 2.

I was nervous. The last ten days had been a chaotic rush of writing, rehearsal, and Rafa, plus daily dog walks, occasional yoga classes, and frequent communications from my family, who seemed to think I was right around the corner and insisted on keeping me up to date on all things Lancaster whether I cared or not about how the roses were blooming in my mother's garden. Out of sight, out of mind didn't really work in my family.

Every morning, Maddie and I went to Noble Coffee to fuel up and debrief on any important news. Maddie fed me daily tidbits, like confirming that Taz was indeed a beast, but a sexy beast, and the whole cast was spellbound. He was pissed because the Jimi Hendrix people wouldn't let him use his music but thrilled that The Band would. Yes, Maddie said, the actor who plays Puck did seem to have a drinking problem, but he was hilarious. And Demetrius and Lysander appeared to be a couple, much to Hermia's chagrin. Sometimes stage manager Lulu joined us, providing other key insider intelligence, most importantly that Taz thought FX was "hot" onstage. She agreed, which, for a lady who preferred ladies, was high praise.

It relieved me to hear that Taz liked FX's performance, because the actor himself was a bit of a basket case. I spent large portions of the day talking him down off the emotional ledge. For a guy who'd made millions at the box office, he sure had a lot of issues about his self-worth. At one point, I even called his agent Hank to say that maybe FX needed someone with more credentials than me to get him emotionally prepared to walk back onstage. Hank sent me an edible fruit bouquet for my efforts, but no psychologist. So I did my best as a stand-in for Sabrina at night when she was onstage in Cinderella and FX wanted to run lines at his Japanese spa home.

In between scenes, FX filled me in on Hollywood gossip and relived every movie he ever made. Some of the stories were riotous; others were navel-gazing road trips with little appeal. One night he said that his career was made by a single shot in the first *Icarus* film, the one in which he stood in a dirty alley, nearly defeated, contemplating the end of the world and his role in its demise. It was at the exact moment that his character decided to rise from the ashes and take on the bad guys that FX hit the perfect head tilt of conviction. "Less than a second, but everyone knows that shot, right? I did fifty takes and only once did I tilt my head to the left, not the right. They used the left tilt. That's all it takes in film, Lizzie. One shot, like a great photo. But onstage, it's so much more."

Finally, after one of these personal pity parties, I blurted out, "For God's sakes! You're playing the king of the Fairies, not Richard III. Get a hold of yourself." Slightly offended by my sudden attack, he pointed out that he was playing two roles: the king of the Fairies *and* the King of Athens. But I guess he understood my point, because after that, he whined less and conversed more.

Our relationship had evolved to the point where we routinely had conversations that weren't loaded with hidden meanings or hurtful memories. We could laugh and fill in the gaps of the last ten years, even wading into the area of bad dates and even worse relationships. Most of the time we were like two old friends, talking. Until, of course, he stripped down to his swimsuit for our daily soak in his personal mineral bath—only then would a touch of longing mixed with melancholy hit me. I stuffed those feelings with the endless supply of toro maki provided by Ming. (So much healthier than my post-divorce diet staple, Mallomars, shipped to me in California by caring friends in New York City.) All physical longing aside, my soak-and-sushi regime had resulted in a five-pound weight loss and glowing skin, a confidence booster during what had become nightly video chats with Rafa.

Rafa. Sitting there in the open-air theater, waiting for the curtain to rise, I missed him. How sad. I missed a guy with whom I'd spent approximately forty-seven minutes face to face. A guy who was seven hundred miles away, worked for my brother-in-law, and, I suspected, preferred women in tailored suits with law degrees, though I had no proof. But digitally, we'd been having a rather serious relationship, which was its own kind of sad.

Our nightly Skype calls consisted of some smokescreen starter chitchat about the house or garden, as if that was the excuse for the connection. From there, the conversation could go anywhere, provided that the sometimes-sketchy connection held up. I talked him through preparing caponata with my eggplants, and he extolled the virtues of chimichurri with my parsley and oregano. I went off on reforming public education and he explained cap and trade and the capital gains tax, two concepts I only pretended to understand. We covered family, pet peeves, and our favorite movies (his, predictably, a toss-up between *The Godfather* and *Air Force One*; mine, just as predictably, *Out of Africa*). As I learned about his life, his transition from farm kid to sophisticated Georgetown student, and how he made the leap from local-issue campaigns to working for high-profile politicians like Ted, I realized that underneath the polished exterior and custom-tailored shirts, he was a loyal and sentimental man. He went to his high school reunions, called his grandmother every Sunday, and got choked up when they played the national anthem at Dodgers games. (I admitted to goose bumps when I heard the

Masterpiece music every Sunday night, but it didn't really resonate in the same way as his reaction to "The Star-Spangled Banner.")

A few days ago, we figured out that we were both Skyping and watching the Wimbledon recap show on mute, so we started to "watch" the show together, commenting on the screaming Russian women and the towering Czechs. Last night, after a long conversation that had nothing to do with first-serve percentages, the time had come to say goodnight. But instead of a quick adieu, we had That Moment. Yes, that prolonged moment of silence where the conversation could go off in a whole deeper direction, possibly involving a declaration of feelings or, if more alcohol had been involved, the removal of clothing. Rafa stared into the camera, smiled, and for the first time in our brief acquaintance, didn't look completely in control of his agenda. Sipping lavender relaxation tea and feeling a surge of romantic bravery, I almost blurted out, "You should come to Ashland."

Yes, please come to Ashland.

Then Puck started barking at an innocent pug out on the street and I was forced to sign off, saving me from taking a chance. As I removed the light makeup I always put on for our chats, I admonished myself. *Rafa is my housesitter. We are bonded by Bumble. There isn't going to be an In Real Life relationship; we're Strictly Skype.* By the time I returned to Pasadena, he'd be back in Washington. It would just be me, the dog, and Sunday nights with Laura Linney.

The bells in the theater brought me back to the present. They signaled the audience members to take their seats. *Here we go. Don't suck.* The house lights came down; the curtain went up. The sound of Richie Havens's Woodstock performance of "Strawberry Fields" blasted through the speakers. The big video screens lit up with images of verdant, mud-free landscapes. And FX Fahey stepped onto a stage for the first time in a decade, this time wearing a Nehru jacket.

The applause was thunderous. You could barely hear the last few lines of Puck's famous soliloquy because the audience was already on its feet, dancing to the Grateful Dead's "Turn on Your Love Light." The production was brilliant: the music, the big-screen stadium-rock-show effects, the hint of nudity that revealed picture-perfect glutes on the men and equally top-notch toppers on the women. It all worked to create a magical, sexy fantasy world. Sabrina was mesmerizing as the queen of the Fairies, and Puck was a comic evildoer. The audience had been enraptured by the lovers' entanglements, the sensuous music and dancing, and the Rude Mechanicals' merriment, but there was no doubt: FX was the unquestionable star.

And he knew it. As he took his bow to adoring hooting and hollering, he was the king. Or Kings, as it were. The look on his face was one of pure joy. I'd seen it before—it was the expression he wore in our one remaining wedding photo. I was happy for him, to feel like that again. I held up my cell phone to capture the moment. It was easier to watch from behind a lens.

As the cast took yet another curtain call, I sent the photo to his agent, Hank, with the message: **Fifth curtain call. We have a hit.**

If the theatrical experience felt like Broadway, the after-party was as close to Hollywood as it was going to get in these parts. FX's temporary home at Chozu Tea Gardens had been turned into a sparkling party venue after some long-distance event planning by Angie, who apparently had commandeered every little white light in Ashland, along with half a dozen food vendors and a deejay playing Motown hits. Several bartenders were on hand, as were enormous bottles of flavor-infused Skyy vodka on ice. In a beer and coffee town, the showy vodka product placement, which the company had no doubt paid for, looked wildly out of place, but the high-spirited actors didn't seem to notice the incongruity. The noise level from the music and enthusiastic conversation was just short of calling-the-police levels. The guests were flying, and not from the vodka or any other substance. It was the intoxication that comes from being part of a hit.

I secured a passionfruit cocktail and stood in the shadows surveying the scene. I caught Maddie's eye and she waved in my direction. She was standing next to FX, his arm around her shoulders, while Dylan and several professional-looking photographers snapped photos. No doubt Dylan's shot would go up on the show's Twitter feed, an account that Maddie had created. Taz was holding court center stage, several females on either side. He was back in his sarong, probably planning on soaking a bit later and not alone, from the way he was eyeing two young actresses.

There was a crowd at the buffet, mostly the character players, scarfing down sushi like they'd never eat again, and maybe some of them wouldn't if they didn't get asked back to be a part of the company next year. And, predictably, a small group of women, not actresses, maybe wives, danced together in bare feet and flowing skirts, somehow turning the slow, sexy beat of "I Heard It Through the Grapevine" into hippie-chick freeform movement with a touch of whirling dervish. I had a strong sense of déjà vu, but I couldn't pinpoint why.

"Hey." FX had snuck up on me and stood behind me. I was startled, both by the fact that he was here so suddenly and that I could hear his voice over the din. "I've been waiting for you."

I colored slightly. *Really?* "I went home to walk the dog." And to remove several layers of fleece and the thick socks I'd put on under my Uggs to survive the outdoor performance in comfort. For the party, I exchanged my outerwear for a cashmere wrap, courtesy of Bumble and Sarah, Christmas 2010. I'm not sure who I was trying to impress, but the night felt filled with possibilities.

Now, with FX resting his head on my shoulder, I was particularly glad I'd made time for the wardrobe upgrade. I turned, putting us face-to-face, and felt that déjà vu again. But this time I knew why. I had been here before. "That was fantastic. You were fantastic."

His eyes were brimming, not filled with joy like onstage but with a deeper emotion. It wasn't what I expected, and the intensity of the moment shot through my whole body.

"I couldn't have done it without you." FX brushed an imaginary strand of hair from my face, leaving his rough left hand on my neck. He bent down and brushed my lips with his. Then he worked a little *Midsummer* magic. "*O, methinks how slow this old moon wanes. She lingers my desires.*"

I was sunk by the Shakespeare. He kissed me deeper and his right hand wrapped around my waist while his left slid down my back. Oh, he felt so good, it felt so good. It had been such a long time since, well, since anything had felt like this.

He pulled back, but not too far back. His hands were still drifting slowly down my backside. There was that lime and mint smell again. I smoothed his black T-shirt with my hands, something I'd been dying to do since the day he walked into my classroom. *What was I thinking?* He nodded his head toward the door of the private bathhouse and switched on his Oberon. "*Come on. I know a bank where the wild thyme blows. Where the oxslips and the nodding violet grows, quite over-canopied with luscious woodbine, with sweet-musk roses and with eglantine....*"

Come on, please. It would be so easy to go with him. No one was looking, no one would know. But as much as I wanted him in that moment, I knew it was, what? Risky? Reckless? Or maybe just too nostalgic. Yes, that was it. If this summer had taught me anything, it was that moving forward was far more exciting than looking back. But FX was here and his body was so warm. I found my own hands reaching behind to touch his forearms, to feel his skin. I closed my eyes to get a handle on my emotions.

"Come on. For old times' sake."

Old times' sake? I opened my eyes. That was definitely not the reason I was searching for. I stepped back and held his hands out in front. "I think you're, like, ten years too late for that."

"I'm sorry. I didn't mean that, I just meant that after tonight...I feel like my old self again."

"And I'm part of your old self?" I said, a touch defensively.

"In the best way." FX's voice was still hopeful that he could salvage the moment. "The best part. The part that's just Francis. You know that's why I had to have you come with me this summer. You brought that part back to me."

"Thanks," I sighed, but I knew the moment had passed. Of course, he was magnetic, but he wasn't what I needed. I dropped one of his hands and took another step back, creating even more space between us. "FX, it's not a good idea for us to relive the past. Even the best parts."

He moved closer. Whether it was real desire or just the emotion of the evening, he wasn't giving up. "You sure? I learned a lot of new things in the last ten years." He raised his eyebrows playfully, indicating that it was the emotion of the evening, not, in fact, some unearthed bond between us.

"Me, too," I said, letting go of his hand. "And one of the things I learned is that you're hard to get over. But I did."

FX leaned in. "Totally over me? You don't have *one night* of curiosity to get out of your system?"

Standing there next to my famous and handsome ex-husband, who was pretty much begging me to sleep with him, the image of a hot, sweaty Rafa mulching my garden flashed through my mind. Oh, I had one night of curiosity to get out of my system, but it wasn't with FX. "Nope, I'm good. I think we're better suited as friends. Wouldn't you say?"

"There's that 'better suited' again."

"But I think Sabrina over there might enjoy the benefits of your experience."

FX Fahey got the message. He shook his head. "You're the best, Lizzie. Let's dance."

Wandering back to Sage Cottage with Maddie well after midnight, I checked my phone. There was a text message from Rafa. It said: Missed you tonight.

I didn't want to cheapen it by texting back.

TEAM ROMEO vs. TEAM

ROMEO MONTAGUE

AGE: About sixteen

HOMETOWN: Verona

OCCUPATION: Heir

PERSONALITY TRAITS: Sensitive, intelligent, passionate

CURRENT RELATIONSHIP STATUS: Secretly married

ATTRACTED TO WOMEN WHO: Happen to be standing in front of him

DISTINGUISHING PHYSICAL CHARACTERISTIC: Whiter than new snow on a raven's back

HOBBIES: Verbal jousting, party crashing, dueling

HANG-UPS: Love, honor, loyalty

OTHER WORLDLY ISSUES: Magical poison; star-crossed relationships

MOST LIKELY TO: Star in a CW show

SIGNATURE LINE: "But soft, what light through yonder window breaks?"

POP CULTURE DOPPELGANGER: Lloyd Dobler

HOTNESS FACTOR: 9 of 10

HAMLET vs. TEAM TWILIGHT

HAMLET	EDWARD CULLEN
Around eighteen	Seventeen (for a century or more)
Denmark	Forks, Washington
Student at University of Wittenberg	Telepathic vampire
Bitter, melancholy, cynical	Protective, gentlemanly, intense
Newly single	Eternally involved
Birthed him; can't swim	Don't bite
First emo guy ever	Sparkles in sunlight
Feigning madness, soliloquizing, stabbing	Classical music, watching people sleep, sucking blood
His mother—big time.	Dogs, dying, Jacob
Talks to ghosts	See Occupation
Listen to Dashboard Confessional	Be arrested for stalking
"To be or not to be: That is the question"	"Go sit down and look pale"
Holden Caulfield, Daniel Radcliffe	Himself
6 of 10	Ice cold

CHAPTER 17

The panicked phones calls started about twenty-four hours later. Hardly enough time for those of us in Ashland to come down off the standing-ovation high, the afterglow of the party, and the gushing review on the *New York Times* website. We'd barely recovered from the morning rehash at Noble Coffee and #midsummer trending on Twitter. The first message came in at 5:43 in the afternoon, while I was at Vitality Yoga, attempting to prolong my vigor with mindful breath and deep-core awareness, or at least that's what the brochure promised. I might have stayed for the restorative class afterward if I'd known there'd be ten frantic messages to listen to on my short walk home. Message number one was a simple "call me" from Bumble. But it was clear by message number three, a classic clip-toned hanging tease from my mother, that something was horribly wrong and I was to blame. "Elizabeth, I'm sure you've heard by now about the situation. It's been decided and I'll be the first one there, boots on the ground, to quell the insurgence. Expect me and the Girls in thirty-six hours."

My mother using military jargon was never a good sign.

I didn't even bother listening to the next seven messages. I called Bumble, who answered on the first ring, a rare occurrence. She didn't bother with pleasantries. "Where have you been?"

"Yoga. What's happening? Is everyone okay?"

"Gee, I don't know Elizabeth. By 'okay,' do you mean 'Will Ted survive if his gubernatorial campaign goes down the drain before it's even started?' Is that what you mean by okay?" Her tone was Full Bumble: the sarcastic rhetorical question followed by a dramatic silence. I was in trouble.

"Bumble, what are you talking about?"

"I'm talking about the X-rated romp in the woods that you've let my stepdaughter participate in. Thanks for letting us know that Maddie was interning for what's essentially an Elizabethan adult film. But with better dialogue."

My head was spinning, "Who called it that? There's a touch of nudity. And Maddie has not been even close to naked people at any point during the production. She's making coffee and getting bottled water, not romping onstage." I was clearly behind in the News According to Bumble. "I don't understand. What's the problem?"

"The problem is that pictures of FX and Maddie are all over the Internet. There she is, the congressman's young daughter, canoodling with FX Fahey, star of the most titillating, and I do mean *titillating*, production of *Midsummer* ever. And those asshats Ron and Ben have connected the dots!"

"First off, there was no canoodling. Really. I was there. FX treats her like his niece. He put his arm around her in paternal affection at the cast party, so let's not mischaracterize what happened." I tried to slow down the speeding bullet that was Bumble.

"Oh! Am I supposed to be thankful for that? Should I send

a fruit basket?" The Sarcastic Rhetorical hits just kept coming. Bumble went on to explain how the conservative talk-show hosts, who already have Ted on their Do Not Support list because of his stance on "lenient" gun control and gay marriage, devoted two hours of their show to taking him down as a horrible parent for letting Maddie participate in "a public pornographic display of nudity and inappropriate behavior." Congressman Ted, in their eyes, was tantamount to a pimp. And imagine what he would do to the education system in California if he were governor. Birth control for all! Sex ed in kindergarten! Callers were whipped into such a frenzy that they were calling for his resignation from Congress.

It was shocking and awful and I thought I was going to throw up. I picked up my pace to get back to Sage Cottage as quickly as I could. "Oh my god, poor Maddie. Have you spoken to her? Bumble, I had no idea anything like this could happen."

Bumble ceased hyperventilating and took a moment to compose herself. I imagined it involved a swig of diet soda. "Fortunately, the current talking point is that Ted is a terrible parent, not that Maddie is the next Lindsay Lohan. But honestly, why didn't you tell us about the production, Elizabeth?"

I hated to remind her that the bulk of our communication over the last month had been about the status of her Sexapalooza. What was a little nudity onstage compared to daily updates about her basal body temperatures and cervical fluid? Plus, I assumed Maddie was filling them in on the details. It hadn't registered with me how the outside world might construe Maddie's participation. Was that my job? "It's so innocent onstage. The whole thing is played for laughs. A quick butt shot, fumbling with the blankets to cover some, um, breasts. I mean, nice ones, but quick, very quick. And the lighting is totally discreet." The truth was that most of the really sexy scenes involve characters that are fully clothed.

"Super. Radio-talk-show hosts are very sensitive to discreet lighting. I'm sure once Ron and Ben are alerted to the nuanced use of theatrical gels, or whatever you call the lights, they'll back off their attacks."

With every remark, I felt worse and worse for Maddie, even for me. "We're kind of in our own world here in Ashland. It's not like Pasadena. We're removed from, you know, the media and you all."

"Well, you're not now."

"Is Ted furious?" Poor Ted. He'd been so generous and kind to me, a wonderful brother-in-law. I never would have done anything to knowingly sink his campaign, or more importantly, his personal reputation. I hoped he knew that.

"I don't know who's more furious: Ted or Rafa."

Oh, damn. Rafa.

"Are you okay?"

Maddie was more than okay; she was defiant. "I am not going home. I turn eighteen next month. They can't make me go home."

Well, technically "they" could, but I didn't want to muddy the argument by pointing out the obvious—that she wasn't a legal adult just yet. But I was hugely relieved that she wasn't a puddle of tears on the couch. She was striding around the tiny living room, gesticulating for dramatic effect. Puck was equally worked up on her behalf. I tried to calm them both down, feigning the sort of wisdom that comes with being an adult and in charge, even though I felt about fifteen and out of control. "I'll back you up on that, but, unfortunately, this may be out of my jurisdiction." Really, I had no idea what might happen next.

I filled her in on the plan, or more correctly, Bumble's plan. (It's incredible what Bumble could pull together over the course of a ninety-minute yoga class.) Team Ted assumed that the brouhaha would subside in a day or two at most. The Ron and Ben Show was local to L.A., and, although FX Fahey was a national media figure, Ted Seymour wasn't yet, so the chances of the national media picking up the story were small. In the meantime, Bumble and Ted would issue a statement supporting Maddie and the concept of exploring the arts, a new position for Ted, thank you very much. Prior to this afternoon, he'd been cool on public funding of the arts and art instruction in classrooms.

The carefully crafted response would also clarify Maddie's role, a lowly intern to her aunt, who happened to be FX Fahey's ex-wife, far away from the action onstage. Then, as icing on the approval cake, Anne Lancaster, a well-respected step-grandmother and education advocate, would arrive in Ashland and act as a Seymour surrogate, attending the play and issuing a statement that declared the play to be a perfectly suitable endeavor for Maddie. Bumble's carefully chosen media outlets were limited to a Ted-friendly non-political talk-radio host and the socially connected and friendly *Look Out Pasadena!* My mother was to issue a discreet statement, do the one radio interview, and pose for a multigenerational photo with Maddie and me backstage after the show. According to Bumble, It Was All Good.

Maddie looked worried. "I hope Dylan doesn't think something's actually going on between me and FX."

Ah, the insulation of being a teenager. And, finally, confirmation that the "just friends" relationship was certainly more than that. An entire political firestorm was brewing around her and she was worried about her boyfriend's reaction to some photos that he himself had taken.

I hope it stayed that way.

A hastily arranged conference call was my first chance to talk to Rafa, a conversation I dreaded but knew I had to face. Bumble presided. "Okay, are we all here? I think so. I heard Rafa, Elizabeth, Suki, and Rob. Suki's the new director of communications for the campaign, Elizabeth, and Rob is the assistant in that office. So what we're clarifying here is Maddie's role. We want to be absolutely clear in our statement. Rafa, go."

So this is how Bumble sounded at work, I thought. Not really that much different than how Bumble sounded planning Thanksgiving.

Rafa jumped in and my heart pounded. I already felt physically nauseous; now I felt emotionally nauseous. "Right, Elizabeth, why don't you talk us through Maddie's day-to-day work?" I certainly wouldn't put his voice in the warm-and-fuzzy category. Or even the slightly cool category. It was glacial. "Elizabeth, are you there?"

"Oh, I'm sorry," I gushed, stalling for time. "Um, technically, Maddie is my intern, but she was pretty much co-opted by the production team to handle lots of menial tasks over the course of the last few weeks. She's been working closely with the director Taz Buchanan and with FX Fahey on everything from basic gofer stuff to launching their social media campaign. During the actual performance, she's nowhere near the action, if you know what I mean." I was hoping to lighten the tone. No such luck.

"But under your direct supervision at all times, correct?" Rafa asked.

"Well...." There was no getting around it. I was now going to have to publicly announce that I'd been banned from the set, that Maddie was not only operating completely independently, but also supplying me with information. It was humiliating, deeply humiliating. "Not exactly under my supervision. At all times. In fact, never really. I mean, we text a lot."

I could sense the phone line freeze and break.

"Knock, knock!" In a celebratory mood, FX showed up at the door, pizza and beer in hand. He'd been sending me links all day of positive press from various sources. (*Hollywood Reporter:* Taz, FX *Midsummer* "Dream" Team. *New York Times: Midsummer* Magic in Ashland.) Clearly he wanted to share the buzz with his entourage—or any entourage. Allowing for the jam-packed schedule of a repertory company, *Midsummer* would run only two nights a week and one weekend matinee, leaving FX plenty of time to wander the streets of Ashland in search of dinner partners while the other actors in the company, including the lovely Sabrina, did other shows. I don't want to say we were his second or third choice, but I'm certain we weren't his first.

While the camera may have caught FX and Maddie together on opening night, it was Sabrina who actually snuck off to the private poolhouse later that night with FX after I shot him down. Well, at least I hadn't made that mistake, I thought as I opened the screen door and let the pizza in. FX followed. "Who wants dinner? No meat in sight! Got a Slammy from Creekside. Our favorite, Maddie."

I marveled at how a guy who'd lived in New York City for the last fifteen years could eat a pizza that featured yams and caramelized onions and still maintain his self-respect. But FX had no shame when it came to his newfound love, the Slammy.

"What does meat matter? I'm probably going to be sent home to the beef capital of America tomorrow anyway!" Maddie said dramatically and erroneously, as Pasadena is not particularly known for its beef consumption.

FX looked confused, so I filled him in on the situation as succinctly as I could, using phrases like "blip on the screen" and "bump in the road"—anything to underscore the small scale of the disaster. He was appalled and right away offered to call his press agent, Heather, who, unbelievably, I hadn't even heard of yet. But I begged off, "Please, this is a nothing thing. And, it's totally Ted's nothing thing. I think the less we say, do, and care, the better. And Bumble warned me, no cross-messaging."

"What does that mean?" Maddie asked.

"It means, let Bumble do the talking. On the conference call, she kept repeating, 'Contain the story. Keep it local.' You're not local news, FX."

"Why are people afraid of pushing the boundaries?" he asked, missing the point entirely. "That is the point of art. And art is life. There's pain, misery, happiness, sex, birth, death, weddings, nudity, emotional vulnerability—it's all in there. Why do people have such a hang-up about digging in and examining the truth?"

Spoken like the Boy in the Plastic Bubble. I used my Professor Lancaster tone to keep the discussion on track. "I'm not sure it's art anyone's afraid of, but there is a certain crowd that seems scared of nudity or anything that slightly resembles sex. Plus, I repeat, this is really about politics. This is about Ted and his stance on immigration or gun control or any of the other issues in which he doesn't toe the party line." I grabbed a beer and a slice. "That being said, it probably wasn't the best idea to have a minor working on the show. The audience had to be over eighteen, and I guess the interns should have been, too. That was my fault."

Maddie looked put out. "I'm only a minor as far as the law is concerned."

FX and I both laughed. I switched back to Aunt Elizabeth. "Actually, as far as everyone's concerned, Maddie. But again, I've been instructed by your father's people to carry on like nothing has happened. You'll be backstage tomorrow night and guess what? Your grandmother arrives tomorrow. So gird your loins, people."

Once again, it was me versus Skype. I stared at the screen and considered calling Rafa. Was it worth it to try to explain to him how

I could have possibly left out such a critical piece of information in our many conversations? Or should I assume that we'd gone back to an "on-demand" relationship and not even bother? Oh, what the hell. I was a grownup, and I really had nothing to hide. I clicked "call" and pinched my cheeks for color.

He didn't pick up the first time, so I tried again three minutes later, guessing that he must have been indisposed. I imagined him out in my garden, pondering his feelings for me and watering the Swiss chard. Still, no answer. A third time was desperate, right? Well, that was a fitting description of my state. Just then, my phone pinged. It was a text from Rafa: Thanks for your time today. Will call if I have questions re: situation.

Apparently he wasn't watering the chard, just ignoring my calls. That was that, I supposed. Right on cue, Puck wandered into my bedroom and rested his head on my lap. "Good dog."

POWER COUPLE #6

Othello & Desdemona

FROM *OTHELLO*

HIM: Damaged and scarred warrior who has risen above his upbringing to find success on the battlefield and then in civic life. But his polished veneer is skin-deep—this guy has a boatload of issues bubbling just under the surface. He's one big emotional red flag.

HER: She thinks she can fix him, foolish girl. No family support, no experience in love, just an overwhelming attraction. She thinks with time, patience, and goodness she can rescue him from his awful past. Sound familiar?

WHY THEY WORK: Oh, they don't. Sure, everyone's rooting for them initially, because wouldn't it be a great love story if these two could pull it off? Different backgrounds, different races, but one great love. But they can't, and really, not everyone's rooting for them. The minute things start to go south, they go south fast.

BEWARE THE JEALOUS FORMER BEST FRIEND: Iago, passed over for a promotion by his boss Othello, vows revenge. And boy does he get it, using any means necessary to destroy Othello and Desdemona's relationship.

IF SHE'D ONLY LISTENED WHEN OTHELLO SAID: "But I do love thee. And when I love thee not, Chaos is come again."

SHAKESPEAREAN COUPLE MOST LIKELY TO: Be featured on *20/20*.

CHEMISTRY FACTOR: 4 OUT OF 5

CHAPTER 18

Anne Lancaster was dressed for battle in what I believe Eileen Fisher calls "soft suiting." Surrounded by the Girls, Funseeker Mary Pat and Dependable Jane, my mother was already commanding the conversation. And even though it was only four in the afternoon, the Girls were already drinking Modest White Wine. (The trio had upgraded from Cheap White Wine about a decade ago.) As I approached their makeshift party on the deck outside their rooms at the Anne Hathaway Garden Suites, I was glad of two things: that I had taken the time to blow-dry my hair, and that I was bearing goat cheese. The former meant that my mother couldn't comment on my need to "pull myself together." With regards to the latter, I've found that good hors d'oeuvres can diffuse almost any tense situation. And if all else failed, I'd brought along Puck. I squared my shoulders, a new pregame ritual I'd picked up from FX, and called out, "Hello!"

"Cheers!" my mother responded, affecting a quasi-British accent, a common side effect of staying in a B&B named after Anne Hathaway.

There was excitement and kisses all around, Mary Pat and Jane hugging me with genuine affection. Because my mother was an only child and my father's family didn't believe in frequent contact, Mary Pat and Jane were like aunts to me, warm and familiar. It was good to see them. They had been stalwarts at graduations, birthday parties, and family weddings. They'd been there to snap pictures on prom night when I'd donned a Jessica McClintock emerald green pouf dress I'd spotted in the late, great *Sassy* magazine. I have almost no memory of my date, David Something, but I remember Jane and Mary Pat fawning over my dyed-to-match shoes *just like the ad.* They had hosted a rip-roaring You Won the Nobel Prize Party with Swedish-themed food and drink, and even my father danced to ABBA. And about twenty minutes after I married FX and realized how furious my mother was going to be, I'd called Jane to seek her advice. She ran the situation past Mary Pat and got right back to me.

"Rip it off like a Band-Aid," Jane said. "Tell your mother right now, the minute you hang up with me. Agree to a lovely cocktail party in your honor over New Year's that Mary Pat can cater, and then go enjoy your honeymoon. I'll swing by your mother's in about a half hour. With martinis." I followed her advice to the letter.

After the dust cleared and my mother was speaking to me again, Mary Pat sent a beautiful silver tray from Greetings, the Pasadena standard bearer for wedding gifts, and Jane sent Tiffany crystal candlesticks. I still use both items regularly, as they graciously urged me to keep the gifts after the divorce.

The Girls brought a sense of fun to every event they attended, and I was hopeful they could keep my mother in check. They seemed at home already. Dependable Jane cooed about the magnificent red and gold OSF banners that hung on Main Street and the inn's scented bath amenities. Mary Pat went to work setting out my basket of farmers' market finds: the herbed goat cheese, raspberries, bread, basil, and several varieties of tomatoes. They chattered on about the two-day drive, their overnight stay in Redding, and the effect the altitude was having on their appearances. (I hated to break it to them, but I didn't think the extra thousand feet of Ashland altitude was the cause for their lackluster Pasadena wash-and-sets.) I had to say, though, that even my mother seemed to be floating in particularly high spirits, and it wasn't just the chenin blanc.

"I can't wait to hold my own press conference," she said, eyes sparkling at the thought of making a statement on behalf of the family. I wasn't sure that the two phone calls Bumble had set up really constituted a press conference, but I didn't want to burst her bubble.

Having been the wind beneath my father's wings for so long, it was clear my mother loved getting a solo mission, Anne Lancaster's own personal Stockholm 2008. While I was suspicious that my mother and her friends were really the best defense against a political takedown, I trusted Bumble. My goal was to lay low and get my mother back to Pasadena as soon as possible with no further damage to Maddie's reputation, or Ted's. Just then, my mother noticed Puck, who'd been sniffing around the other side of the courtyard. "Who's this adorable thing?"

"My dog." All eyes were on Puck, and he was thrilled to get some attention, greeting the ladies with a wagging tail and wiggles. They cooed in response. I explained that he was a stray that found me instead of vice versa. There was unanimous approval, though my mother did express some concern that not all men love dogs. But Dependable Jane, the group's needlepoint-pillow philosopher, retorted, "Dogs come into our lives for a reason."

So true! One dog and my mother had turned into a pussycat. Not a single comment on my clothes. Or how pale I looked and was I getting enough iron. Extra string cheese for Puck tonight. He'd earned it.

Once the dog was sufficiently praised, we settled around the table to discuss the next course of action. My mother took out a leather-bound monogrammed book that served as her calendar, address book, and notes to self. The pages were jammed with articles she had clipped, business cards, and dental appointment reminders. She was not in any hurry to go digital, but she was quick to assess blame. "Let me say, Elizabeth, that no one thinks this mess is all your fault." The Girls nodded. And I nearly choked on a cherry tomato.

All my fault? I wasn't the one with the radio show or the political ambitions! My eyes teared up a bit as I tried to work the fruit down my throat. My mother misread my blocked airway for emotion. "Don't cry, dear. We're here for you. We know you didn't intend on ruining Ted's career. Let's face it, whenever FX is involved, it's not good for you. But we'll fix it. We'll go to the show. We'll love it. I'll tell the reporter how wonderful the play is and how Maddie is thriving and Ted and Bumble are wonderful parents, and no one will blame you anymore."

My mother's pseudo-sympathetic version of the situation was harder to hear than Bumble's sarcasm. "Can I get a glass of that wine, Mary Pat?"

Commander Anne flipped a page in her notepad, revealing her well-ordered checklist. "Now, have you arranged for us to meet the cast after the performance tonight? Bumble needs a photo of us all backstage. She's hired a local photographer, I believe."

I was completely prepared for this. In the middle of the night, after I'd spent a good hour lying in bed analyzing the Rafa text (he was busy, stressed; he'll come around, right?), I'd moved onto Misconceptions I'd Allow to Go on for the Sake of Self-preservation. The idea that I was intimately involved in a smash-hit play was one such misconception. Sure, Bumble and Rafa knew the truth, but there was no reason to come clean with my mother. She'd be gone in thirty-six hours tops, and I could continue with the rest of my summer.

I responded, "Here's what I thought. Maddie is really close to the cast, and she's very proud of her work as a production assistant. She secured you three great seats for tonight, and I gave her the task of arranging the meet-and-greet after the performance. It'll be a chance for you to see how much she's grown and matured. I think observing her in her role will help inform your statements to the press." I was borrowing the language that Rafa used on the conference call. My mother was hanging on every word. "I'll be there, of course, and we'll get our multigenerational photo."

The idea was roundly applauded. My status as advisor to the famous director was preserved. This wasn't going to be so bad. Funseeker Mary Pat stood up and expertly refilled the four glasses, draining the bottle and immediately opening another. I added, because I could, "Mom, you might want to slow down on the vino. It could be a long day."

My mother's nose was a touch out of joint.

When the phone rang and Rafa's name popped up on the screen, my heart did a little flip-flop. *He was calling me!* See, we could work through this minor misunderstanding. I let it ring two more times before I answered, buying time to compose myself. Deep breath. "Hello, this is Elizabeth."

"And this is Bumble, Miss Sexy and Sultry. Who were you expecting on the other end of the phone? Wait, Rafa?"

"I didn't know who it was," I lied. "I'm a little out of breath. Running home to get changed before tonight." Actually, I was sitting in the front seat of my car checking Wimbledon results, responding to a text from Pierce DeVine about countertops, and drinking a cup of strong coffee to counteract the effects of the late-afternoon wine. "Why would Rafa call me? Is something wrong at the house?"

"I don't think so, other than this mess. The house looks fine," Bumble said, giving me nada about Rafa. I had no doubt her list of action items was long and her patience for small talk was short. "What's Mom's status? Is she up to the task?"

Now the whole family was using military jargon. Well, I'd buck the trend. "She's grand. I just left them at the B&B. She and the Girls are freshening up, as they would say, and then they'll head over to the play. Believe me, she's ready for her closeup."

"Well, keep her contained, Elizabeth. I really think we'll be able to ride this out. Ron and Ben only did one segment today on Ted. And Fourth of July weekend is coming up. People don't care about this stuff over a holiday. Ted's confident, I'm confident. But I think it's scared Rafa off."

Again with the irrational physical reaction to the name. "What do you mean?"

"Well, he's really Ted's chief of staff, a policy guy, and this aspect of politics is not really his thing." Oh good, nothing to do with me, and yet I was a little disappointed my name hadn't come up in their discussions. "Ted was hoping Rafa could be persuaded to run the campaign because of his strong California connection. But I don't think so now. Rafa can't wait to get back to DC after this."

I took this news personally, even though I had no reason to assume that any percentage of Rafa's decision was because of my lapse in disclosure. Is that a thing, lapse of disclosure? It should be. "Well, maybe he'll change his mind."

"Hmmm."

"I am sorry, Bumble. I had no idea anything like this could happen."

Bumble softened for the first time in twenty-four hours. "It's not your fault. I begged you to take Maddie. And really, if it wasn't this issue, those vultures would have found something else to attack. They can't stand Ted. Remember Slategate? How ridiculous was that? Ted can't win with these two. Even more reason to let this thing go. Once you start feeding their hate machine, they'll never stop. How is Maddie?"

"Righteous. Really. She may not be Lancaster flesh and blood, but some of our appreciation for martyrdom seems to have rubbed off. She's ready to go up in flames for what she believes." I told Bumble about the line of Free Maddie T-shirts that Maddie and Dylan were designing last night at Sage Cottage. A quote from Shakespeare's *Cymbeline* was to be emblazoned on the front: *Boldness be my friend.*

"What exactly is it that she believes in so deeply?"

"That she should be allowed to stay in Oregon with her boyfriend for the rest of the summer."

"Everybody needs a cause. Okay, I'll let you go. Check your e-mail for names and contact information in case the cell phone connections are bad and you have to call them back," Bumble instructed. "Remember to tell Mom to stick to the script."

"What script?"

"The script we gave her about how much she enjoyed the show, how important exposure to the arts is, blah, blah, blah. The script!" Down-to-business Bumble was back. Her tone suggested I was a low-level intern who was also hard of hearing. *Dear Bumble, thanks for treating me with such contempt. I've learned a valuable lesson from this and I'm sure someday I'll be able to identify what that lesson is. Your sister, Elizabeth.* I could never work for Bumble.

Still, I seized the opportunity to improve my standing in the eyes of Team Ted. At no point in my mother's review of the plan did she mention a script. I was worried Anne Lancaster was going rogue. "You'd better e-mail me the script, too. I'll make sure she sticks to the talking points tonight." Then, adopting the language of my mission, I signed off, "Over and out."

"Is that what an acid trip is really like? Maybe I should have tried drugs in the '60s instead of mastering the art of French cooking!" My mother appeared to be hallucinating at this very moment.

She was gushing, *gushing* to FX backstage after the performance, using what I assume she thought was a stage whisper but really turned out to be just a very loud voice. Dependable Jane and Funseeker Mary Pat provided a Greek chorus of "We loved it, too!" chants in the background. What was in the intermission coffee anyway? Or had the magic of the theater finally rubbed off on my mother and her posse? One thing I knew for sure: The family surrogate for a potential Republican candidate for governor taking a pro-drug stance was not in the script. That would be a bridge too far for the electorate, so I stepped into the picture, literally.

"Let's focus here." The photographer who Bumble had hired was snapping away, getting shots of an exuberant Anne Lancaster congratulating a dashiki-wearing FX Fahey. The kid with the camera looked like a sophomore in high school, maybe college, who must have overstated his qualifications to get the gig, and he'd brought a few friends along, one of whom was sporting a sad little soul patch and an *Icarus* T-shirt. Soul Patch Boy was using his phone to record every move FX made. They were carrying some equipment bags that looked empty but must have been useful in getting past security. I didn't like it at all.

I half-remembered Bumble's words to me, something about keeping the comments contained and getting out without any further controversy. "Okay, let's get Maddie in there with her grandmother and FX. I'll tuck in on the end. Oh, Mom, why don't you stand in the middle next to FX?"

"Listen to her, bossing us around!" My mother gave her former son-in-law a playful poke. She was transformed, giddier even than the day my divorce became final and she gave me a bright red Coach day planner as a gift. "Good planning makes for good decisions," my mother had written on the gift card. I used that damn planner for a decade. Now here was my cautionary mother throwing caution to the wind. I know the production was the ultimate in "feel good" theater, but really, she needed to put a little Pasadena back into her personality. FX laughed conspiratorially with her and gave me a look that indicated he had no idea what was happening. I returned the confusion. "Somebody really liked the play."

"That's a cozy group, FX and three generations of lovely ladies." Dressed in all black and sporting a freshly waxed pate, Taz Buchanan entered backstage left. Oh great. How did he even know the woman was my mother? Maybe FX had mentioned the situation, which made me nervous. Between Taz and Soul Patch Boy, I felt the need to get out of there as quickly as possible, so I latched onto my mother and called to the photographer to finish up.

But Anne Lancaster broke ranks and offered the director a double-handed shake with three extra pumps for the camera. "Oh, Mr. Buchanan, the play was simply wonderful. So delightful," she cooed, starstruck. "You're a magician. Did you get that?" She turned to the college kid with the Nikon and he nodded.

"Thank you. I understand you're Maddie's grandmother. Although that's hard to believe, you look more like an aunt," Taz purred in his exaggerated Outback accent with a wicked grin. My mother totally fell for it. "Maddie has been absolutely terrific to work with. And I'm sorry if her involvement in our little production has caused any issues."

FX must have talked. I jumped in because I was pretty sure my mother didn't have a script for this part of the evening, and the way her eyes glazed over with every syllable from the Australian, I didn't think she had enough composure left to think on her feet. "How kind of you to say that, Taz," I said, my voice rising in volume to drown out anything my mother might add. "My mother, my father, and our entire family, including my brother-in-law, Congressman Ted Seymour, support the arts and Maddie's participation in this production. I teach Shakespeare to students like Maddie, and what they learn is that the issues they face in their own lives aren't new, and they're not alone in struggling with them. The themes in *Midsummer* are universal and timeless, as potent today as when the play was written. Rebelling against authority. Expanding your mind-set and your world. Learning about the true nature of love. Shakespeare's work is both revered and relevant today for a reason: It speaks to all of us, no matter our background or position. We can all learn from the Immortal Bard. Ted Seymour is a great dad. He raised Maddie as a single parent for many years and she's a wonderful girl. He should be commended for letting her experience Shakespeare up close. Every student should have a summer with Shakespeare." I concluded the speech with an earnest nod and a brief wave, as if I were a candidate for Educator of the Year. *What was that?*

The Girls turned to me with stunned faces. My mother snapped back from her delirium and was clearly not pleased that I had stolen portions of her script for my speech. She gave me the same look I saw when I declared that I wouldn't be trying out for Rose Queen in 1992: slight disgust at my lack of respect for tradition mixed with a touch of envy for my nonconformity.

"Hear, hear, Professor Lancaster!" FX proclaimed, stepping up next to me and planting a big kiss on my cheek, then wrapping his arm over my shoulder. "I couldn't have said it better myself. I fully support Maddie, her father Ted Seymour, and her aunt Elizabeth Lancaster. Elizabeth taught me to love Shakespeare. And she is a woman of exceptional propriety who has uncanny radar for the moral high ground. I'm honored to have had the chance to help pass along the gift of Shakespeare to her niece Maddie. I, too, commend Congressman Ted Seymour."

The little crowd of onlookers burst into applause. FX acknowledged his people with a wave and then grabbed my hand and kissed it in a highly theatrical gesture that gave me the willies. Did he have to make me sound like an uptight British headmistress from a PBS miniseries? A woman of "exceptional propriety"? Seriously?

Out of the corner of my eye, I caught Soul Patch Boy with the cell phone camera nodding with excitement. We have got to get out of here, I thought. "I think we're done here," I announced to no one in particular and everyone within earshot.

I gathered up Maddie, my mother, and the Girls and tried to usher them to the door, but Taz wasn't quite finished. "I'm glad to hear you say that, Elizabeth, because that's exactly what FX and I told that reporter today. Although I think you said it much more eloquently."

I stopped dead in my tracks, with my mother, Dependable Jane, and Funseeker Mary Pat crashing into me Keystone Cops–style. "What reporter?" I said slowly, turning my glare from Taz to FX.

"What was her name, FX? Bambi?" Taz turned to FX, who was already signing programs.

"No, Candy. Your friend Candy. From that website, candysdish. com. She gave me her card at that party, so we called her and told her what was happening. Don't worry, we said lots of nice things about Maddie and Ted. Just trying to be helpful." FX smiled broadly, waiting for some props or perhaps a doggie treat. It took all the strength I had not to run at him brandishing my clog and beat him with it.

Taz grinned and said, *"What's done can't be undone."*

Just then my cell phone rang. I didn't even have to look at the screen to know who was on the other end of the line. But I did because, like a wreck on the road, I couldn't look away. It was Bumble.

FAKE THE SHAKE

3 Surefire Lines to Get What You Want

Boys, we know sometimes you want a night out with the guys. Or to get out of doing the dishes to watch the game. Or maybe you remembered the birthday but failed to get a gift—not even a card! Want to win over your girl, no matter what the circumstances?
Try one of these three opening lines:

"Let all the number of the stars give light to thy fair way!"

Antony & Cleopatra

"The fairest hand I ever touched. Oh beauty, till now I never knew thee."

Henry VIII

"The brightness of her cheek would shame the stars, as daylight doth lamp."

Antony & Cleopatra

CHAPTER 19

I've only been scared for my life twice. The first was Lollapalooza 1994, when I made the mistake of thinking it would be great to be in the front row for the Beastie Boys' set, requiring hours of time on my feet in the hot August sun without food or drink. By the time Mike D launched into "Fight for Your Right to Party," I was lightheaded, nauseous, and in danger of being trampled by the fully hydrated Beastie Boys fans rushing the stage. My friend Lila Montoya-Hidalgo picked up on my panic (maybe it was the gasping for breath and my high-pitched cry of "Help!") and cleared a path to the edge of the crowd before I was sucked under a carpet of combat boots. "She's going to puke!" Lila warned in her British-by-way-of-Bogotá accent, as she cleared a path using her vintage Bermuda bag as a machete. I made it out alive, barely. It took me a good hour to convince the medics that there had been no drugs of any sort involved.

Lila was a good friend, I thought. I really should have kept in touch after she graduated from Duke, married that DuPont, and moved to Delaware to a town my mother assured me was "not as dreadful as it sounds." I knew that if anybody in Delaware lived in a decent zip code it was a DuPont and Lila, but that was the sort of response my mother didn't appreciate, so I kept it to myself. All I know is Lila saved my life that day, and I vowed to look her up on Facebook.

If I survived this day, that is.

What had been a small local controversy only two days ago was now part of the crawl on *Good Morning America:* FX Fahey Defends Racy *Midsummer* as Part of the "Fabric of Life." (Early in his career, FX had appeared in one of those long-running cotton ads, a daily source of pain post-divorce, as they often ran during the soaps my grandmother and I watched. Publicly, he was still in my doghouse for talking to Candy, but privately, I had to laugh at his homage to the famous campaign.) Once the national media had picked up Taz and FX's interview at candysdish.com, the situation had spiraled beyond the capabilities of my mother, the Girls, and me to control anything.

Reinforcements were arriving from Pasadena. They were setting up a tactical headquarters in Ashland over Fourth of July weekend. Their mission was to create the impression that Ted was an excellent father, Maddie was a grounded and well-educated daughter, and the whole controversy was nothing but a mountain out of a molehill. All of those things were true, but that didn't mean they were easy to prove in the eyes of the press. Or so Bumble had warned me.

The public debate now covered every angle, from Ted's fitness as a father to public funding of the arts to the appropriateness of teaching the more bawdy Shakespeare plays in public schools. In other words, pundits from both sides of the aisle and in the middle were involved, and the cable news chatter was deafening. And right there in the middle of it all was Taz Buchanan, who was certainly relishing his role as rebel director and defender of the arts on every

TV talk show I happened to catch last night. I was convinced it was Taz's plan from the get-go to stir up controversy for this production. Once FX *au natural* was out, he found another innocent to use: Maddie. It infuriated me, but my theory muddied the waters so much that I kept it to myself. Maddie first; that was my mantra.

I watched as the entirety of Team Ted, including Ted himself, deplaned at Ashland Airport. That former career in real estate development came in handy under circumstances like this, when flying commercial would just be tedious. Private is the only way to go to the middle of nowhere on a holiday weekend, I imagined Bumble informing Ted as they planned the logistics. Watching Bumble and Ted, or as I'd come to think of them, the Macbeths, make their way down the stairs in matching crisp navy blue outfits and expensive accessories, I felt a surge of resentment that shamed me a tiny bit. They were a walking Coach ad. What were they doing here? This was supposed to be my summer of writing and snacking and finding myself. Alone. Now, one by one, my family was invading, and even though it was partly my fault, I didn't appreciate it. Although I must say, Bumble and Ted looked rested and ready, as if this was the fight they'd been gearing up for all their lives. Clearly, the Macbeths ruled.

Next down the stairs was Suki Kim, the new campaign communications director, looking as if she'd just come from the set of a hit political drama in which she played a campaign communications director. She weighed about eighty pounds and was wearing impossibly high heels. Her assistant Rob was loaded down with computer equipment and a bad haircut. They may not be relatives, but their presence reminded me again of how out of my league my own family was. I seemed to be the only person who didn't have "people." Even my mother had the Girls.

Then, inexplicably, my father got off the small jet, wearing a blazer and a white floppy tennis hat and carrying a briefcase. *My father? What help could he possibly provide?* He squinted into the sunlight and located me in the distance. At least he waved with genuine affection, then pointed behind him at the next passenger down the stairs, my sister Sarah, solo. No kids, no husband, just a canvas bag filled with books and a yoga mat, no doubt.

Last off was Rafa. He was wearing sunglasses and absorbed in his phone as he made his way down the stairs, a feat that impressed me. I couldn't help but notice that his hair was a little mussed, which in retrospect, seemed like a tiny thing given the dire circumstances of the political situation. Watching him make his way toward me, white shirt gleaming, I tried to hold my nerves in check. Skype did not do this man justice, I thought.

How had this happened? How was it possible that all these people needed to be here because of me? Oh, right, because I wanted to remodel my kitchen. I considered yelling "I'm gonna puke!" and running from the tarmac but realized at some point, I was going to have to face the music. And my family. Plus I was wearing my sheath dress, so I was never going to be more ready than now.

Bumble waved and brought her hand to her mouth, shouting over the engine, "We're here. Wherever the hell that is."

My sisters were the first to reach me. "Wow, nobody told me that everybody was coming," I said, hugging Sarah fully and Bumble carefully so as not to wrinkle her pressed pinstriped shirt. "Well, everybody except Pierce DeVine and your hairdresser, Bumble."

"Pierce is in Montecito and my hairdresser's afraid to fly. I asked her," she responded, and I was pretty sure she was telling the truth. Sarah chimed in that the girls were at camp on Catalina and Steven's annual snorkeling trip with his college buddies was scheduled for Fourth of July weekend because the one divorced guy made the arrangements, so she figured why not come to Oregon? "Hey, Bumble offered a private jet and a room at the best hotel in town. How could I say no?" Sarah squeezed my hand a bit, and I knew she would have come if she had to fly in the middle seat and sleep in a tent.

Then, because the two minutes of small talk had taken two minutes too long, Bumble inquired about the distance to the hotel and the running time of the "play we have to freaking sit through." Somebody's taken her hormone shots today, I noted but kept to myself. "It'll take twenty minutes to get to the hotel, and the play is three-plus hours long."

"For God's sakes."

Bumble was about to blow a gasket when Ted greeted me with a rush of assurances that everything was going to be okay and told his wife to put on a happy face. He said he was looking forward to taking in a show. I'm pretty sure the last time he'd sat through five acts of Shakespeare was never.

My father, who'd been waiting for his rolling bag even though the ground crew was in charge of luggage, pecked me on the cheek and said, "Good to see you Elizabeth. I hope you have an HDTV. Breakfast at Wimbledon!"

After Bumble introduced me to Suki and Rob, she asked, "Where's Maddie?"

"Working," I lied. Maddie had begged me to go alone so she had a few more hours to be with Dylan, "Before the curtain comes down and I'm forced to go home on that stupid plane." I trumped up some book research and gave Maddie a grocery list to kill a couple of hours. To the assembled crowd at the airport, I announced, "We're carrying on here, as directed. You picked a great weekend to come to Ashland. Big Fourth of July celebration here! A real parade, games in the park, there's even a reading of the Declaration of Independence. And then, of course, there's the *Midsummer* matinee and then fireworks, so, you'll be very busy tomorrow. But, Maddie and I would love it if everybody came to our house for dinner tonight. And of course, Suki, Ron, and Rafa, we'd love to have you as well. You're...like family."

Finally, my eyes locked with Rafa's for the first time since his arrival. He'd pushed his sunglasses on top of his head and was staring back at me. His expression was unrevealing *but not uninterested*. Was that a glint in his eye? I held his gaze for an extra moment, hoping to match his confidence. Maybe all was not lost and at least we could be Skype friends again. Then I realized how pathetic that sounded, even in my own brain. "So…backyard get-together tonight at my place?"

Bumble raised an eyebrow, about to object to my Pollyanna Has a Barbecue in the Middle of a Political Crisis plan, but Ted spoke first. "I think that's a great idea. We have a little work to do this afternoon, but we're all free tonight. Besides, that's all this is, a family visit. Just a normal family visit to check in with my nearly eighteen-year-old daughter. So your plan is perfect, Elizabeth. Thank you." God bless Ted; he really was a good man.

Rafa nodded, too. "Sounds great." I was very pleased with myself. Rafa sidled up to me, speaking quietly. "It's good to see you again *in person*. Call anymore of your own press conferences lately? Like while we were on the plane?" he said with a grin, handing me his tablet. There was my little Summer with Shakespeare speech on YouTube, thanks to Soul Patch Boy. "I wouldn't answer my phone if I were you. It could be CNN. Or, worst of all, Ron and Ben. You're on the verge of going viral. You're very good on camera. A natural." He leaned in closer and whispered, "But I knew that."

A thousand watts of electricity ran through me. "I had no idea I was being filmed," I fibbed, secretly relieved to see that I did look pretty good on camera. The V-neck was a smart choice, very slimming.

"Obviously, you didn't know," Bumble said, looking over my shoulder at the image on the screen. "Or else you'd never have worn that shade of lipstick. Good God, is it frosted?"

The closest thing we could scare up to a motorcade was a rented SUV and my humble hatchback. Rob was behind the wheel of car one, transporting Ted, Bumble, Rafa, and Suki to the elegant and beautifully restored Ashland Springs Hotel in the quaint downtown area, in full bloom for the Fourth with overflowing planters hanging on every lamppost and American flags over every shop door. Even though it was a holiday weekend and the hotels were booked to overflowing, Bumble had scored a block of rooms thanks to a canceled wedding, because that's the sort of luck she possesses. Tough break for the bride but good news for Bumble. She and Ted would be in the Honeymoon Suite, of course, with views of the mountains. The rest of the team had their own guest suites and would set up a war room in a conference room where Ted could do TV remotes if necessary. What had Ted called this trip? A family visit? There's a euphemism for you.

That left me alone in the car with Sarah and my father, who were also headed to the Ashland Springs Hotel. "You know I hate B&Bs," my father explained succinctly, and I did. He barely enjoyed making conversation with longtime colleagues before noon, never mind strangers at a breakfast buffet. And the last people he ever wanted to talk to were innkeepers—unlike my mother, who used an opportunity like that to pretend to care about local history but really managed to talk about her own family. "I wanted a proper hotel. Your mother can join me if she'd like, but I don't want to intrude on her girls' weekend. You know how she feels about those." He'd learned a lot in forty years of marriage; I'd give him credit for that. Or he was simply afraid of her.

"I thought about staying with you, Elizabeth, but then I found out there's a spa at the hotel," Sarah confessed. "I'm spending the afternoon at the Waterstone, soaking in an Oregon berry bath and having a sandalwood and ginger body polish and massage. I can't wait."

I laughed. "So you're here for the free room and the spa! Why did you come, Dad? You're not exactly a fan of theater, spa treatments, or humanity, for that matter. You could have stayed home with your work and your good TV."

My father and Sarah exchanged nervous glances. "Well, guess who called me this week?" he said uncharacteristically. He wasn't exactly a guessing-game sort of person. In fact, when I was a child, he'd often force me to reason out the answer to one of my own questions, and believe me, it was no game. He'd grill me for a full half hour, working my way backward through the logic, before I figured out how a remote control garage door worked or why the air pollution was worse in the summer. It was torture. And he wonders why I didn't go into the sciences?

"I can't imagine who called," I said, shaking my head and hitting the brakes. One road into town and one road out meant traffic as Ashland filled with eager tourists searching for parking spots. "Who?"

"Duff Miller. My college roommate. The president of Redfield."

My suspicion meter went up to eleven. "Really? Like an out-of-the-blue, how's-it-going-roomie kind of phone call? Or what?"

"Well, as it turns out, he heard about your involvement in the play through the news. And coincidentally, your mother had sent him your CV. So he happened to be coming to Ashland this weekend, as he does every year on the Fourth of July, and he thought he'd look you up. He has a place here. I thought I'd come up and introduce the two of you myself." My father was talking at twice his normal speed, so it actually took me a minute or two to let the reality sink in. When it did, I looked in my rearview mirror at Sarah, who was grimacing and nodding. "Dad filled me in."

"*Wait, what?*" I was literally speechless.

"Ah well...." He went on to explain the timeline of events with a little prompting from Sarah. Apparently my mother didn't trust my father or me to take action on the possibility of teaching at Redfield. She was so convinced that I couldn't have changed my mind so quickly after my initial refusal that she took matters into her own hands. She dug up a CV I'd sent her a few years ago when I was doing a speech at the Caltech Women's Club and she needed to introduce me.

According to my father, she updated it with a few items like my book idea and my work in Ashland and sent it to Duff's personal e-mail with a charming note, "in case he hadn't been made aware of my interest in teaching at Redfield." My father concluded, "I'm sorry. I couldn't explain to Duff what had actually transpired, and it didn't seem right to explain it to you on the phone, so I got on the plane."

The idea of my mother "freshening up" my academic resume was terrifying. With what? My groundbreaking research on Elizabethan Bad Boyfriends? And the reality of her sending it off to a college president, like I was a junior in high school looking for a summer internship, was simply humiliating. Couldn't she leave my career alone? Although really, I realized, my father and I had brought this on ourselves by not coming clean to my mother. I couldn't get mad. In fact, I was having a hard time not laughing. "So on top of everything else—like bringing down Ted's political career—I have a job interview this weekend? And my dad is coming with me? Super!" He started to chuckle, too. We were a pathetic pair.

Sarah joined us. "Don't think of it as a job interview, think of it as coffee. Dad already set it up for tomorrow morning."

"Oh, good. Sarah, do you want to come along with us? We can wear matching outfits. Maybe Mom can get you a teaching gig there, too?"

"Are you kidding? My job is to distract Mom while you two get yourselves out of this mess. I'm taking her to the parade."

"Hold on," I said, looking at my brilliant, clueless father. "Mom doesn't know you're here, and she doesn't know this is happening?"

"I thought we could tell her together. Tonight. She'll be at dinner at your place, right?" Apparently he wasn't as clueless as I thought.

We arrived at the hotel. "You know, maybe I do want a job at Redfield. I'm beginning to think getting away from my family is a good idea."

If I had any doubt that my Summer with Shakespeare monologue was indeed going viral, it was put aside when I heard the voicemail left by apoplectic junior agent Melissa Bergstrom-Bennett. "Elizabeth, love the video. Fantastic! Get that book proposal done now! Call me." Followed by another from the producer of the Ron and Ben show, wondering if I'd like to come on the air for "a quick interview."

I saved the first and deleted the second.

One of my mother's mantras was, "When the going gets tough, the tough get mowing." As a teenager, I cringed every time she said it to my sisters and me. It was corny and not a particularly accurate pun, one of my persnickety pet peeves when it came to the English language. We never actually mowed our own lawn, the perks of living in an area with an endless supply of affordable gardeners, but my mother used the term "mowing" generically, as in anything that needed a little elbow grease. She'd hand us a broom or a vacuum or a trowel and require us to clean the house or wash down the patio furniture to get ready for some big event at the house. It seemed like our childhood was an endless round of preparations for an endless number of faculty dinners and holiday parties.

True to our characters, the Lancaster sisters interpreted "the tough get mowing" differently. Sarah did one small task thoroughly and completely over the course of an afternoon. Bumble hid in the bathroom applying lip gloss until the hard work was over. And I did the bulk of the chores and then put away the supplies. Like my mother, I found inner peace in physical labor.

Now, as an adult, I often find myself muttering, "When the going gets tough, the tough get mowing." Like at that very moment, in the backyard of Sage Cottage, as I did a quick clean up and set up for the barbecue. Let others worry about political ramifications; I preferred to spend my energy raking stray leaves and setting out the high-end paper goods I secured at Prize in Ashland. Like my mother, I coped by planning. Plus I was hoping the lilac-themed cocktail napkins might distract the guests from the crisis at hand. Or at the very least send a subliminal message to Rafa that I was sorry for any trouble I had inadvertently caused.

Why William Shakespeare Would Be a Bad Boyfriend

FELON
Prosecuted for illegal wool trading and money lending

PLAGIARIZER
Based many plays on already existing works

SECRET LOVER
Who were all those sonnets written for, Will? *Who?*

ACTOR/WRITER
Not a stable career path

FLAWED CHARACTER
Shades of bigotry, racism, anti-Semitism, and misogyny

ALREADY MARRIED
Never a good bet

WORE AN EARRING
So last millennium

CHAPTER 20

"More of these, please—they're divine." Mary Pat stood before me, holding an empty serving platter, which had been filled with my patented grilled pizzas. "You make them, I'll toss them on the fire."

"Thanks," I said, taking a moment to look out on the scene in the backyard. Miraculously, it was a simple family party, like I had suggested and Ted had wanted. My parents sat in the corner, chatting with Dependable Jane and Sarah, who was blissed out from her afternoon of pampering. I could see they weren't speaking to each other, though; my mother's laundry list of grievances included my father's appearance overshadowing her big moment and her girls' weekend simultaneously; my YouTube appearance trumping her front-page interview with *Look Out Pasadena!*; and my father forbidding her from joining the coffee/interview with Duff Miller, even though she'd made it happen. It was clear his strategy for the evening was to wait out her bad mood and keep replenishing her wine glass, not a bad call.

In that moment, the two had appeared to reach détente and were listening to Dependable Jane recall her Greatest Moments in Real Estate, the foreclosure version. Dependable Jane really didn't subscribe to client/realtor confidentiality, at least not after her self-imposed six-month statute of limitations had expired. She started a lot of stories with, "Well, you know, I held my breath hoping the sale would go through, and I really shouldn't say, but the sellers…" and ended many a story with, "but you didn't hear that from me." In fact, she really shouldn't have said, and we did hear it from her, but the tales were often so juicy we didn't care.

In the other grouping, Ted and Bumble were doing some grilling of their own. They had poor Dylan of Klamath Falls in their sights, but he appeared to be holding up under questioning from the congressman and the flack. I gave him credit for that, as those two intimidated me on occasion. Maddie, a student of her stepmother's, had done an excellent job prepping Dylan on safe areas of conversation while the two of them were setting up the bar for me. It seemed that both Dylan and Ted were fans of Lou Reed's music and admired his influence on world political leaders like Vaclav Havel. (That must have been a short detour in Ted's musical journey, because most of his campaign theme songs had come from one-name, early '80s bands like Kansas or Styx.) How Maddie had happened upon this conversation starter, I'll never know, but the foursome was deep in conversation.

So far, none of the rest of Team Ted had shown up, including Rafa. I hoped my face hadn't fallen too far when I opened the door to just Ted and Bumble, searching beyond them for the man in the white shirt. Bumble mumbled something about a new press release and "maybe later," then thrust a couple of bottles of wine into my hands and made her way to the backyard.

All that waxing for nothing.

"Elizabeth…" Mary Pat said sharply, jolting me from my reverie. "The pizzas?"

"Oh, of course, another round. I'll get them ready. And then we can throw on the salmon. I made a cilantro-citrus coleslaw, too, and some all-American potato salad. It's delicious, if I do say so myself." I took the platter from Mary Pat, who gave me and my black maxi dress the once-over. I could tell she approved.

The retired caterer laughed. "I like an immodest cook."

"Tis an ill cook who cannot lick his own finger," I quoted. *"Romeo & Juliet."*

"True, but still, I think you missed your calling. You should have come and worked for me."

Then I thought about the job interview in the morning and my botched summer of Shakespeare and responded, "Maybe I should have."

"Hey."

He was here. Rafa was standing in my kitchen in person, not on a screen, and it was no surprise that he seemed larger in person. He'd brought a lush bouquet of lilacs, the last of the season, and their scent filled the room.

"Aren't you a *dulce viento* blowing into town?" I managed to get out, referring to the flowers.

He handed them to me. "For you. Your favorites, I think. Sorry, didn't mean to startle you. The front door was open. I let myself in." Puck greeted him like he was a long-lost friend, his voice familiar from the hours of conversation earlier in the summer. Rafa returned the affection. "Hey, Puck, how ya doin', buddy?"

I found a glass vase, made a fresh cut, and put the lilacs in water. "These are beautiful, thank you. I'm glad you could make it. Bumble said something about work." I covered my nerves by pouring him a glass of Prosecco. He accepted it, and I wished for the millionth time that day that my family would disappear into thin air. "Has Brian Williams called for me yet? Because I definitely want to talk to him."

Rafa laughed. "Public relations is really Suki's territory, not mine. She and Rob are handling the interview requests and statements. I'll let them know your interest."

"So you just came along for the private jet and the free hotel room like Sarah?"

"I couldn't come all this way and not see Sage Cottage." He checked out the kitchen and refocused on me. "Well, that and a few other perks." He held my gaze, then let his eyes wander to the island, spotting the pizza dough I'd pre-grilled. "Need help? I mean, we've cooked together before, right?" He put down his glass and rolled up his sleeves, then moved over to the sink to wash his hands, a protocol I appreciated. "What kind of pizzas are we making?"

Food prep was a comfort zone. "I have red pepper, roasted eggplant, and fresh mozzarella for those with a savory palette. And marionberry, fig, and chèvre for those who want something a little sweeter. Take your pick. Which ones do you want to assemble?"

"I'm disturbed at the thought of eating a Marion Barry pizza, so I'll take the eggplant," he said, like a true Washingtonian.

"That's kind of your veggie, isn't it?" I said, recalling one of our first Skype conversations.

"I think the early Greeks cultivated the first eggplants," he mocked in return, as he expertly tossed the toppings onto the dough. I was hugely relieved that the chill I'd perceived on the phone had dissipated. In my fantasy world, where Rafa had come to Ashland for a visit, not political containment, this was how I imagined a conversation between us would be. Except, of course, that a crowd of nosy relatives was sitting fifty feet away waiting for pizza. Recognizing that it may be our only moment alone all weekend, I seized the opportunity to explain.

"I know you think it's unbelievable that I didn't mention anything about the production in our conversations. I'm sorry. It wasn't intentional." I carefully dried off the berries to avoid his eyes.

He studied me, then spoke. "I know that. It was just a shocker to have this come out of the blue when we'd...been in contact." Oh, so that's what he was calling it. But he continued, "When you asked my advice about how to get what you want out of somebody, was it related to this somehow? Because I've been thinking that it must have been."

He'd been thinking about me! I answered carefully. "It was. Here's the thing, my real purpose here this summer is to protect FX and his professional reputation. Actually, my job isn't unlike yours. You protect Ted; I protect FX."

Rafa considered my analogy for just a second. "But Ted isn't my ex-husband. Or *People's* Sexiest Man Alive." I gave him a surprised look. "I can Google, too," he added.

I went on to explain the whole situation, from FX's anxiety to Taz's demands to my own banishment. I added that, after hours of talking about FX and to FX every day, I really didn't want to spend a lot of time talking about FX at night. "I never considered the fallout. I was so wrapped up in making sure FX didn't make any mistakes in judgment that I made one concerning Maddie. She was so happy with her work, and it seemed so harmless."

"So how'd you get FX out of the—what'd you call it, gratuitous?—striptease? What did you have that Taz wanted?"

"Um, I let it slip that FX was, um, half a man. You know, in the parts department." I was as red as the roasted peppers and suddenly fascinated by the distribution of chèvre on the dough.

There was silence from Rafa, then a sharp burst of laughter as the picture became crystal clear, "Wow, Elizabeth Lancaster, you are a shark! Unbelievable! You should come to Washington, because you have no shame!"

Thrilled by his approval, but pretending to be humble, I shook my head. "I know. I'm awful."

"Is it true?"

Now it was my turn to burst out laughing. "No!"

"Damn, that would have been great inside information. Does FX know?"

"No!"

"You're good." He looked at me in admiration or maybe something stronger. Who knew subterfuge could be such as aphrodisiac?

"Well, there's a lot of gamesmanship in Shakespeare. Call me Iago." And that is as close as I, Elizabeth Lancaster, could get to flirting, evoking Othello and tossing my hair, even though it was tied back in a ponytail.

Just then the front door opened and I heard the unmistakable voice of FX Fahey. "Hello, the house!"

Oh, for God's sake, what was he doing here? He strolled into the kitchen like he was coming home after a day on the job, loaded down with beer, wine, and his agent, Hank. "Maddie told us to be here by seven, so we are. And look who's here—Hank!" He announced this factoid like it was the news we'd all been awaiting for weeks. Then he noticed Rafa and our pizza making. Was that a territorial look on FX's face?

Hank, on the other hand, literally looked like a fish out of water in his fitted suit and his Hermès tie, not the usual backyard-barbecue outfit, in Ashland or anywhere. FX dropped the beverages on the counter and extended his hand to shake Rafa's, clearly sizing up my company. "Hi, I'm FX Fahey."

I interjected, doing the introductions like my mother had taught me in middle school when I'd answer the door at her garden-club gatherings. "FX Fahey, this is Rafa Moreno, the chief of staff for my brother-in-law." Then I turned to the bespoke Hank. "Hank Goldberg, Rafa Moreno. Hank is FX's agent." Rafa wiped his hands and gave both men a firm handshake.

Hank moved in with a double kiss for me, like we were the best of friends after one meeting, several phone calls, and an edible arrangement, so I played along. "Good to see you again, Hank. You look like you're headed somewhere later tonight, but my mother always says that's the trick to partygoing: dress like you're off to a better event, even if it isn't true. Then you can leave if you want to." All the men laughed.

Then it was Hank's chance to be overly friendly, "How big a fan are we of Elizabeth's? You've done it, Professor! Created a hit play and a political controversy to boot. I had no idea the scope of your capabilities. I was skeptical when FX told me about this arrangement, but you're the best. Unbelievable job here."

"Well…" I said lamely, because really, I had done nothing except be in the right place at the wrong time.

"Are you kidding me? There's no such thing as bad publicity, and this is no such thing as bad publicity," Hank carried on without shame. "Who would have thought we'd get everyone from *Access Hollywood* to network news to cover our little summer project? Not me. Shakespeare? Who cares? But FX on the crawl? Brilliant."

I'll admit I was reveling in my moment as an accidental mastermind, but it was short-lived. Hank's agenda was not complete. "And Rafa, you're just the person I want to talk to. FX and I have a pitch for the congressman. Or should I say governor? Let's grab a beer and talk."

"Huh, okay." Rafa hesitated a bit then wasted no time to go off and talk shop with his new best buddy. My house, my man, and yet the plan was out of my control.

"Are those pizzas ready yet? What's happening in here?" Mary Pat walked into the kitchen. "Oh, hello, FX!" Ever since seeing the play, the Girls had changed their tune on my ex. She gave him a big hug, scooped up the pies, and headed outside, leaving FX and me alone in the kitchen.

He popped open a beer and leaned back against the counter. "Oh, so—Rafa, is it? Seemed very cozy in here. Chief of *staff*, huh?"

"What are you? Fifteen?"

"Some days."

"You were right. This was a good idea," Bumble admitted as she, Sarah, and I stood on the deck overlooking the scene. "We should have more normal family things, you know, instead of fundraisers or campaign stops or speeches." Bumble meant that sincerely. Since she'd joined the ranks of the political spouse and my father won that Nobel, the majority of our "family'" events revolved around something other than family and usually involved a microphone, a silent auction, and/or a call to action. Even cancer researcher Sarah was constantly on the lookout for funding, relying on family to attend luncheons and rubber-chicken dinners. But tonight, even the presence of Rafa, FX, and Hank didn't seem out of place. It was a beautiful night, the cedar-planked salmon had been perfect, and the wine FX had brought along was better than we deserved.

"Okay, Elizabeth, you're in charge of all events from now on," Sarah commanded. "Especially once you get that new kitchen."

"Yes, because clearly I'll never win a large prize, run a state, or need to fundraise for anything important. The new dishwasher will open up a whole frontier of event planning for me: family dinners. Unless I'm offered that chairmanship of the English Department at Redfield based on my leading-edge work on Shakespearean characters and their equivalents from the cast of *Friends*."

"Is that really what you're working on? *Friends* as a cultural touchstone?" Sarah asked, looking skeptical.

"Do not mock *Friends*. You know how I feel about the entire cast. Did you know you can pretty much find every character from *Friends* in *As You Like It?* Upon careful analysis, I can posit that Rachel is Rosalind." My sisters laughed while I couldn't help but notice the foursome in the corner of the yard. Ted, Hank, FX, and Rafa were getting along like frat brothers at a reunion. It made me nervous. I redirected my sisters' attention. "What's that all about?"

Bumble nodded knowingly. "They're plotting some endorsement

strategy or something. That Hank is slick, and Rafa's smart enough to know he can't pass up an opportunity to connect with Hollywood. Ted will need to win some of them over, even though he's a Republican. Looks like this might be Rafa's last act before he heads back to DC."

Breathe, breathe. "Oh, he's not staying on with the campaign here in California?" I tried to sound nonchalant.

"No, like I said before, he prefers policy to politics," said Bumble. "He's a behind-the-scenes guy, making deals and working on legislation. He really doesn't care about slogans or the ground game. Plus I think he's a little sick of our family, and being isolated in your house hasn't helped. He started doing weird things, like planting stuff, and making gazpacho. He needs the city. He's going back before Congress goes into session."

I must have let out a tiny groan because Bumble looked over at me. "Are you okay?"

"Just losing a housesitter, that's all." And all hope of a romantic future.

"Hey, Steven's brother Sam is coming into town for a few weeks with his kids. Maybe they can stay there," Sarah said. "I can't deal with three boys under five. I just can't."

I envisioned my perfect August tomatoes as the weapons of choice for Sam's brood. No way. "Yeah. Maybe."

On cue, Puck trotted over and nuzzled his nose against my hand, providing comfort and support. Bumble looked down. "I never really saw you as a dog person. You're not going to become one of those sad single people who send out Christmas cards with pictures of themselves and the dog, are you?"

Well, not if you say it like *that*.

The text from Rafa came in just as I was getting into bed: Let's meet in the park at the reading of the Declaration of Independence. Need to talk to you.

Maybe Bumble was wrong. Apparently he wasn't so sick of my family after all. At least, not the part with me in it.

Friends
vs.
As You Like It

	AS YOU LIKE IT	FRIENDS
COMEDY	✔	✔
LONG-RUNNING FAN FAVE	✔	✔
LOVE AS MAIN THEME	✔	✔
BEVERAGE OF PREFERENCE	Wine	Coffee
HEROINE WHO FLEES PERSECUTION	Rosalind	Rachel
NOBLE, CHARMING HERO	Orlando	Ross
LOYAL FRIEND TO HEROINE	Celia	Monica
SAD SACK TRANSFORMED BY LOVE	Oliver	Chandler
THE FOOL	Jacques	Joey
PROUD SHEPHERDESS	Phoebe	Phoebe

CHAPTER 21

"I'm glad we could squeeze this in. My wife marches in the parade with the Macaroni Noodle Band every year, and I don't want to miss her. She plays the clarinet, and this year, they're all wearing won ton costumes. Isn't that great?" Duff Miller was regaling my father and me over coffee in the lobby of the Ashland Springs Hotel, his voice tinged with excitement at the prospect of people dressed as pasta. The soft, warm colors of the grand lobby were a striking contrast to the red, white, and blue crowds outside gearing up for the Fourth of July, Ashland-style. Thousands already lined the street in anticipation of the homegrown parade, which featured every Little League team in the county, a large number of dogs in costumes, and floats sponsored by places like hair salons. It was a point of civic pride. "You've never seen a parade like Ashland's, Richard. Never. It's the best."

We were, in fact, a family of parade snobs. I'm sure my father had never sat through what my mother would certainly call "a complete free-for-all," not when you're used to the majestic Rose Parade every New Year's Day. Instead of carefully constructed commercial floats lavished in flowers and corporate sponsorships and hand-chosen bands of hundreds, the Ashland parade was a hodge-podge of ordinary citizens, a smattering of musical instruments, and a variety of livestock and people in gorilla suits. Of course, we were too polite to point out the obvious: Decorated shopping carts don't exactly impress Pasadenans. Still, my father was enjoying reconnecting with his old friend, sharing memories and smoothing over any miscommunication, so he simply said, "I'm looking forward to it. Anne is saving us a seat." Actually, he was headed right back up to his room to watch the women's finals from Centre Court.

I was just hugely relieved that Duff Miller wasn't going to charge me with academic fraud as a result of the trumped-up curriculum vitae my mother had sent along. Really, it could have been a very embarrassing and potentially career-ending situation, if Duff hadn't been such a good sport.

I was honest and told him about my mother's enthusiasm for Redfield and my own satisfaction with my position in the community college system. To clarify the depth of my body of research, I reeled off a few chapter ideas from the book, which got a laugh out of him. Truth is, Duff just wanted to meet me and have coffee. There was never any job at Redfield, and he was way too complimentary of my teaching at PCC to consider luring me away, even if there had been. "I was struck by your passion for teaching, as evidenced by that video on YouTube. Obviously, you care about your students, and I think the Summer with Shakespeare is a great idea. When does that get under way?"

"Um…I'm not sure I know what you mean?" I said, trying not to sound too stupid, because really, it wasn't a very complicated sentence, but damned if I knew what he was talking about.

"The program you mentioned, Summer with Shakespeare. That's a great idea, and if we at Redfield can be of any help administering your vision, let me know. I have connections here at Southern Oregon University, too. Maybe we can help you with dorms or faculty, anything you need."

For the second time that summer, I had a creative flash. If Duff thought Summer with Shakespeare was real, why couldn't it be? I could make that happen, maybe. "I will keep that in mind. We're in the initial planning stages," I said, hoping he didn't ask who "we" was, beyond me and Puck. "And I'm sure we could use support here in those areas."

"Diversity is our watchword at Redfield, and it sounds like an opportunity for us to connect with some of your students who might be first-generation college attendees. Lure them to Oregon, get them interested in Shakespeare, and maybe even our school." Duff was one hundred percent sincere, unapologetic about wanting to recruit "diverse" students, which is admissions code for kids who don't wear North Face jackets, hire private college counselors, and drive baby BMWs. Basically, he wanted to attract more kids like my students to the wilds of Oregon. "So when you're ready to launch, please be in touch."

I looked at my dad; he completely understood the implications of Duff's offer. I said, "We will, Duff. We will." And my father nodded in agreement.

⁂

As it turned out, costumed dogs do make for a terrific parade, and I regretted any smug remarks I might have made about kazoo bands in the past. Duff's enthusiasm had rubbed off on my father and me, and we missed tennis to sit through the entire spectacle alongside my mother, Sarah, and the Girls. Like veteran parade-goers, they'd staked out a good spot on the shady side of the street near their B&B, with access to bathrooms and coffee.

My mother's demeanor was a cross between insanely curious about our conversation with Duff and insanely put out that she'd been left out of said conversation. I admit that I enjoyed watching her squirm before I doled out spoonfuls of information in between animal acts and baseball teams. "There really isn't a job there. And you know, Mom, he's the college president. He doesn't even do the faculty searches."

"I think I know how academia works, Elizabeth," she snapped back. "Although I hardly think it could hurt your chances to have the support of the man who is the public face of the school, even if he doesn't actually check the references. Oh look, people dressed in deer heads. How…clever."

It was really the best of both worlds for our relationship: She felt justified forging my CV and contacting Duff Miller behind my back, and I didn't have to interview for a job I didn't want. We would move forward from there, but I did have to add one last point. I waited for a break in the action and got one, thanks to a stubborn mule and the 4-H club. "You know, Mom, you can't do that again for *so many* reasons. Prison, for one, because I think falsifying documents is a felony. And really, I don't know how many times I have to say it, so I'll only say it once more: I like my job. I like my students. I like my house. I'm not going anywhere."

To which she responded, "Fine. I was only thinking of you, but I can see you can take care of yourself and your professional life. Look what you've accomplished this summer."

Touché, Martyr Mom, touché. I caught Sarah rolling her eyes, a rare sight for my hyper-polite sister. A few months ago, I might have blurted out the possibility of a real Summer with Shakespeare program as a defense. But I'd been down that path before, so I held my tongue and let Anne Lancaster have the last word.

Satisfied that the conversation was over because she'd deemed it so, my mother turned back to the Girls. "Is that a Chihuahua suspended by balloons?"

I spotted Rafa at the park bandshell, standing off to the side, arms folded over his chest, waiting for me. Okay, here we go. He said he needs to talk to me. "Needs" is a great word. I debated the greeting: Kiss on the check? Fist bump? Tiny wave? He made it easy, whipping out miniature American flags and handing one to me. "Happy Fourth of July!"

I guess that's what a Congressional chief of staff considers a romantic gesture. "Wow, you're quite a patriot. Flags, the Declaration of Independence…."

"I love America," Rafa said. "Look who's reading the D of I? Your man Icarus."

Oh, no. "Really?" I tried to sound generous, but I was completely annoyed. Yet another one of my people falling for the charms of FX Fahey.

"Usually the high school history teacher does the whole thing, but the mayor asked FX this year. It's slightly controversial," Rafa informed me in a tone that implied he had inside information.

"You really have your finger on the Ashland pulse after only a day on the ground."

"That's my job," he concluded. "You know, FX isn't such a bad guy."

"Yeah, I know." But he was the last thing I wanted to talk about.

"What happened to you guys?" The question surprised me, because up until this moment, we'd both gone out of our way not to mention the movie star in the room. So I told him the short version. "We were college sweethearts who couldn't make it in the real world. It's an old story. Can you imagine being married to your college girlfriend?"

Rafa shook his head. "Patsy Doyle? No."

More surprises. "You dated a girl named Patsy Doyle?"

"I went to Georgetown. It's full of Patsy Doyles."

Now I was curious. "And did you make it past graduation?"

"Barely. That night, we were out at the Tombs with our parents. Her dad, this Wall Street bond trader, Big Jim Doyle, holds up a glass, nods at my family, and then toasts in the loudest voice possible, 'Viva Mexico!'"

"Oh, that's bad."

"Believe me, it's happened before. And don't get me wrong: I like Mexico. But besides the obvious fact that we're Argentine, I think my family's been in the country two generations longer than the Doyles. It was a sign that we weren't from the same worlds. I was from a world of good people and she was from a world of assholes. We broke up that night."

Decisive. I liked that. "What's Patsy Doyle up to now?"

"She married a bond trader from Connecticut named McManus."

"In other words, she married her father."

"Yup." Rafa seemed rather proud of himself that he'd called that one.

I aimed for the same light tone. "Well, our disintegration took a little bit longer and required a few more legal documents. And there were some co-stars involved—his, not mine—but at least I didn't turn around and marry my father. Not that my mother hasn't tried to set me up with a few physicists." I shook my head.

"That doesn't seem to be your type," he said. Now we're getting somewhere, I thought.

Just then, the mayor of Ashland introduced FX Fahey, who bounded onto the stage, wearing blue jeans and a vaguely Colonial white cotton shirt with a leather cord tie that I'm guessing Zadie, the costumer designer, cooked up for him. The crowd went wild and FX beamed. The poor history teacher in the cheesy tri-corner hat, who was now relegated to orating the list of grievances against the King, was completely outmatched onstage. FX took his position behind the podium and launched into a rabble-rousing version of the Declaration of Independence: "When in the course of human events it becomes necessary for one people to dissolve the political bands which have connected them with another...."

We listened for a little while longer and I noticed that Rafa was actually mouthing the words along with FX. He really was a patriot. He leaned in. "Speaking of political bands, I need to talk to you about something. Let's take a walk." He took my elbow gently and led me toward a stand of trees. Maybe this really was a Congressional chief of staff's idea of a romantic rendezvous.

He found a place in the shade that was out of the direct line of the sound system. Instead of the full effect of FX's voice, the oration provided a sort-of soundtrack in the background. Rafa looked me straight in the eye. "I have a proposal for you, Professor Lancaster."

"Oh..." I said, surprised at his frankness, and then I realized those words sounded vaguely familiar. The sensory memory of my reunion with FX in my office at PCC came flooding back to me. My heart sank a little bit. "Yes?"

"Actually, it's more correct to say we have a proposal for you," Rafa clarified, even more to my chagrin. "Ted, FX, Hank, and I have an idea, and we'd like you to be involved. In fact, we think your involvement is critical to the success of the idea."

So this really wasn't a date at all.

Rafa led me to the Ashland Springs Hotel, where Hank was waiting in the conference room that Team Ted had booked for the weekend. Suki and Rob worked quietly on their computers, but there was no sign of Bumble and Ted. Apparently the media didn't care about bad parenting or book banning on the Fourth of July—too many stories about the dangers of fireworks to report. The remnants of what must have been a strategy meeting—coffee, a picked-over fruit plate, and Hank's trademark muffin basket—had yet to be cleared by room service. Once again, I hated to see those muffins go to waste, but the situation had a feeling of formality and scarfing a zucchini-carrot combo seemed ill-advised.

Hank kicked off the conversation without any preamble. "Elizabeth, we need you to like this." Then the two of them sprung their big idea on me: make Summer with Shakespeare a reality. Yes, a real live education foundation providing instruction and internships for high school and community college students at Shakespeare festivals all over the world. Of course, in the future, to avoid any controversy, all students would have to be at least eighteen, but that was a small detail. The foundation would be funded and chaired by FX Fahey and Congressman Ted Seymour with a board of directors that included Taz Buchanan, agent Hank, and me. If all went as planned, the formation of the foundation would be announced immediately after the performance tonight, and there'd be a kick-off event in Los Angeles, timed to enhance FX's Oscar campaign and Ted's gubernatorial campaign. Hank punctuated his pitch by saying, "You've brought us all together, Elizabeth. You're the glue."

I was speechless. I had never been the glue before, *of anything!* Of course, the core idea was exactly what I'd been thinking about since my conversation with Duff Miller. But in my world of endless classes, limited connections, and low salaries, it would have taken me years to get it off the ground, if I ever got motivated to do anything at all. Here in this world of fruit plates, strategists, and daily polling, it took twelve hours.

I owed Soul Patch Boy a high five.

"It's a win-win for FX and Ted," Hank continued. "FX has been looking for an opportunity to do a Brad Pitt–Rebuild–New Orleans–type deal for a while, but he thought all the good causes were taken. We did a little tsunami stuff because he loves to vacation in Thailand, but he didn't feel that connected to the material. But this, your idea, your passion, has reignited his passion for Shakespeare and for being a part of something bigger, like a cast. He wants to take it to the next level, lead the fight for arts education, particularly theater. He's totally into this."

Truthfully, being part of a cast wasn't really being a part of something that much bigger, but in the context of an FX-centered life, I guess it was. I nodded a lot and waited for Rafa to speak.

Rafa did, in full chief-of-staff mode. "Ted wants to support education reform and the idea of giving an underserved population of students a brighter future, but signing some of those reforms into legislation can be very difficult politically and take a long time to negotiate. With this, he can make a statement that studying the arts is an important way to expand a student's knowledge of history, politics, language, relationships, you name it. He's impressed with how Maddie seems to have matured this summer. And an alliance with someone of FX's stature is beneficial, given Ted's political aspirations. A high-profile, privately funded foundation is the perfect middle-ground solution." Nothing had ever sounded sexier to me than the words "high-profile, privately funded foundation" coming out of Rafa's mouth. I needed some air.

"We're going Bono on this. Totally bipartisan. No rancor, just turning kids on to Shakespeare," Hank added. Then he went on to explain that I would be onboard to help steer the "education and selection piece." Hank and Rafa would take care of the business end of the foundation. "Our legal team sets up foundations for our clients all the time, because, like every day, some actor wants to cure something. Leave this to us."

Clearly, the majority of the celeb foundations Hank's agency set up were in name only. It appeared that Congressman Ted and FX wanted this one to be different, to actually be a foundation serving students with an interest in the Bard. Rafa nodded in agreement, as if they'd actually had a lengthy conversation about how to convince me to do this. Convince me? Where do I sign up?!

"Think about it, Elizabeth. It will be a time commitment on your part. You'll have to be involved on a monthly, even weekly basis, if we want this to really work. And you might have to oversee the summer portion of the program for the first few years. Of course, we can give you a salary for that. We've already talked to Gus Grant here at the Oregon Shakespeare Festival, and they would love to be a part of the pilot season next year, so that may mean coming back here next year." Hank spoke in such a serious tone for a guy wearing seersucker pants.

If they were trying to scare me off, threatening me with another summer in Ashland wasn't the way to do it. First, though, I wanted to confirm my interest and let them know they weren't the only big thinkers in town. "As a matter of fact, I was working on a similar plan. To that end, I've already had a meeting with the president of Redfield College about Summer with Shakespeare. He's very taken with the idea and interested in possibly providing dorms and staffing." Both men murmured approval. "So it goes without saying, I'd love to be involved, at whatever level you need me."

Hank gave me the thumbs up, a gesture that never fails to amuse me.

Thanks to the sun slanting through the hotel shades, I had to turn my head sharply and found myself staring straight at Rafa. There was admiration in his eyes. "Well done."

3 Simple Steps to Be a Cleopatra in the Bedroom

"Age cannot wither her, nor custom stale
Her infinite variety. Other women cloy
The appetites they feed, But she makes hungry
Where she most satisfies."

Antony & Cleopatra

1. CHOOSE WISELY You don't need to have sex with a lot of men, just the right men. According to her biographer, Cleopatra only slept with two men. Thousands of years of gossip and scandalous rumors, and only two men! Of course, they were Julius Caesar and Mark Antony, both powerful (and married) Romans. But the queen chose wisely: one for power and one for love.

2. BUY REALLY GOOD SHEETS According to historians, Cleopatra used to wrap herself in bed linens and then have the bundle delivered to Mark Antony to unwrap. (So much classier than the naked-under-the-raincoat trick.) While you might not have the household staff to pull off a Wrap and Deliver, you can spend a few bucks on good sheets.

3. MAKE THE MOST OF WHAT YOUR MAMA GAVE YOU Experts agree that Cleopatra was no great beauty, but she managed to pretty much define female sexual power for thousands of years. How? She worked it. Charisma and confidence, ladies, are the most powerful aphrodisiacs.

CHAPTER 22

The October day in 2008 when my father was awarded the Nobel Prize, my mother called a few minutes after five in the morning and simply said, "Your father won. He won." There wasn't any doubt about exactly what he had won. It was October and it was five in the morning, which could mean only one thing: Sweden called.

The rumors that maybe, just maybe, his work was significant enough to get noticed by the Swedes had been in circulation for several years, his research having reached maturation and fulfilling the Nobel's "test of time" standard. But with the Nobel, there's no public list of finalists, just cocktail-party speculation, and then, one October morning very early if you live in the Pacific time zone, you receive a phone call from Gunnar Oquist, secretary of the Royal Swedish Academy of Sciences. My father had gotten his call for what the Academy declared "groundbreaking experimental methods in measuring and manipulation of individual quantum systems."

In other words, I told my fellow PCC instructors later that day in the break room, he had figured out something nobody else had before: how to measure ultra-tiny particles without changing the basic nature of ultra-tiny particles, which normally liked to morph when measured. No follow-up questions please, I begged the room full of English majors and history geeks, because that's as deep as my understanding runs, except I can tell you that he used powerful magnets and lasers to measure those little quantum buggers.

Immediately after my mother called, I threw on some clothes, jumped in my car and stopped at Eurocafe, my dad's favorite coffee shop, for a large to-go container of Sumatra and some croissants to bring to my parents' house. Of course, I blurted out to the gracious owner, Kim, "My dad was awarded the Nobel Prize!" at which point she promptly declared the coffee and pastries on the house and told me to tell my father, one of her favorite grumpy old men, that he'd "never pay for coffee again at Eurocafe." When I arrived, Bumble and Maddie were already there, and Sarah, Steven, and the girls tumbled in minutes later. We sat around the kitchen table, hanging on every word as my father recounted what would become his oft-told Getting the Call Story. ("I couldn't find my glasses and I was so distracted looking for them, Gunter or Gomer or Gunner Whatshisname had to repeat the news three times. I mean, I didn't really need my glasses to talk on the phone, did I?") We celebrated with coffee and champagne, laughing and toasting, in our sweats and bathrobes.

Then I told my father the good news about coffee on the house for life and he was overcome with emotion. Honestly, tears sprung to his eyes, as if the entirety of his efforts had finally been justly rewarded with *free coffee for life!*

By ten that morning, my father was whisked off by the Caltech Office of Communications, which was experienced in exactly this sort of press inundation, for a day filled with interviews by journalists who pretended to understand what my father was talking about when he described his work. By late that afternoon, he had told his

Getting the Call Story to everyone from the *New York Times* to NPR to Diane Sawyer with the charm and self-effacing humor he could turn on when he wanted, which wasn't often. Most embarrassing question? Larry King asked if his work had any relationship to the TV show *Quantum Leap*. For real. After a producer saw my father nail his Anderson Cooper segment, he was booked on *The Daily Show* for his first post-ceremony interview. Bumble was beside herself. "He'll be the new Michio Kaku."

That never materialized, but the weeks that followed were a blur. My father was feted and honored by everyone from the President of the United States to the president of the Pasadena Rotary Club. In between accolades, he worked on his half-hour mini lecture that he was obligated to give before both accepting the prize and making the required five-minute toast to honor the King of Sweden. The lecture was easy; the toast had him in a tizzy. He asked me for help. "I need one great quote," he begged. "That's your area." I introduced him to YouTube, where he studied the dozen previous banquet toasts posted there. (And where he also discovered the entertaining world of unfortunate skateboard and snowboard accidents, which amused him to no end.) Then I told him to go with Yeats, because you can't go wrong with Yeats.

My mother took in every good wish as if she herself had been in a lab for thirty years, using the imperial "we" to describe the experience—and I will say, she really did deserve some credit. Her sacrifices for my father's career were well documented, particularly by her. She had put up with countless dinners alone, faculty politics, and being solely responsible for creating a childhood for us while he concentrated on his work. As a reward, she intended to put that Nobel money to immediate use. After years of "dressing like the French," she was done with buying one or two good outfits to get though a season. She was taking a steamer trunk to Stockholm.

By the time he descended the steps of the Blue Hall in Stockholm, looking like an elegant Alan Alda with his medal, the official diploma, a check for 1.7 million dollars, and Princess Sophia on his arm, it was clear his life would never be the same. Unlike the atoms he works with, he was fundamentally changed. (And, for the record, hats off to the Swedish royal family. There's not much going on in the frozen north these days, with Volvo and Saab gone, but they really put on a fabulous show in honor of Alfred Nobel, et al. The slate of parties, lectures, balls, and banquets was top-notch pomp and circumstance, and every member of the royal family sported a sash all week long. Bravo.)

When my father returned to his Pasadena lab, settling back into life's natural rhythms, Dependable Jane stopped by with all the newspaper clippings carefully laminated for posterity and a new needlepoint pillow that featured the phrase: Got Nobel? She wanted every detail and scooped up all the official programs for future lamination. She asked breathlessly, "What was the best part of the experience?"

Richard Lancaster, Nobel laureate, didn't hesitate a bit. "Oh, the morning I found out and Elizabeth brought the free coffee. That was great."

Now, in the kitchen of Sage Cottage contemplating the events of the last thirty-six hours, I was having my own free-coffee moment. Except for me, it was the tuna sandwich I'd ordered from the Ashland Springs room service menu and charged to Hank's room after nailing down the details of my participation in Summer with Shakespeare. Hank offered lunch and I said, "Yes." It had been a triumphant day, and it wasn't even over yet. Had any tuna sandwich ever tasted better? I think not.

I hadn't exactly won the Nobel Prize, but I felt fundamentally changed. Like a million fractured components that had constituted my life up to this point had come together to create one clear path. When I decided to go to Ashland, I vowed to say yes to opportunities that in the past I might have blown off out of fear or sheer laziness. Now those yeses had paid off. I suppose my methods didn't impress with their lack of predetermination, but somehow I'd put myself in the right place at the right time, a professional and personal first.

The play, the book, and the potential of the foundation was the sort of career path I wouldn't have dreamed possible six months ago, and it was exactly right for me.

On top of that, I'd managed to handle the arrival of my entire family with what I'd like to call wit and grace while standing up to my mother and impressing my sisters. And my father and I had reached a new level of understanding.

And Rafa? Well, that was yet to be determined, but there was something there, I knew it. Maybe I just had to say, "Yes" one more time to find out.

But at that moment, I was sure enjoying that tuna sandwich.

The scene at Chozu Tea Gardens unfolded like one of those really long Steadicam shots in a Martin Scorsese movie, with characters from my past, present, and future interacting in unexpected ways in what appeared to be slow motion. The music, food, and white lights were all familiar, but everything else in the picture was new. From morning until night, the day had been a blur of activity, ending with an amazing performance of *Midsummer* that had captivated my skeptical family. Even they couldn't resist being swept up in the peace, love, and fairy dust. Now, at the after-party at FX's place, my family and the cast and crew mingled like longtime friends.

My parents stood shoulder to shoulder with Taz Buchanan, all three fully engaged in conversation about the effects of hallucinogens on lab rats. Agent Hank was exchanging cards with his new ally, Duff Miller, and his wife, Grace, now sans clarinet and won ton costume. Sarah was clearly giving free medical advice to Lulu and several members of the cast who were revealing inappropriate body parts. Dependable Jane was dancing with Drunk Puck (the actor, not the dog), and Funseeker Mary Pat was flirting with Lysander and Demetrius, oblivious to the fact that the two men were gay, or maybe it didn't matter to her. Maddie and Dylan were taking pictures of themselves on their phones, clearly having learned nothing from the last few days.

In the middle of it all, of course, were Bumble and Congressman Ted. They were toasting, *toasting* with FX and his co-star, Sabrina, who couldn't have looked more intimidating in her body-hugging red dress and several blue glow-stick necklaces. The reporters who had been around for the short announcement about the foundation were long gone, so there were no unfriendly photographers to catch anyone off guard. The beer, wine, and tuna rolls were flowing. All around me, harmony was breaking out and spirits were high, another night of the *Midsummer* dream.

Watching my serious family come together in this spirit of fun and adventure was an added bonus to the already satisfying day. I felt like for once I wasn't the odd man out in the Lancaster clan, the bantamweight in the ring with heavyweights. Now I was in the center of the action. I was the glue.

The only one who didn't seem swept up in the moment was Rafa, who was tucked in a corner of the garden on his phone. Who was he calling on the Fourth of July? Was there some kind of Wonks Anonymous group he checked in with when he missed discussing the latest from Politico?

Taz didn't leave me much time for contemplation, as he bounded over with energy and purpose. He was leaving in the morning, his work in Ashland done. For its final performances, he'd leave the play in the hands of the stage manager, Lulu. Maddie had told me that he was going back to Sydney to start preproduction on his next film, a modern-day version of *The Odyssey* starring Chris Hemsworth, every girl's favorite Aussie and no stranger to skirt-and-sword epics. But at this moment, Taz was carefree, beer in hand and sarong in place; no doubt he'd be in the soaking tub within minutes. My only hope was that Dependable Jane wouldn't be involved. "So, Lizzie, nice boots."

Yes, I was wearing red cowboy boots and a white sundress, figuring I had one last shot with Rafa before he got back on that private jet to leave my time zone. I ignored Taz's remark completely, as he no longer intimidated me. "It looks like we'll be working together in perpetuity on this Shakespeare thing, Tazzie," I said. "Shall we call a truce?"

"Oh, we're not enemies," he said with an actual wink. "We're worthy adversaries. You played me to your advantage. I played you a bit. And look how it all worked out: I got a hit play; you got a foundation. *Go to your bosom; Knock there, and ask your heart what it doth know.*"

"*Measure for Measure.* A play about power, sex, political scandal, and false accusations. Very nice." Then I took advantage of our intimacy and confessed. "As long as we're friends now, I should tell you, FX…is really a whole man."

"Bah! You think I didn't know that? Okay, maybe I fell for it in the bar, but by the morning, I knew you'd had me. But I admired your spirit," he said. "I was just testing him, seeing how far he would go. I was never going through with it."

"Liar. You were testing him, which I knew. But you would have gone through with it, because why not? A naked FX Fahey? That's only good for box office," I shot back, and by the look on his smug face, I knew I was right. "And I know you deliberately stirred the pot in the Maddie scandal. But I gotta give it to you. You sold a lot of tickets, got a lot of press, created a lot of buzz. Just remember: *Tis excellent to have a giant's strength. But it is tyrannous to use it like a giant.*"

"You got me!" he barked. "But guess what, milady? Sorry to offend your sensibilities, but our *Midsummer* may be going to

Lincoln Center." I gasped. "Full production. Musical numbers! Dancers! Giant projection slide show! And lots and lots of nudity! You'll love it."

"I'll hate it, but congratulations," I said, giving him a hug and getting a tad too close to his sarong opening. "And I want two tickets to opening night."

"Two? I thought you could be my date?" Taz held on to the hug.

"I don't think so. Not feeling that good about our relationship, Taz." I backed way off. "I'll take Maddie to New York as her graduation gift."

Just then Ming appeared with blowers and sparklers, announcing, "Ten minutes to the fireworks! Ten minutes! Best spot to watch is on the rooftop deck. One at a time, please!" The crowd started to move toward the narrow staircase with great enthusiasm, and I took that as my cue to leave.

"I have to head home and protect my dog," I said by way of explanation, not really caring if the Bald One understood. I considered saying goodbye to my sisters and to Maddie, who was spending the night at the hotel with Bumble and Ted, but I didn't feel like getting waylaid in a sea of hugs and kisses. I'd only be gone for a bit anyway.

"Hurry back. I'm in the soaking tub later." Taz did a little shuffle for my benefit. Yeah, definitely nothing under that sarong.

"Where are you going?" Rafa caught me on my way out the door, his hand catching my forearm and his gaze taking in my red cowboy boots for the first time.

"I don't want to leave Puck alone during the fireworks," I explained, hoping I didn't sound like one of those me-and-my-dog-on-a-Christmas-card people that Bumble warned me about. "The local paper ran all these articles about how dogs go nuts on the Fourth of July. I don't think I should leave him alone."

"Want some company?"

I didn't hesitate. "Yes."

POWER COUPLE #7

Beatrice & Benedick

FROM *MUCH ADO ABOUT NOTHING*

HER: Smart, good-looking gal who mocks marriage whenever she gets the chance. Never met a pun she didn't like and is always ready to engage in a battle of wits. Underneath that tough exterior is a vulnerable heart.

HIM: Smart, good-looking guy who mocks marriage whenever he gets the chance. Never met a pun he didn't like and is always ready to engage in a battle of wits. Underneath that tough exterior is a vulnerable heart.

RELATIONSHIP HISTORY: They had a moment in the past, perhaps even a one-night stand Elizabethan-style. But it appears that he led her on and then let her go. And she has not forgotten.

RELATIONSHIP HURDLES: Both are subject to gossip, innuendo, eavesdropping, disguises, false accusations, and fear of commitment. Plus she's not crazy about his beard.

MEET CUTE: He returns from war, triumphant and cocky. She re-engages in what observers call a "merry war" of wits. His first words? "What, my dear Lady Disdain! Are you yet living?" And it is on.

HER SIGNATURE LINE: "I had rather hear my dog bark at a crow than a man swear he loves me."

HIS TRANSFORMATIVE LINE: "I may chance have some odd quirks and remnants of wit broken on me because I have railed so long against marriage. But doth not the appetite alter? A man loves the meat in his youth that he cannot endure in his age."

WHY THEY WORK: Both are unwilling to "settle" just to be married. And they engage in really sexy pillow talk.

SHAKESPEAREAN COUPLE MOST LIKELY TO: Celebrate their golden anniversary.

CHAPTER 23

I was much more nervous than the dog. Puck couldn't have been more relaxed, lounging on the bent willow love seat, oblivious to the booms and the bursts of red, white, and blue. Honestly, he could barely keep his eyes open, the sound of the fireworks acting like a canine sleep machine. I was the jumpy one. Rafa and I sat on the front porch steps of Sage Cottage, taking in the pyrotechnics, which were slightly obstructed by the huge trees on my street. The fireworks peeked over the tops of the branches—enough magic to cast a spell over the evening, but not so much that I could hear violins (self-consciously) in the background. For that I was thankful; I still had no idea where all this was headed.

Normally, I was an "oooh-er" and an "ahh-er," but that seemed too goofy for the moment. After all, I was trying to impress a guy who I'd spied lip-synching the Declaration of Independence; maybe he wouldn't have minded my enthusiasm. Still, I tried to keep it in, but one gasp escaped my lips after a giant burst of stars. "I love fireworks," I explained.

"I'd expect no less," Rafa said, not taking his eyes from the sky. Another giant burst of color, this time blue to hot white. "You like the dramatic."

"Be not afeard; the isle is full of noises. Sounds and sweet airs, that give delight and hurt not," I quoted from *The Tempest*, regretting it immediately. "I'm sorry. It's a terrible habit that I picked up this summer. It's how people talk here. I used to be normal."

"Don't apologize. Most of the people I hang around with quote from the quarterly economic indicator reports, so I'm happy to listen to a fresh source." Now a red explosion with screamers, my favorites. We sat in silence, watching the blazing tails trail off. The air was cooling off from the heat of the day.

"I have something to tell you." Rafa turned to me, now our knees grazing, his hand resting gently on my thigh. An accident? "I have to go back to DC in a few days. For good. The office there needs me."

I need you. "I figured something was up. You were on the phone all night." Another burst of light illuminated his face, intense and focused.

He nodded, "Making arrangements. I'll go back to Pasadena tomorrow and pack my stuff. Then I'll eat all the ripe tomatoes in your garden with a little bit of olive oil and some really good salt. I'll spend exactly twenty-four hours with my family so my mother doesn't disown me and then catch a flight home." He let his hand drift up and down my leg as he spoke, smoothing the fabric of my dress against my skin. There was nothing accidental about his actions.

The heat was immediate. I dipped my head to compose myself. Home. His home, on the other side of the country. "That's a tight schedule. But it sounds like you're free tonight?"

"I am. Wide open." His hand gently pushed the hair out of my eyes.

"Me, too." Rafa leaned in and kissed me, his white linen shirt grazing my bare shoulders, his lips soft and dry. I brushed my hand against the side of his face, slightly rough with stubble, then ran my finger across his jaw line and down his neck. I heard an easy intake of breath as he pulled back. I kept my right hand on his chest and combed through his hair with my left. His eyes were closed, but mine weren't. My god, he was a handsome man.

Then I felt a wet nose.

It seemed Puck wasn't too keen on someone moving in on his girl. Rafa laughed, the moment gone. He stood up, his athletic body moving gracefully, and he reached for my hand, "You smell good. Him, not so much."

"I think he's jealous," I said, as I let Rafa pull me up next to him and wrap his arms around me, his own scent a mix of pine and warm earth. As his hands found their way down my back, he said, "Well, by my calculation, I got here first. Remember the day you answered the door in your bathrobe? All professor-y with your glasses on and your hair up, talking about artichokes? That's the day I marked my territory. Remember, I gave you my card? That dog didn't show up until weeks later."

That day? In my fleece bathrobe and camisole? Not exactly a top choice for my get-the-guy outfit. That's something for my book, I thought, as I absorbed the sensation of his body so close to mine. "*Marked your territory?* I guess you win." Rafa bent down and kissed my collarbone once, twice. Oh, poor Puck, trying to wedge himself between Rafa and me on the steps, unaware that he had no chance, despite his adorable face. Now it was my turn to breathe deeply. "Okay, dog, you're going to sleep in the crate," I said, as I reluctantly freed myself from Rafa's arms and grabbed Puck's collar, heading into the house. I turned back to see Rafa, watching my every move. "And you, lucky dog," I said, "get to sleep on the bed tonight."

❧

This never gets any easier. I scrambled around my bedroom, lighting a few candles and contemplating musical choices while Rafa bought some time in the kitchen opening a bottle of wine. *Is Alicia Keyes setting the bar too high? Should I go with alt country to match my boots?* One of the great benefits of being in a marriage or any long-term relationship would be never having to go through these awkward first encounters ever again. At least, I imagined that to be true when I weighed my makeshift life against Sarah's or Bumble's. They knew what would happen when the lights went out, for better or worse. My own marriage was so short, we never really achieved a familiar bedtime rhythm. And the few relationships since had never even come close to settling into a routine. I know this was supposed to be the spice of single life, but I lacked the "go with it" attitude of those girls I read about in *Cosmo.* Definitely alt country tonight. I put on Allison Moorer and waited. *Please, please, let this be great.*

"Here you go," Rafa handed me a glass of pinot gris and took quite a slug of his own. *Is he nervous, too?* That surprised me. He seemed in control on the front porch; now, as he stood a little awkwardly in my bedroom, a kind of shyness had crept into his manner.

"Are you okay?" I asked, setting the glass on the bedside table after taking a sip.

"Of course, Elizabeth, it's just…" he trailed off, reluctant to complete the thought. "You know, you're…."

"Your boss's sister-in-law?"

"Yes, but that's not it."

"Bumble's sister?"

"True, though she doesn't scare me. Much. Anymore."

"Still, we should probably not mention this to them. Or anyone, right now." He shook his head in agreement. But he still looked uncomfortable, which I'd never seen before. "Then what is it?"

"This is dumb," he said, letting out a sigh. "But you were married to FX Fahey. Icarus. Sexiest Man Alive. That's a little intimidating."

My jaw almost dropped open, because he was clearly serious. "Rafa, you really don't have to worry." *Have you seen your forearms in those white shirts with the sleeves rolled up? Believe me, FX Who?*

"You must have heard this before." He sipped his wine again, this time with less urgency.

"Actually no," I said gently, recalling the motley collection of divorced lawyers, depressed colleagues, and closeted gay men that made up my romantic history, a half-dozen lesser specimens who'd never uttered my ex-husband's name. *Thank God it had never come up before this*, I thought. *My sex life would have been even grimmer.* That Rafa was the one with insecurity issues almost made me laugh out loud, but I tried to be sensitive. "The men I've dated since FX never met him like you have. In fact, I probably never even mentioned him, so it wasn't an issue. He's not the kind of ex you talk about on a first date. Or a twelfth. And, honestly, it's been almost fifteen years since…that part of my life."

"But I saw him onstage tonight."

"Onstage, he's a star. But, remember, that's not who I fell for. I fell for the cute guy in my dorm freshman year. He's my Patsy Doyle. And if there's anything I've learned this summer, it's that I still think of him that way. As a friend, a really charming friend, a guy I used to be crazy about, but not anymore." Rafa's vulnerability gave me confidence. I took his hand and led him over to the side of bed. I lifted the wine glass out of his hand, set it on the table and unbuttoned his shirt like I'd wanted to do for months. My lips brushed his temples. Oh, those cheekbones. His shoulders relaxed, then the rest of his chest, his hips. I felt my own hips go with his. "Besides, I can tell you this, from the preview downstairs, you're better at this than he is."

That perked him up. "Really?" Rafa kissed me deeply, then deeper. I responded with my whole body.

"Much better," I said, as he opened the top buttons of my dress, one at a time, exposing my bare skin underneath. His hands felt warm, exploring.

"Is this better?" he whispered into my neck.

"Uh-huh."

He flicked his finger across my breast and followed with his mouth. I closed my eyes. After a short while, he raised his head slightly. "And this? How's this?" he asked. "Is this better?"

"Oh, yes."

"Good morning!" A voice woke me and it took me a few seconds to shake off the night. Is it possible to be both a tiny bit embarrassed and proud at the same time? My face was flushed. The cotton sheets felt crisp against my skin as I rolled over and spied the empty pillow next to me. Empty except for a note: Went to get coffee. Rafa.

What a good man.

"Elizabeth? Hello!" a voiced boomed out from downstairs.

Wait, that wasn't Rafa. It was my father, my freaking father. What the hell? I squinted at the clock. 6:32 in the morning. 6:32!

"Breakfast at Wimbledon. Let's go. The match has already started. How do you turn this TV on?" Freaking Nobel Prize and he can't even work the remote.

Good God, I couldn't get one morning to myself? How about a few more hours to be a grownup, making omelets for the attractive man I managed to lure back to my cottage after months of self-improvement and carefully applied natural-look makeup? "I'll be down in a second," I yelled through gritted teeth. I scrambled to put some clothes on, detangle my hair, and text Rafa a warning. Ping!

His phone was still on the bedside table next to the empty glass of wine. Not ideal, of course, but it did amuse me to think that he might be having his own out-of-body experience. I'd never seen him without his phone.

"Look, it's my dad! He's here to watch Wimbledon, too!" I said in an unnaturally loud voice coupled with cartoonish hand gestures as I intercepted Rafa, bearer of lattes, in the front hall. Fortunately, he'd managed to shower, dress, and buy breakfast, so it looked like he was just arriving. I mouthed the words, "I'm so sorry," as I took a coffee out of his hands and handed him his phone.

"You look beautiful," Rafa whispered and kissed me lightly, then said for all in a three-block radius to hear, "Oh, great. I'm here to watch the finals, too. Had I known, I would have brought coffee for you, Dr. Lancaster." Unlike my ex, Rafa was possibly the world's worst actor, but my clueless father didn't notice. He wouldn't be suspicious of Rafa's appearance at all. To him, it was perfectly normal to show up at the crack of dawn at somebody's house for possibly the last Nadal-Federer final ever.

"Rafa!" my father called out. "Good to see you. They're on serve in the first set. Elizabeth, I ran into Sarah on the way out of the hotel. She's going for a run and then she'll stop by afterward." My father had made himself at home in the leather chair, bringing his own coffee and a single scone that he was already eating. Rafa parked himself on the couch, as if this had been the plan all along, so I flopped down next to him. "Oh, and Rafa, I don't know if you've heard, but I ran into Ted in the lobby this morning and we're, um, wings up at two."

"It's wheels up, Dad."

"That makes more sense," he said, not taking his eyes from the TV. "Oh, what a forehand. Let's go, Roger. Your mother insists on driving home with the Girls, Elizabeth, but I'll be on the plane."

"So will I," Rafa said, because there was no getting around it. He reached over and squeezed my hand, then quickly let go.

It wasn't how I pictured spending my last few hours with Rafa, both of us watching tennis with my dad as the rest of my family filtered in over the course of the morning, first Sarah, then Maddie, soon followed by Dylan, and, eventually, my mother and the Girls, who announced they had stopped by to leave me several half-bottles of wine and boxes of Triscuits before they hit the road, but then they decided to keep the snacks and wine for the trip home, because God forbid my mother should drive more than a half hour without provisions. There'd be no chance to talk to Rafa about what next, to answer the question, "So what are we doing here?" No walking the dog together or reading the *New York Times* in bed after who knows what. Instead, there'd be conversation, cross-talk, and noise, including lively commentary on Federer's ability to look good in everything from tennis whites to black tie, a breakdown of the gossip from last night's party, and a pledge from me to send along contact information for the cast, particularly Taz, so the Girls could send thank-you notes. More coffee and pastries arrived along with FX, who looked slightly put out when he spotted Rafa in his spot on the couch, but he recovered when my father extended his hand in greeting. Instead of a languid parting with deep silences and long-held gazes, we'd manage a group goodbye after a four-set match, and Rafa would dash to check out of his hotel and make the plane after several texts from Ted that they were moving up the departure time an hour. I wanted promises and plans. Instead, I got a text from the airport: Skype soon.

No, that morning wasn't at all how I would have scripted our first, and only, morning together, but then again, nothing about the last few months had been quite what I expected. My work, my family, my relationships—all had taken turns in directions I'd never have predicted six months ago, which was, I guess, the real reason

I agreed to come to Ashland in the first place, to make something happen. Well, that and new countertops.

Maybe the chaos of the morning was a sign, a sign that maybe this time, I was on the right track. As I'd heard dozens of times that summer: *The course of true love never did run smooth.*

RIGHTEOUS ROLE MODEL

Elizabeth I

WHO SHE IS: Queen of England and Ireland from 1558 to 1603.

NICKNAMES: The Virgin Queen, Gloriana, Good Queen Bess.

WHY SHE IS RIGHTEOUS: Daughter of Anne Boleyn and Henry VIII, reviled by her father and later abused by her (sort of) stepfather, she nonetheless became the Queen of England. She overcame a prison stay to rule with an iron fist and usher in a new age of wealth and discovery. Noted for heeding the advice of trusted advisors, enriching her country, and founding a precursor to the Church of England. Enjoyed Shakespeare's lofty opinion of her goodness and purity. Not every ruler gets his or her own "age."

OFFICIAL MOTTO: *Video et taceo* (I see, and say nothing).

UNOFFICIAL MOTTO: A woman needs a man like a fish needs a bicycle.

WHAT TO STEAL FROM HER:

☙ Supported the arts and artists like Shakespeare, Spenser, and Marlowe

☙ Didn't let the fact that she never produced an heir get in the way of a good reign

☙ Relied on makeup, wigs, and that giant neck ruff to hide the signs of aging

☙ Proved that men and women can be friends by keeping the love of her life, Robert Dudley, Earl of Leicester, on as an advisor long after the romance ended

WHAT TO SKIP: A noted anti-Catholic, she imprisoned and executed her sister, Mary Queen of Scots, as well as many others, on the basis of religion.

HER WORDS TO LIVE BY: "Though the sex to which I belong is considered weak, you will nevertheless find me a rock that bends to no wind."

GIRLS' WEEKEND: Vegas with Angela Merkel and Betty White.

CHAPTER 24

"So, Elizabeth, who are you taking as your date on the big night?" The question came from Candy McKenna but inspired a roomful of well-accessorized women to turn their eyes on me. Like so many times before, my sister jumped in before I had a chance to answer. This time I was grateful for the surrogate. My anxiety level about the "big night" was sky high, thanks to questions about my date, my dress, and my speech, in that order.

"Yes, who are you taking as your date? Must be someone special—those are fresh highlights," Bumble said as we stood around the island in her Pasadena kitchen after the final committee meeting before the Summer with Shakespeare benefit. We were surrounded by a dozen members of the newly formed Elizabethan Guild, the auxiliary to the foundation charged with throwing parties and raising money for my worthy cause. Bumble winked at the collective brain trust. "Elizabeth's been holed up for months working on her book and the selection process. We've barely seen her. Maybe she has a new guy she's been hiding."

"Hardly." I laughed off the accusation. In the six months since the SWS had come into being, I'd found myself in a lot of first-time situations, not the least of which was being part of the inner circle of the Elizabethan Guild. Add to the list finishing a book proposal currently being shopped to publishers by Melissa Bergstrom-Bennett and teaching an enthusiastic classroom filled to capacity with students, thanks to the fact that I was integrating all the new pop-culture research into my classroom lectures. (How had I not thought of a *Twilight* versus *Romeo & Juliet* character-analysis mashup before? An educational breakthrough.) My new kitchen was being painted a smoky sage in homage to the summer cottage, and I had indeed recently gotten highlights, but I wasn't ready for full disclosure with the Elizabethan Guild.

My mother, who'd been on a sabbatical from volunteer work, hatched the idea of an auxiliary group, even coming up with the double-entendre name, declaring, "It may be the only public acknowledgment you get in this lifetime, so I'd take it." *Well, when you put it that way.* The Girls gave it their stamp of approval, so I caved to the cuteness, provided that Bumble took the lead assembling the guild. "Why do I even have to be involved in this? I'm picking the students for the program, not the caterer for the gala," I'd snapped when Bumble invited me way back in September.

At the time, Bumble heartily agreed, imagining the ineffective and unconnected groups of locals that I might invite. "Yes, please, you stick to Shakespeare, because your people can barely organize a potluck," she said, invoking the memory of my thirtieth birthday and the eight vats of spinach-artichoke dip but no crackers. "I'll bring the movers and shakers, but to get the members to care and to join, you have to report on what's happening in your classroom, how your students are responding to the idea. Your job is to get these women invested emotionally, and I'll get them invested in other ways. The Elizabethan Guild will be the new charity to work on here in Pasadena. I'm only asking fun, smart women who won't spend every meeting talking about their hormone-pellet regimen."

Speaking of hormones, Bumble was awash in estrogen, nearing her last trimester of pregnancy and enjoying the full benefit of the surge with glowing skin and lush hair that was beautifully set off by her deep raspberry Rosie Pope maternity dress. Fortunately for me, she had exercised a rare bit of caution, holding back the details of the miracle conception, except for that fact that she and Ted were going to name the baby, boy or girl, "Ashland," so I felt like I had all the insider information I really needed.

Bumble did look beautiful. She and Ted, now officially in the race for governor of California, were thrilled at the prospect of a new baby in the house just as Maddie was heading off to Wesleyan. (Yes, FX had used his powers of persuasion to convince Maddie that our alma mater, not some place in the middle of Pennsylvania, was the right school for her. The admissions office had agreed, accepting her early decision.) In fact, Bumble had been so distracted by the baby, the campaign, and the benefit that she'd barely mocked my love life at all lately, so I was a little surprised she was asking now. I sidestepped the question as best I could. "Oh, I'm still working on a date. I'm more nervous about the speech."

Bumble opened another bottle of seltzer water with ease. "I hope you don't resort to bringing one of those divorced sitcom writers. This town is crawling with them, and those guys are such downers."

The Elizabethan Guild collectively howled and shook their blown-out heads in agreement. After months of planning, a star-studded evening of theater, fundraising, and photo ops was to take place Saturday night at the famed Pasadena Playhouse. The event had been timed to highlight FX's recent Oscar nomination and to take advantage of all the actors in town for the Golden Globes. (It would no doubt be the largest collection of town cars to ever head from LA's celebrity-filled westside to celebrity-free Pasadena.) With help from Agent Hank and Taz, who also called in all their professional favors, FX had lined up a serious who's who of stars to perform, from *SNL* comics to members of the Royal Shakespeare Company, to perform material from *Henry V, Much Ado About Nothing, Romeo & Juliet, The Tempest,* and, of course, *Midsummer.* In between the performances, Congressman Ted and FX would co-host, and Maddie would speak about her experience. Near the end, I'd be called upon to provide what Hank called a *"Stand and Deliver/Dead Poets Society* moment" by introducing several of the students going to Ashland this summer. Finally, the evening would end with a spectacular live auction, the centerpiece item being a chance to appear onstage at opening night of Taz Buchanan's production of *A Midsummer Night's Dream* at Lincoln Center. Winner take all: a part in the chorus, your name in the program, and a dressing room next to FX Fahey and his as-yet-unnamed co-star.

The evening was so far beyond anything I'd ever been a part of, putting me in the big leagues with Bumble and Congressman Ted, or perhaps even my father in Stockholm. Okay, maybe it wasn't Nobel Prize level, but I was following Patrick Stewart onstage. And panic was starting to creep into every cell of my being. I'd been a behind-the-scenes sort of person for my entire life, not the star. I wasn't even the star of my own life most days. "Oh, don't worry," Agent Hank assured me after running down the confirmed performers and guests from FX's list. "These people love to love teachers. It makes them feel normal. Look at you, you're so real."

It will be real all right. A real letdown after Sir Patrick Stewart brings down the house with Prospero's big speech. Yes indeed, we are such stuff as dreams are made of, except of course, if you're the one following Captain Jean-Luc Picard, then it's the stuff nightmares are made of. I never got nervous speaking to a classroom, but the stakes seemed very high for this event. I remembered my father before his Stockholm speech, reaching out to me for advice. I needed someone like that, someone to talk me down off the cliff, to run my material by, to be there that night.

It was hard to explain the depth of my terror to the Elizabethan Guild, so I stuck with the topic of my mystery date and my dress. "Don't worry, I have a no-sitcom-writer rule in effect for the whole month of January," I assured them. "But what do you think I should wear?"

I needed to redirect the conversation, and wardrobe seemed like a sure bet with this crowd. After hours of discussion, the Elizabethan Guild, or the "Lizzies" as Candy had started to call them, decided to include the words "Festive Attire" on the invitations, a bold step forward in the area of party wear in Pasadena. It was a risky move to abandon "Cocktail Attire" for something a little more interpretive to appeal to the theater crowd. But the Lizzies were fearless.

If any good had come out of my brief sojourn into Bumble's world, it's that I knew once and for all that I didn't want to be Bumble. Give me my books, my cramped office, and my underpaid colleagues in their oversize sweaters. I'd rather prepare a dozen lectures on sexual slang in Shakespeare than have one more discussion about the color of the typeface on the invitations. Not that they weren't lovely women doing lovely things for deserving students, but I was much happier in my bubble than theirs. For the last decade, my status as unmarried and childless had disqualified me from so many local traditions, like the high-stakes preschool application process and the mandatory charity work, that I often wondered what I was missing. Now I knew.

When Bumble sensed my discontent a few months ago, she'd warned, "Do not disparage these ladies. When all those fancy friends of FX tire of this cause, and they will, these are the ground troops who will keep the foundation afloat with their work and their money. Watch and learn. These women are fundraising killers."

Bumble had used the pregnancy and the campaign as worthy excuses to bring in two of Pasadena's most notorious social assassins to plan the event, Candy McKenna and Zizi Rinaldi. Zizi, a lithe, raven-haired local legend, was heiress to a chain of auto-supply stores. Zizi's job in the family business was to spread the wealth among the area charities, and when she took a personal interest in your cause, like she had with SWS, watch out—she could grind sponsorship dollars out of a stone. If her violet eyes didn't manage to mesmerize potential donors, then a few shakes of her well-done chest certainly would. Men were powerless and women were scared. It was rumored that her entire garage was filled with silent auction items that she had not only donated but also bought back in order to get the money rolling. "She even has spare yellow lab puppies in there," Bumble had whispered during a previous meeting. There was no doubt that Zizi Rinaldi was going to be onstage at Lincoln Center, snagging the ultimate auction item. The only question was how much she would pay for the privilege. After all, the license plate on her Jag read GOTCHEX.

Normally a media celebrity like Candy would have stayed on the sidelines for such an event, preferring to report for candysdish.com than actually get her hands dirty with planning decisions, but this was such a rare and delicious mix of Hollywood, politics, and old Pasadena money that even Candy couldn't resist. "Plus, I think that thing FX had with Scarlet Josephson is over, so he's available. I think maybe I have a shot with him. We've established a certain rapport. You don't mind, do you, Elizabeth?"

I didn't mind, but it wasn't over with Ms. Josephson. FX was on location in Prague with ScarJo filming a CIA thriller and had become my new text buddy, as he was completely oblivious to the cost of international messaging. Most of our contact was about the foundation and the event, but he occasionally let some relationship intelligence slip, like: Off to Paris with S. Adieu. But I didn't want to burst Candy's bubble. No one knew better than me how slim the pickings were in town, so I let her think she had a shot with FX. Anything to make the event a success, a trick I'd learned from Bumble.

Candy had brought her people to the Lizzies: a whip smart lawyer/life coach by the name of Tina Chau-Swenson, whom I discovered had a photographic memory and a contact list that covered all the best zip codes in Southern California; and the much-whispered-about Helen Fairchild, a widow who'd become a modern-day heroine around town when she replaced her philandering husband, unfortunately plowed over by a Rose Parade float while sexting his mistress, with a handsome archaeology professor. Helen was the producer of a TV show called *The Dirty Archaeologist* and managed to live in Pasadena in the winter and on the coast of Turkey in the summer, lucky girl. She was a frustrated academic who was working on a book herself, some historical fiction about Troy. I liked Helen, and we'd actually made plans to have coffee once the madness was over so I could reveal everything I knew about the book world, which was almost nothing.

Rounding out the committee were the assorted wives of bankers and business owners who themselves were bankers and business owners and somehow managed to work by day, raise honor-roll-worthy children by night, and spend their spare time stuffing envelopes and filling gift bags. Bumble was right, I had come to appreciate their work ethic, even if I could never live up to their grooming standards and shopping expertise, as evidenced by the fact that it took Tina Chau-Swenson about three seconds to come up with a solution to my faux fashion dilemma: "Missoni! Vintage! Floral!" She whipped out her tablet, brought up an Etsy page (I knew I liked Tina), and pointed right at the perfect dress, a muted floral-print maxi with V-straps and a touch of metallic. "I almost bought this for me, but it's so much better for you. You're young, hip, and have really nice collarbones. And look, you can move in it, maybe even sit down. It says, 'I teach but I have style.' Click here," she ordered, leaving me almost no choice. Fortunately, it was beautiful.

"Trust her. Tina knows what she's talking about," Helen said. "It's pathological."

A chorus of agreement encouraged me to find my credit card for what would be my last splurge. The remodel had tapped out every dime I'd made last summer, and now it was back to my regularly scheduled modest lifestyle. The dress was worth it, though. It meant at least one aspect of the evening was a known quantity.

That Saturday, the texts started coming in at about four in the afternoon, as I was sitting in the salon getting the hair and makeup that Bumble had insisted on. "You need your face to last for hours on a night like tonight, and the only way that's going to happen is if you have Lenore spray paint it on. Just shellac that foundation right on. I'll treat." So I was in the chair having my eyelids airbrushed with color when the first one popped up: Meeting over. SFO fogged in. Plane late.

An hour later, I was slipping into my binding underwear and my fabulous dress that was (thank you, Tina) exactly right when the next one came in: Delayed again. I showed the text to Puck, who threw himself back down on the hardwood floor with a sigh. I felt the same way. "I know, little guy, me too."

And I was standing in the courtyard of the Pasadena Playhouse, nursing a glass of chardonnay and making conversation with a group of locals who'd spent five hundred dollars a ticket to get a glimpse of FX and his pals, when the last text arrived: Think we're taking off.

Please get here, I thought as I surveyed the tented courtyard, marveling that all these people were here because of my idea. The Lizzies were the very definition of festive—no tasteful sequined T-shirt was spared. Candy, Helen, and Tina were being photographed by *Look Out Pasadena!* while Zizi, needless to say, was posing/auditioning for FX and Taz for some higher-profile publication.

I spotted my parents holding hands and chatting with the Girls and Pierce DeVine, resplendent in a midnight-blue velvet blazer.

264 | LIAN DOLAN

Earlier in the evening, my mother had weighed in with a trademark comment: "I wasn't too sure of that dress when you described it earlier, but it works on you." Ted and Bumble were holding court with a cabal of well-suited Friends of Hank, using the event to secure new supporters. Sarah and Steven observed from the corner; they'd brought Hope and Honor, because Elle Fanning was performing the *Romeo & Juliet* balcony scene with one of the boys from One Direction, and for that the twins were willing to sit through "some guy named Jude" doing the St. Crispin's Day speech.

Even Maddie was paired up, introducing Dylan, a surprise guest, to the Emmas, whose parents had thrown down the cash to get their daughters on the guest list—the next generation of the Elizabethan Guild. Dylan, on the other hand, was there courtesy of FX, who'd paid for his ticket and encouraged him to join Maddie onstage to speak about his summer experience. ("Ever since *Portlandia*, everyone loves people from Oregon," Hank had assured me in a conference call when he told me the secret plan.)

Oh well, I thought, chances are that no one even notices I'm solo, because I usually am at social events. Besides, my immediate issue was stage fright, not singledom.

"You ready?" FX tapped me on the shoulder.

I turned my ashen face to my ex-husband and started to speak but couldn't get much out. "I'm a little nervous...."

Now it was FX's turn to be my cheerleader. Or to get revenge. He pecked me on the cheek, took both my hands in his, and mimicked, "Oh for God's sakes, Elizabeth, it's hardly *Hamlet.*" Then he broke into his Oscar-nominated grin.

"Thank you. That's very helpful." FX was still holding my hands, warmly and gently, without the slightest hint of anything more, like an old friend. Which, I guess, he was now.

"You'll be great," he said, looking right at me, then letting his eyes drift around the room. "This is great. Right? You should have no worries. You're in the right spot. We're in the right spot."

I teared up slightly, realizing that never in a million years did I think I'd get here, we'd get here. To the right spot. I pulled myself together and nodded. "Yup."

"Showtime."

Backstage was a reunion of sorts, with Taz embracing me like a long-lost lover and Lulu following suit and gushing over my Missoni. Drunk Puck was there to reprise his role and, yes, he was slightly drunk. I waved to the young lighting director and the costumer from Taz's crew who were catching up with Dylan and Maddie. I searched for Sabrina, only to discover that she'd been replaced in the Titania/Hippolyta role by Scarlet. Yes, that Scarlet. I guess she hadn't bothered with the pre-party out front, rubbing shoulders with strangers. She'd slipped in the back and was in her dressing room. "Their chemistry is insane! Rehearsal blew my mind," Lulu told me. "I think she's committed to Lincoln Center, too." Poor Candy. At least the extensive dermabrasion had taken five years off her face, even if it wasn't going to lead to FX.

I felt bad for poor Sabrina, jilted for the bigger name. But, of course, Lulu had the scoop. "Sabrina's fine. FX got her an audition for a TV pilot and she got it. Some doctor-lawyer show. I think she actually plays a character that's both a doctor and a lawyer. That's all she ever wanted from FX anyway. A new agent and a shot at a pilot."

I smiled at the thought of someone using FX instead of vice versa, then remembered my new European extra-quiet, low-flow dishwasher and didn't feel so superior. Sabrina and I do have something in common.

I excused myself to collect my nerves in a dark corner, like I'd seen FX do last summer. I don't know how these actors do it, I thought. Maybe Drunk Puck was onto something.

My phone pinged: In the cab.

And then: Don't worry. Just be yourself.

I was wrong. My appearance following Sir Patrick Stewart wasn't just a letdown, it was a complete plonking meltdown. FX's effusive introduction included the fiction, "Elizabeth and I were married for a short time, and I think once you hear her speak about her work, you'll understand why it didn't last. She's way too good for me." The audience ate it up, like we were the alt Demi and Bruce, and I made my entrance on the applause.

I took a deep breath, squared my shoulders, looked out at the audience and was immediately blinded by the stage lights. Every word of my carefully crafted two-minute speech that I'd worked on for weeks flew from my head, and I was pretty sure my paralysis lasted longer than the cocktail hour. Slowly, as I adjusted to being onstage and my eyes adapted to the wattage, I began to make out the faces of my family, the Lizzies, that guy from the BBC version of *Sherlock Holmes*. FX looked on encouragingly but with concern in his eyes, as if he were going to jump in at any second if the silence went on for any longer.

A flash of white entering the back of the theater caught my eye. My racing heartbeat slowed a bit. Fighting the glare, I could make out a figure coming down the aisle and taking a seat in the back. He made it. It was Rafa, in his white shirt, not the slightest bit festive but one hundred percent solid. He smiled, encouraging me with his expression.

Just be yourself.

Be great in act as you have been in thought. "My name is Elizabeth Lancaster, or as FX thinks of me, Elizabeth the First...Wife." The whole audience laughed, but I kept eye contact with Rafa. "I teach Shakespeare, and I can't think of a better job...."

EPILOGUE

"No one was surprised?"

"Nope."

"Really?"

"Not a bit."

"How long have you all known?" The after-party had moved to my house, and Bumble, Sarah, and I were sitting at the new breakfast bar in the kitchen, staring out the new picture window at the garden, having one last glass of our beverage of choice—either champagne or Martinelli's—and snacking on a charcuterie platter we'd snagged from the event. The crowd had thinned to the three of us, along with Ted, Steven, and Rafa, who were camped out on the couch in the living room. And, of course, Puck, who was lounging by the fire.

"Since the Fourth of July. I had my suspicions before that, but Sarah confirmed that you left that party at FX's place together."

My mouth dropped open. I was sure no one had seen us leave.

"I'm a mother. Eyes in the back of my head," Sarah said by way of explanation.

All our effort to keep the relationship secret had been wasted. The faux work conferences I'd cooked up when Rafa was in town. The "trip to New York to meet my agent," which was really a getaway to DC. I'd even come down with "the flu" over Thanksgiving so Rafa and I could spend a long weekend in Santa Fe. All for naught.

Well, not really for naught, because it had been a lot of fun.

But now I understood the reaction when Rafa had kissed me in full view of my family, FX, Taz, and half of Pasadena after my speech. We had thought that appearing together for the first time as a couple at such a public event would cause at least a little stir. Instead, the moment invoked amusement, not surprise, and only FX let out a few courtesy catcalls. Everyone else acted like it was an everyday event that I had an attractive man at my side. My mother, not a fan of PDA, simply said, "Oh, Elizabeth, dear!"

I still didn't believe them. "Maddie knew?"

"She told us you'd been Skyping him all summer. 'Worse than Dylan and me,' she said."

"Now I'm embarrassed. I thought she hadn't noticed. What about Dad?"

"Please, Rafa showing up at the crack of dawn to watch Wimbledon? Even Dad's not that clueless."

"Why didn't anyone say anything? I can't believe Mom didn't make a comment. One of her patented hanging teases, like 'Elizabeth, I think you have something to share with us?' I cannot believe she kept quiet."

"Oh, she said something, just not to you!" Bumble laughed. "About every three days, I'd get a call. 'Is it still on? Or is he after some lobbyist now?' You can thank Sarah for the privacy. She read us all the riot act if we interfered. She said we owed you six months to yourself after this summer. She practically made us sign a contract. Although faking the flu over Thanksgiving was really quite desperate.

That really made us laugh. We mocked you the entire meal."

"Well, I was desperate!" I turned to Sarah, ever-steady Sarah. "Thank you."

"You're welcome." She pushed her glass away. "We were shocked you could keep it quiet that long. Very impressive. That's when we knew it was serious. That and the lilacs."

She nodded out the new window toward the back of the garden, where Rafa and I had spent a glorious weekend in October planting a staggered row of lilac bushes along the back wall. "These are called Blue Skies. They'll thrive here," he'd said, wiping his dirty hands on his jeans after finishing the job. "I'll make sure of it." I flushed at the memory.

On cue, Rafa strolled over with more champagne. "Anybody need a refill?"

Sarah stood up. "No, we're leaving, aren't we, Bumble?"

Bumble rumbled out of the chair, pregnant-woman style. "I'm exhausted. We'll need our sleep if Ted's going to get elected and Rafa's going to move to Sacramento!" She winked, and I had no doubt there would be a million more such comments coming Rafa's way. She was right, though; Ted had better win.

Rafa stood behind me, his hands rubbing my shoulders as we watched the foursome let themselves out, the house suddenly quiet. Now it was just the two of us, three if you counted Puck, looking out at the garden and beyond to the lilacs. Rafa leaned down and whispered, *"I do love nothing in the world so well as you. Is that not strange?"*

"*Much Ado*. How long did it take you to memorize that?"

"Pretty much the whole plane flight." Rafa reached for my hand, his lips against my neck.

"Well, it is perfect." The rose-colored votive glowed, the shadows playing against the imperfect walls. *I love you with so much of my heart that none is left to protest.* "And good news: That's the only quote you'll ever need to memorize."

Q & A WITH AUTHOR LIAN DOLAN

In *Helen of Pasadena*, your protagonist was a woman roughly your age, with a teenage son about the age of one of your sons. She even majored in the same thing in college that you did. But Elizabeth Lancaster is younger, single, childless, and a Shakespeare professor. Was it more of a challenge to write her?

Actually, it was a lot more fun to write Elizabeth than Helen. With Helen, there were so many obvious parallels to my life that I really had to work to make it clear she wasn't me. (I thought I'd done a fine job, but I can't tell you how many people have called me "Helen" since the book has come out. Or introduced me by saying, "This is Helen of Pasadena!" Um, no.)

Elizabeth's the cool, slightly cynical single gal that I'd like to think I would have been had I not gotten married and if I had a PhD. I had a fantastic Shakespeare professor in college who brought the material to life with her passion and sometimes brought us to tears with her lectures. Elizabeth is an homage to her, but she comes with more emotional baggage and a funkier wardrobe than my former professor.

One similarity you have to Elizabeth is being the youngest of the family—in her case, a highly accomplished family, and in your case, a very large family, also with its share of accomplishments. How has being a youngest shaped you as a writer?

When you're the youngest in a big family—or probably any family—you end up observing more than contributing for years of your life. No one wants to talk to the youngest or hear what you have to say at the dinner table. So I spent a lot of years listening, laughing, and making copious mental notes about people, behavior, and conversations—all very helpful for a writer. Also, you have plenty of "lives" to borrow material from. Was that funny story about the bad date mine? Or my big sister's? Ultimately, it doesn't really matter who went on the bad date, I can still use it in my writing.

Shakespeare looms large in _Elizabeth the First Wife_. Have you always been interested in the Bard?

I grew up in Connecticut near a town called Stratford, which is home to an "official" Shakespearean theater, so from elementary school through high school, seeing a play was an annual field trip. And I can still remember the discussion about _The Taming of the Shrew_ in my eighth-grade English class with my groovy, feminist teacher. I think that early exposure gave me an interest and a comfort level with the material. Let's face it, the first few Shakespeare plays you see, you barely have a clue what's happening. But the more you read and watch, the more you understand.

In high school, I also loved going into New York City in the summer to see Shakespeare in the Park with friends, because that was a whole happening, from waiting in line for the tickets to seeing great actors in an outdoor setting with a raucous audience. By college, I eagerly signed up for a full-year class, reading a dozen plays and even playing Hamlet in our in-class production.

But my lifelong fascination with the Bard was really cemented during my junior year abroad in Athens. I had the opportunity to see an amazing Royal Shakespeare Company/Peter Hall production of *Coriolanus* with Ian McKellen in the title role. The production was staged in the ancient amphitheater on the Acropolis. There was no need for a set, because it was the ancient amphitheater on the Acropolis! Just the words, the acting, and the lighting—and with Shakespeare, you don't need any more. It was mind-blowing, to steal a phrase from the book. Just one of those experiences that connected me to thousands of years of theater, words, and the whole human experience in a single night. Made me a lifelong believer in the power of the Bard.

How challenging was it to write about Shakespeare, the most influential literary figure of all time?

Very. The more I researched for the book, the more I realized I didn't know jack about Shakespeare. At first, I thought I'd weave some Shakespearean mystery into the plot, something to do with the writing of *Midsummer* and the noble family for whom it was written. But after dipping into my research, it became very clear that there were lots and lots of serious Shakespeare scholars and ten times more enthusiasts who would bust me if I didn't get the research exactly right. That reality was sobering! That's why I decided that Elizabeth's research for her book would have a pop-culture slant and be more accessible and fun than arcane. That was a critical decision in the creation of Elizabeth's character and the plot. As a writer, I felt inspired when I decided to go in that direction.

Which brings up Elizabeth's book-within-a-book, *All's Fair*. What inspired that?

Once I decided to ditch a super-serious scholarly focus on the Shakespearean material, I worked on creating pseudo-scholarly material that any reader could enjoy. The idea hit me in the shower—where I do my best thinking—and I immediately got out and searched for contemporary relationship books based on Shakespeare. There weren't any! I was shocked, but thrilled. It seemed like a really contemporary way to use the material, and I like writing about contemporary women and their lives.

Plus, let's face it, even for educated readers, for many of us our last exposure to a Shakespeare play was in high school or college. Details get fuzzy. And who's kidding who? Life is busy, and nobody sits down to read *The Tempest* after they put the kids to bed. But I thought, readers might have read or seen *The Tempest* at some point and would like a little refresher class. I hope *All's Fair*, the book-within-a-book, helps readers feel a little more on top of their Shakespeare again. Like they're back in the literary game, able to drop references and quote quotes without having to work too hard!

Is there a Shakespearean heroine you most identify with?

Before I wrote the book, I probably would have said Beatrice from *Much Ado About Nothing*, just because she is fabulous and easy to like. The Elizabeth Bennet of the canon. But doing the research on all the Righteous Role Models made me appreciate so many more of the female characters for various reasons. Juliet was one tough teenager. Cleopatra worked it. Portia made a feminist statement in an age when those didn't come easily. There's a lot to admire in almost all of the women of Shakespeare, especially when viewed through the perspective of time.

In this era of extremely heated political debate, you've created a world in which Democrats and Republicans not only get along, but also love each other. Is this literary wishful thinking or actually possible?

When I conceived of the book, we had a Republican governor of California who was a fiscal conservative, a social liberal, and a bodybuilding movie star married to a Kennedy clan member! Clearly, here in California, anything IS possible.

Elizabeth Lancaster sticks to her career guns and doesn't do what her mother wants her to do. Is this an essential message for you?

One of the themes I wanted to explore in *Elizabeth the First Wife* was the idea of breaking free of your family's expectations and being your own person. (That's definitely the baby of the family in me!) But I've observed in my own life and the lives of others that being your own person is not that easy, even as you slide into midlife. And ironically, it can be even harder to carve out an adult identity if you have a close family where you can get stuck, never really evolving from the role you played when you were twelve.

In Elizabeth Lancaster, I wanted to explore a woman sticking up to not only her mother, but really her whole family, who have plenty of ideas of how she should be living, what she should be doing, and how she should be dressing. The Lancasters are purposefully an intimidating bunch, high profile and high powered, making it even tougher for Elizabeth to strike out on a new path. Plus, she is stuck romantically at age twenty-three, when she got totally burned, so that's not helping her forward momentum. The book focuses on Elizabeth, in her mid-thirties, defining who she is and finally making choices as she sees fit, not to please her family.

And I do feel that finding a professional path is critical for women to establish their adult identities. We have a lot of roles we play in society or in a family—wife, mother, sister, aunt, caretaker—and by definition those roles rely on others in our family. But in our professional lives, we get to create our own persona. Be who we really are when our mother isn't watching. I think that's important in a woman's self-identity.

Once again, Pasadena serves as a major setting and theme. Has your vision of Pasadena evolved since writing *Helen of Pasadena*? Can we expect to see you escaping to Ashland any time soon?

I know so much more now about Pasadena than I did when I wrote *Helen of Pasadena*. Wow, since that book came out, lifelong Pasadenans have dished the dirt on all kinds of scandals and local lore. I won't be walking away from Pasadena anytime soon, because there's too much good stuff to mine and great cultural institutions to explore. But I did like bringing in another locale. It keeps my writing fresh and provides a comparative setting for Pasadena, which is steeped in tradition. The next book will be Pasadena and somewhere in Europe, because I can write the trip off as research, right?

That being said, Ashland is an amazing town with a wonderful spirit and a creative soul. I'd love to find my own little Sage Cottage there one day.

Helen Fairchild swoons over the manly forearms on the sexy archaeologist. Elizabeth Lancaster swoons over the manly forearms on the sexy political operative. Is it safe to say you have a thing for masculine forearms?

Guilty as charged. Forearms are revealing. I think as a gender, women have focused on men's backsides and abs for too long. Six-packs don't tell us anything except that the guy spends a lot of time in the gym and probably doesn't eat pasta. A man's forearms say a lot about his life choices. Are they tanned and muscular? Then the guy must get outside and move dirt around, figuratively or literally. Are they pale and slim? Too much time in the office! Could be dull. There's a story in every forearm, and all you need is for the guy to roll up his sleeve to get a good look.

Does writing a novel get any easier the second time around?

Nope.

BOOK CLUB
DISCUSSION TOPICS

1. When we meet Elizabeth, she seems perfectly contented with her life, although her family of high achievers encourages her to be more ambitious. Do you think she was denying her ambitions out of fear?

2. Setting plays a large role. Could Ashland and Pasadena be considered characters of their own? Does Elizabeth's relationship with each of these places change over the course of the book?

3. The title *Elizabeth the First Wife* ties our protagonist to Elizabeth the First of England. Which of her aspects draw inspiration from Queen Elizabeth? How is she a modern-day Elizabeth?

4. Did you think Elizabeth and FX were going to get back together at the end? Were you hoping they would?

5. What is the significance of an all-consuming "first love"? Compare Elizabeth and FX's relationship to the one with Rafa. Do you remember your first love as vividly as she does?

6. Each chapter begins with an excerpt from Elizabeth's book proposal, *All's Fair.* How did these affect your reading of the main storyline?

7. Elizabeth struggles to create her own identity within her family, and ultimately triumphs. Is that a common issue?

ACKNOWLEDGMENTS

Is it easier to write a second novel? Sadly, no. You still have to write every word, and it's just as difficult to stay out of the fridge as it was the first time around. But if you're lucky, you have a team to get you through the good days and the rough ones. I'm one of the lucky ones, so thanks go to:

My publisher, Prospect Park Books, and its positive and patient brain trust: Colleen Dunn Bates, Patty O'Sullivan, Jennifer Bastien, Caroline Purvis, and the sales and distribution team at Consortium. This one's for you. Thanks to book designer Kathy Kikkert for her lovely work.

My multimedia empire builders, if writing in your bedroom and recording a podcast in your closet can be called an empire, including my agents, Yfat Reiss Gendell at Foundry Literary in New York and Katie Cates at Kaplan/Stahler in Los Angeles; my webmaster and designer, Emily Tellez; my photographer, Dana Bouton; and my hairdresser/life coach, Trina Mor.

My sources for the book: the California Institute of Technology, the Pasadena Showcase House for the Arts, and the Oregon Shakespeare Festival. At Caltech, many thanks to my friend Leslie Maxfield, the director of Academic Media Technology, and to the impressive bunch at the Caltech Women's Club, including Dr. Carol Carmichael, who provided inspiration, encouragement, and some good dirt. Also, my gratitude to Dr. Robert Spero of the Jet Propulsion Lab, who factchecked my physics and found it wanting. Thanks for those helpful hints, Robert—now get back to work on those Laser Interferometer Space Antennae! All hail to the tireless volunteers and designers of the Pasadena Showcase House for the Arts, who raise money for children's music programs, especially president Beverly Marksbury, who graciously showed me around the house. And thanks to the terrific press office at OSF for behind-the-scenes information, tickets, and tours.

My writing teacher, Erika Mailman at mediabistro.com, and my fellow classmates, who helped me to shape the book from page one, including Jenny Williams, Sharon Jessup Joyce, Nicola Ruiz, Ann Turnicky, and Julie Flakstad. Every writer needs a gut-check group.

My name donors, Mary Pat Brandmeyer and Bumble Ward. Now that I've stolen your names for posterity, we should become better friends. Thank you for loaning me your monikers.

My hometown and the many Pasadena locals who have embraced my work with grace and good humor, allowing me into their homes, book groups, and previously unattainable private clubs. Special thanks to Larry Wilson, Patt Diroll, and Charlie Plowman of Pasadena's fourth estate.

My own Pasadena Posse of friends who have supported me through my writing and so much more in the last year, especially Ryan Newman, Susan Pai, Sally Mann, and Danielle Waldschmidt-Gay. Plus the many excellent friends from afar who've cheered me on, including Alyssa Isreal, Andrew Ferren, Chris Connor, and my fellow Sagehens.

My readers, listeners, and the online community of the Satellite Sisterhood and the Chaos Crew, who keep me motivated and connected. Thank you for supporting my work, posting funny pictures of your dogs, and listening to the show. Who says virtual friends aren't real?

My brothers and sisters and my entire extended family. It was an extraordinary year in which we lost both our parents but never our sense of humor. Remember the family motto: Stay low and brace for impact.

Finally to my boys: my husband, Berick Treidler, and my sons, Brookes and Colin. You're the best.

Lian Dolan
Pasadena
February, 2013

ABOUT THE AUTHOR

Lian Dolan is a writer and broadcaster. Her first novel, *Helen of Pasadena*, was on the *Los Angeles Times* bestseller list for more than a year and was nominated for Best Fiction by the Southern California Independent Booksellers Association. In addition, she's written for TV, radio, and magazines, including regular columns in *O, The Oprah Magazine, Working Mother,* and Oprah.com. She is the co-creator and host of the Gracie Award–winning radio show Satellite Sisters, now a podcast and blog. Her musings about modern motherhood are found on the podcast and blog called *The Chaos Chronicles*, which was developed for TV by Nickelodeon.

Lian graduated from Pomona College with a degree in Classics. A Connecticut native, she now lives in Pasadena, California with her husband and two sons.

2/14